Praise for *Tijuana Straits*

"A compelling little crucible of evil and nascent love, succeeding on the strength of its characters, the velocity of the plot, its location on *la frontera,* and the terrific surfing back story. . . . Nunn infuses the formula with enough energy, intelligence, and indignation to drive us to the last page in a single sitting. . . . The Miltonian arc of Nunn's prose, the heroic metaphors, the vertiginous plunge of his sentences—long, dark, syntactical labyrinths—make *Tijuana Straits* thrilling to read. Clearly, part of the pleasure of this book is watching Nunn construct the story, so that when you're a little more than halfway through and the characters are nearly upon one another, he puts a careful distance between them, driving expectations and anxiety higher. Like an uncut diamond, *Tijuana Straits* is all the more beautiful for its slight imperfections. . . . While Nunn obviously knows the landscape of lost dreams, his writing and storytelling stay well above the fray, so that in the end, when he creates moments so satisfying and wonderful, you're left to hope that this book is being read out loud—by firelight or flashlight—somewhere on an open beach."

—*Los Angeles Times*

"If there is a literature of surfing, *Tijuana Straits* is surely one of its classics."

—*The Washington Post Book World*

"*Tijuana Straits* is darkly funny and deeply moving, horrifying and lyrical, profane and almost biblical."

—*Fort Myers News-Press*

"*Tijuana Straits* is an uncommonly thoughtful thriller whose outrage over the environmental pillaging of the California coastline gives it a wicked undertow . . . a terrifically atmospheric chunk of prose, with any good writer's panopticon gift for swooping in on a large event's most visual traces."

—*San Francisco Chronicle*

"Kem Nunn is an immensely talented writer whose baroque prose style [is] at times re of Cormac McCarthy."

"Kem Nunn is an accomplished storyteller and a first-rate writer. In *Tijuana Straits* he has sounded depths that are all too real; his quietly lyrical, terrifying, and utterly absorbing novel is a classic examination of people clinging to one of the world's most potent frontiers, the darkly promising, often treacherous intersection of Mexico, California, and the Pacific Ocean. Nunn knows the subcultures and strategies through which people there survive and he has wrought a harrowing and moving story of unforgettable characters living, literally, on the edges."

—Robert Stone

"His characters may be in dire straits, but his readers are comfortable in the hands of an exciting novelist working with fascinating material."

—*The Sunday Oregonian*

"Nunn has a weird genius for villains. Like a great surfboard, form follows function in Kem Nunn's book. As hell comes to the valley, the language follows."

—*The San Diego Union-Tribune*

"Nunn is a different sort of artist altogether."

—*The Orange County Register*

"Nunn lays down a crime-thriller plot and charges it with grisly violence, doomed love, an obsession with sin and redemption, and of course, the swell of the decade. . . . Nunn's voice has become overtly literary; he's clearly schooled himself in the more violent strains of American literature. . . . Add the SoCal surf lore and a satisfying dose of natural history and you've got a truly strange amalgam of a book, at once a heart-pounding gorefest and a disturbing look at the dark side of the California dream."

—*Outside*

"Nunn shares with Carl Hiaasen a deep moral outrage and a flair for creating, in surrealistic fashion, exaggeratedly malevolent villains amid a stewing, toxic landscape. . . . There's no denying his talent, and it comes shining through in the novel's best passages—the climactic pulse-pounding race through the dunes, the near-mystical surfing scenes."

—*Booklist*

KEM NUNN

Tijuana Straits

⇥ A NOVEL ⇤

SCRIBNER

New York   London   Toronto   Sydney

SCRIBNER
1230 Avenue of the Americas
New York, NY 10020

First Scribner trade paperback edition 2005

SCRIBNER and design are trademarks of Macmillan Library Reference USA, Inc., used under license by Simon & Schuster, the publisher of this work.

For information about special discounts for bulk purchases, please contact Simon & Schuster Special Sales: 1-800-456-6798 or business@simonandschuster.com

Designed by Kyoko Watanabe

Text set in New Baskerville

Manufactured in the United States of America

3 5 7 9 10 8 6 4 2

Library of Congress Control Number: 2004041622

ISBN-13: 978-0-684-84305-6
ISBN-10: 0-684-84305-6
ISBN-13: 978-0-7432-7982-6 (Pbk)
ISBN-10: 0-7432-7982-4 (Pbk)

For Lisa Marks, with love

In the margins of the community, at the gates of the cities, there stretched great zones . . . soliciting with strange incantations a new incarnation of evil . . .

—Michel Foucault, *Madness and Civilization*

Do not neglect to show hospitality to strangers, for by this some have entertained angels without knowing it.

—Hebrews 13:2

PART ONE

1

THE WOMAN appeared with the first light, struggling across the dunes, a figure from the Revelation. Fahey saw her from the beach. There was a pack of feral dogs loose in the valley and Fahey had been hunting them for the better part of three days, without success. To complicate matters, he'd attempted to work behind a little crystal meth and it had left him in a bad place. He supposed that buying in the parking lot of the Palm Avenue 7-Eleven from a kid with a head shaped like a peanut and a hoop through his nose had not been the best of ideas. He watched as the figure crested a dune then disappeared from sight, still too distant to be properly identified as a woman. From the beach she appeared as little more than a hole in the dawn, a spidery black cutout in the faint yellow light just now beginning to seep from the summit of Cerro Colorado on the Mexican side of the fence that cut the valley into halves, and Fahey took her for one more clueless pilgrim stumbling toward the river that would most likely mark the end of the road. She might weep in bewilderment upon its banks or drown in its toxic waters. In either case there was little he could do, for he'd accepted as his charge the protection of certain migratory birds, most notably the western snowy plover and light-footed clapper rail, and within this jurisdiction the ubiquitous pilgrim was hardly a concern. Still, on the morning in question, Fahey found his obduracy mitigated by a kind of relief. It was, he believed, helpful to share the dawn with someone whose prospects were at least as fucked up as his own.

As if on cue, Fahey's heart resumed hammering at an absurd rate. Earlier, at about that point when it was becoming clear the bargain-basement chemical intended to do him wrong, he'd considered seeking help. The thought, however, of actually presenting himself in the emergency room in San Ysidro, along with such theaters of humiliation as were bound to follow, was so appalling he'd abandoned the idea almost at once. One might, after all, have expected more from a man of Fahey's age. But then one would have been disappointed.

Fahey put the pilgrim from his mind and knelt to examine the tracks. To his great disappointment, the prints were diamond-shaped and spaced to suggest the short, even gait of coyotes as opposed to dogs. The dogs' tracks would be rounder and farther apart. There would also be more of them. There were four dogs in the pack Fahey was hunting. He guessed the impressions before him to have been made by no more than two animals. He rose unsteadily in the soft sand. He'd glimpsed the tracks in his head-lights from the opposite bank, then driven around for a closer look, slow going in the old valley's predawn Stygian gloom, his clutch beginning to smoke as the truck churned through the long beach in approach to the mouth of the river. He stared after the tracks as they veered into the dunes before losing themselves in shadow. Fahey considered himself a competent tracker. That he had been chasing the same four dogs for the better part of a week did not speak positively for his state of mind or, by extension of that logic, portend well for the future.

He walked the short distance to his truck, a battered 1981 Toyota, nearly half as old as Fahey himself, of indiscernible color. The bed was a jumble of poorly maintained tools, a variety of traps, nets, and poles, remnants of a time when these sorts of outings had been what he'd done to earn a living. His preferred method of dealing with feral animals had always been to trap them and he'd hoped to catch one or more of the dogs in the same way. He had accordingly run two dozen cages and another half dozen leg holds. The leg hold traps were, strictly speaking, illegal in the state of California but Fahey was not anticipating complaints. The dogs were an unusually bad lot and Fahey could not remember any quite like them. Already they had mauled a border patrolman and wiped out a dozen of the least-tern nests. They had also killed an old female coyote that had managed to snare herself in one of the illegal traps.

Fahey took a bottle of water from the cooler near the tailgate in the bed of his truck. The drug had left his mouth dry as cotton. He uncapped the bottle and drank. At his back the lights of Imperial Beach still flickered above the grasses of the great saltwater estuary that formed the northwest corner of the valley. Before him, across a wide swath of land known as Border Field State Park, were the dark cliffs of the Mexican mesas, the lights of Las Playas de Tijuana, and the great rounded edge of the Tijuana bullring, which might, he thought, in the aqueous coastal airs, have passed for the mother ship of some extraterrestrial and conquering race, settled there to survey its holdings. East lay the bulk of the valley, still dark with shadow. To the west, however, a thundering Pacific had begun to catch fire in the early light as Fahey looked to the sea. He had begun to think about the coyote he had trapped and was trying not to. He studied glassy swell lines beyond crackling shore break and churning lines of white water, sweeping south toward the fence and the beaches beyond. The animal had tried unsuccessfully to chew off its own foot in an effort to escape its fate. Seeking to drive the image from his mind, Fahey called forth the admonition of Mother Maybelle Carter, to keep on the sunny side of life. Unhappily, his gaze swung south, toward the mesas and their blood-soaked canyons.

Fucking Mexico. For some it was still a slice of the Old West, all whores and cowboys. For Fahey it remained an unfathomable din of fear and corruption, the wellspring of barbarous histories, none more iniquitous than his own. Of course Fahey's perception of the place ran to his youth, high school and the Island Express, when it had been his experience that only bad things happened south of the border. Subsequent experience had led to the revised conviction that only bad things happened pretty much everywhere. Still, the shit was always creepier in a foreign tongue, and he kept to his side of the valley, as familiar now as the face of a lover, though in point of fact Fahey had been without lovers for some time. Lovers, he had concluded, were like Mexico herself, little more than instruments of grief. Better to go it alone, on one's own side of the fence, where at the very least, Fahey reasoned, one might hear them coming.

Returning the water bottle to the cooler in the bed of his truck, he took in a coloring sky, thick scrim of smog going crimson above the Mexican hills. The dogs he tracked were from over there, out of the canyons. He had glimpsed them just once, on the first day, running single file across the top of Spooner's Mesa, three pit bull mixes and a border collie. He ran his traps that evening, found the coyote the next day. He had not seen the dogs since, nothing more than tracks in the sand, and for the last twenty-four hours even those had eluded him. Earlier in the week, when Bill Daniels from Fish and Game had come around to his trailer wanting to know if he would be willing to hunt some bad dogs for them, a one-time gig, like what he used to do before the job became federal, ruling out known drug runners and convicted felons, he had accepted for want of scratch, but in the last four days something had turned. Maybe it was the old coyote, half eaten, trapped by the leg hold Fahey himself had run. The hunt had gotten personal.

He was about to get into the Toyota and drive away when several birds—too small to be anything but snowy plovers—rose suddenly from the sand near the base of the dunes, beating the air in frantic circles. He hadn't known of any scrapings this far north on the beach and he went down to the wet sand, then walked along its edge, hoping for a better view of the birds' nesting place, wondering at what might have spooked them when, to his great consternation, the clueless pilgrim he had all but forgotten about reappeared once more, not fifty yards from where he stood.

He could see now that she was a woman. A mane of black hair held aloft by offshore winds flew like a pennant in the direction of the sea. To his horror, Fahey watched as she raised a hand and started toward him, setting a path that would lead directly into that part of the beach from which the birds had risen. Fahey raised both hands and pushed them toward her in what he imagined as some internationally recognizable signal to stop and go back. The woman came on. Fahey shouted into the wind, repeating the signal several times. Still the pilgrim stumbled toward him, toward the delicate nests that would house the even more delicate eggs. The plovers rose high above the dunes then dropped in unison, swooping toward the woman. It was the bird's nature to defecate upon approaching predators. The woman threw up her arms and began to run, still in Fahey's direction. Fahey cursed, ran to his truck and reached inside, going for that narrow space between the seat and the rear wall of the cab, banging his hand against the door jamb with enough force to peel a strip of skin from his knuckles, but managing to extract the short-barreled shotgun he housed there, pointed the weapon toward that place where the sky met the sea and discharged a round.

The blast seemed to get the woman's attention. She sank to her knees, her hands upon her ears, then rose and stumbled back the way she had come, vanishing among the dunes. Fahey stood wheezing on the beach. He had not fired a weapon in some time and he found that doing so just now seemed to have aggravated his condition. His heart thundered erratically in the hollow of his chest, as meanwhile, the plovers, driven to even greater levels of panic at the sound of his gun, widened their circles above the beach, the morning made horrible with their cries.

Fahey wiped at his brow with the sleeve of his shirt, bent forward to retrieve the spent casing, and was surprised to find it dancing away upon an eddy of swirling white water. He splashed after it, snatched it from the sea, stuffed it dripping into the pocket of his shirt, then stood to gaze upon the crashing waves, remembering the phase of the moon and the tide it would engender, only to be reminded in turn of a time when such prompts would have been wholly unnecessary for he would have known the tide and the swell with it, as a matter of course. And for just that instant, sea water seeping into his socks, gun held loosely in the crook of an arm, was thoroughly transported . . . and beheld the boy, not yet sixteen, hunkered at the foot of these selfsame dunes, and the old Dakota Badlander right there beside him, surfboards like graven images of wood and fiberglass set before them, tail blocks sunk into the very sand upon which Fahey now stood, and the boy watching, as the old man waves toward the sea with a stick held at the end of one long arm corded with muscle, burnt by the sun, then uses the stick to trace in the sand the route they will follow and the lineups they will use to find their way among the shifting peaks that stretch into the ocean for as far as the eye can see, wave crests capped by tongues of flame as the mist of feathering lips flies before the light of an approaching sunrise . . . and this when the light was still pure, before the smog, before the fence at the heart of the valley, before the shit had hit the fan.

At which point a faint cry issued from the dunes in which the pilgrim had vanished—the present visited upon Fahey once more, in all its fine clarity. Raising the gun, he slogged onto the dry sand to stand looking into the folds of a dune. It was Fahey's philosophy, in a general sort of way, to leave what pilgrims he happened to cross paths with to their own devices and he was inclined to do so now. He took it as something like the Prime Directive from those early episodes of *Star Trek* he'd watched as a boy. Alien life forms were simply too foreign to be adequately known. Interfering was to invite consequences that were sure to be unforeseen, possibly dire. The Prime Directive now called for him to go to his truck and drive away. Fahey remained where he was. He could not have said why. An image presented itself to his mind's eye—that of a slender young woman, his figure of the Revelation, a shapely arm raised above ragged clothes in what could only be interpreted as a gesture of supplication. Pilgrims generally ran at the approach of Americans, particularly those in uniform. This one had actually tried to get Fahey's attention and he saw once more that mane of hair, held fluttering upon the wind, black as the wing of a bird. His eyes searched the dunes into which she had fled and which, along this particular two-mile stretch of sand separating Las Playas de Tijuana from the town of Imperial Beach, were quite shallow. But there was no further sign of the pilgrim. The beach was silent, save for the crack of the shore break and the cries of the birds that continued to circle.

Odd, he thought, that the birds had not yet returned to their nests, as if they now sensed some new danger. He scanned the beach in both directions but found nothing. Perhaps it was his presence to which the creatures objected. "I'm here to help," Fahey told them. But the plovers maintained their frantic patterns.

He continued to stand facing the dunes. It was of course quite possible that the woman would return to the beach, that she still posed some threat to the nesting birds. The plovers were tiny creatures, no larger than a child's fist. Their method of self-defense, as the woman had discovered, was to take to the sky, then dive bomb the offending predator, most often a coyote or fox, shitting in unison till the enemy fled in what Fahey could only imagine as some state of profound disgust. The strategy had apparently worked well enough when the birds numbered into the hundreds. For the last few years, however, the plover had occupied a place on California's endangered species list. To date—and they were already well into the mating season—no more than a dozen of the small egg-bearing nests, little more than shallow scrapings in the sand, had been found and half of those already lost to the dogs Fahey tracked. But now, here at the mouth of the river, he had found a few more of the birds, clearly protecting what might at least be two, possibly three, nests, and it was incumbent upon him to defend them as best he could, be it from marauding animals or clueless pilgrims, hence Fahey's indecision. Or at least that was what he told himself, moving now in what he deemed to be a wide enough circle to avoid the nests, but angling toward the fold in the dunes through which the young woman had vanished. He was either looking out for the birds or violating his own Prime Directive. Fahey took it as one of life's little lessons that people were rarely doing what they claimed to be doing, even when that claim was made to none but themselves.

He climbed a dune then worked his way along the top, its summit crested with a sparse covering of ice plant, till he had come to that place where her footprints were plainly visible in the sandy hollow below. The prints led from the beach to the valley, sunk deep across a narrow salt pan still damp in the early light before vanishing into a small stand of mule fat and sandbar willow that grew near the bank of the river, where it curved away to the south.

A second decision was now called for. Finding her among the dunes would have been one thing. To follow her beneath the trees was another. The thicket into which she'd vanished was something of an aberration, as the greater part of these riparian woodlands lay farther east at the heart of the floodplain. Between this thicket and the bulk of the forest was cordgrass and brackish marsh and all of it, both woods and marshland alike, cut by such footpaths as the uncounted feet of migrants and smugglers had worn there over decades of use. And though he knew the valley, and the trails with it, he was loath to go where he could not see what waited. Or perhaps his very knowing was what brought him up short, that and the dubious nature of his enterprise. For who could say with certainty that the woman was not the bait in some elaborate and malevolent scheme?

A plover rose high into the air above Fahey's head before falling away toward the sea. At almost the same instant a naval helicopter broke from the training field at the edge of Imperial Beach in the northeast corner of the valley, rising above the marshes in gross mimicry of its tiny counterpart, then chugging northward, the length of the town, whose residents were encouraged to think of such disturbances as the sounds of freedom. He watched as the huge ship beat lazily at the sky then veered seaward before reaching the more affluent homes of Coronado Island, a community in which the sounds of freedom were less than welcome. He waited till the helicopter was gone, heard in its absence the frantic cry of a bird, the distant thunder of big surf, the rattle of his own heart. He was reminded of a father's lamentations, a man he had scarcely known: "Foolishness is tied up in the heart of a boy. The rod of discipline is what will drive it from him." He came off the dune in the direction of the valley—the direction taken by the woman, moving laterally so as to control the speed of his descent, skirting the salt pan so as to save his boots, entering at last among the trees, where he had not gone twenty feet before finding her . . . huddled near the base of a metal sign posted to warn potential bathers of polluted water, as if the reek of raw sewage rising from the river itself would not have been enough.

"Please," she said. And her English was quite perfect. "I need your help."

It was not the greeting he had expected and Fahey, days at a time without human intercourse, was still considering a response when he saw the woman's eyes tick to a spot somewhere beyond his left shoulder, even as the cry of one more plover split the morning, and he felt it then, knew without seeing what had frightened the birds, beyond the approach of the woman or the report of the gun, and turned, and saw the dogs—three pit bull mixes and a border collie, the pack of murderers he'd glimpsed on Spooner's Mesa, the same that had eluded him now for the better part of a week, all four of them, hunkered like gargoyles in the slatted shadows of the trees, the river at their backs.

2

THE SHOTGUN held five rounds. Fahey had wasted one trying to scare the woman away from the birds. He watched now as one of the pit bulls, a no-neck brute with dull eyes and a dirty white diamond shape beneath its throat, dropped to its stomach. Two more dogs hunkered down as well. The collie remained standing, a short distance behind the others, shifting its weight, skittish, the weakest of the pack.

Fahey, who had not been called upon to hit a moving target for more than a year, took a step closer to the woman. He hooked a thumb into the gun strap slung over his shoulder and very slowly allowed the strap to slide down his arm, at the same time, bringing the gun to bear. He spoke to the woman without looking at her.

"Can you walk?" he asked.

"I don't know," she said.

He could scarcely hear above the rush of blood in his ears. The prospect of bringing down the four dogs with four shells for a man in Fahey's delicate state was a daunting proposition. Nor were the conditions in his favor. The rising sun had yet to penetrate the willows and the trees were even thicker near the water, the muddy bank upon which the dogs waited dark with shadow, the entire setting shot through with a musty green light, together with the reek of whatever it was that flowed from the mesas of Tijuana with their myriad of polluting, foreign-owned factories, from her hills and canyons where the huddled masses waited.

Fahey felt a pain in his left wrist. It snaked its way up his arm and into his jaw. Christ, he thought, I'm having a heart attack. He appeared to be viewing the animals before him from within the confines of a Lava lamp. Still, it was his belief that the dogs would be reluctant to charge two adult humans. He believed that if he could get the woman to her feet, that if they moved slowly, they might back toward the beach, where his truck was waiting. With luck, perhaps, the dogs might follow at a distance. With real luck, Fahey thought, he might even get a shot at them from the safety of his cab. The woman, however, was slow in rising. Fahey slid his eyes in her direction, in time to see that she was favoring an ankle. When she tried to put weight on it, the ankle gave way altogether. She let out a little gasp then sank to the ground. Fahey made a lateral movement, put out a hand to steady her. She took him by the wrist in an icy grip, surprising in its strength, but she was already going down and Fahey, caught off balance, shuffled to keep his footing. All things considered, he imagined it an unfortunate display, and when he looked again, the dogs were coming.

Fahey wrested his hand from the woman's frozen grasp, sank to one knee, and began to shoot. The dogs came in low and fast, bouncing like hailstones, tongues on fire, trailing drool. Fahey took them head on. In the end, he supposed, it was a question of time. The last of the pit bulls went down not ten feet from where he knelt.

Had the collie been as eager for blood his time would have run out and she would have reached him before he could fire again. As it was, Fahey found her standing maybe thirty feet away, circling, spooked, wild-eyed in the silence that followed in the wake of the shooting, the loss of the pack. This time he took aim, shot, and missed. The animal stared in dumb wonder then made for the river, yipping plaintively, a tiny plover in hot pursuit.

Fahey lurched to his feet, light-headed, sucking wind. He stared at the gun in his hand, as full of dumb wonder as the dog itself. The dead pit bulls were staggered across the ground in the order he had shot them, gaping holes already drawing flies. Fahey stared into the shadow of the willows after the departed dog then turned to the woman. He found her shivering on the ground, covered in the ragged canvas tarp she had apparently acquired somewhere in the course of her journey, for he was at this point imagining that she had come to him by way of Yogurt Canyon—a popular route of passage whose entrance to the valley was near the beach and so named for the frozen yogurt stand that stood at its head in Las Playas de Tijuana on the other side of the fence.

"It's okay," Fahey told her. "It's okay now." It occurred to him that he was speaking as much to himself as to the pilgrim before him.

The woman pulled the tarp from her head, brought herself to one elbow, and looked around. He could see now that she had been badly beaten. There were fresh bruises on one side of her face together with a collection of tiny cuts still oozing blood. Beneath the tarp were the remains of a sweater, a dirty pair of jeans and a single Nike running shoe. The clothes were wet, caked with sand. The woman continued to shiver in the cool light. He supposed that she had been the victim of bandits. Perhaps there had been others in her party, now dead or scattered. He wondered how far she had come and if the bandits were still in the neighborhood. Bandits in the valley might be from either side of the fence, though most often they were comprised of gang members from the neighboring towns of San Ysidro and Chula Vista. The shotgun in his hand was now empty. His truck remained unattended on the beach, subject to both miscreants and a rising tide. Fahey consulted a watch then went to his haunches at the woman's side.

"You want to try again?"

The woman threw a frightened look across one shoulder in the direction of the country from which she had come then tried to stand. Fahey rose with her. Standing, she was a head shorter than Fahey, slight and dark. He watched as she worked with her tarp, rolling it about her head and shoulders, holding it to her chest. The article was long enough to trail on the ground and done up in it she was once again the biblical figure he had glimpsed from the beach, a daughter of Lot at the edge of the plain. He waited till she had arranged the material to her satisfaction then turned to the dunes. The woman responded by fainting dead away. She went to the sand amid the folds of her tarp much like a collapsing circus tent, the maneuver accomplished in total silence.

Fahey looked on, aghast, at the entrance to the trees. The blood was still pounding in his temples but having survived the dogs he was beginning to believe that he would probably outlast the drugs as well. He had, after all, outlasted them in the past. Having arrived at this observation, others followed in its wake. He had been two days without sleep. Back at the ranch his windrows would be in need of water. The dogs he had killed would have to be delivered to Fish and Game to fetch their bounty, then taken to the animal shelter for disposal. Fahey considered the rag heap before him. On the one hand she had led him to the dogs, albeit unwittingly. On the other hand she might well be involving him in some drama, the likes of which he'd spent most of his life trying to avoid. He supposed it was no less than one should expect, in violation of the Prime Directive.

He stood amid the buzz of insects, the reek of the river, the sunlight finding its way among the branches to warm his shoulders, a victim yet again of his own vicissitudes. The second helicopter of the morning could be heard above the willows, pounding the sky, and it occurred to him that if he lingered here much longer he might well be forced to explain himself. At the very least he might expect a visit from any border patrolmen close enough to have heard the shots. Fahey knew a number of the officers by name and could show good cause to be here. Still, he was not anxious to make conversation in his present condition. He could imagine his appearance—the ruddy, sweat-streaked face of an amphetamine junkie, days without sleep. God knew what his pupils looked like. Fahey was not generally liked. And still there was the pilgrim to consider. She was not your run-of-the-mill pilgrim. Her English was far too good. Perhaps she was not even illegal, just some woman taken by bandits while walking in the valley. He looked down on the pitiful pile at his feet. She was obviously going nowhere under her own power. In the end, he gathered her to his chest as one might collect a pile of dirty laundry and staggered from the willows, through the dunes and back to the beach, where the plovers were waiting.

She rode by his side like a sleeping child as Fahey nursed the old truck through the soft sand at the foot of the dunes, the river mouth at their backs, a late south swell pounding like cannon fire along steeply banked beaches as empty as the moon. Seabirds scattered at their approach. A flock of white pelicans rose awkwardly into the blue before soaring on snowy wings tipped with black. Offshore, a number of dolphins were at play among the waves, primordial shapes suspended in translucent faces—such were the wonders of the Tijuana River Valley, where sights and sounds all but obliterated from the southern half of the state might yet be found—God's script, written among the detritus of two countries.

The Toyota's clutch was smoking once more by the time they reached the mouth of Monument Road at the edge of Border Field State Park. Above them loomed the Tijuana bullring and its attendant lighthouse, a bleached shinbone set before the morning, and beyond these the red-tiled roofs and gaudy pastels of Las Playas, one of the city's few high-rent districts, home to her businessmen and drug lords. Fahey turned inland here, driving now in the shade of the mesas, where the great steel fence rode the hills like an amusement park ride.

His intention was to deliver her to the emergency room at the hospital in San Ysidro. Later, he would return for the dogs. The road was of hard-packed dirt and he'd just hit third gear for the first time since leaving the river when the woman opened an eye. "Where are you taking me?" she asked.

"For help," Fahey said.

There followed a moment of silence, and then the woman's fingers on his arm, as cold as they had been on the beach. He could feel the chill through the fabric of his shirt. Christ, he thought, she must be frozen to the bone.

"That won't work," the pilgrim told him.

Fahey glanced in her direction. She made for a somewhat alarming spectacle—one eye swollen nearly shut, the skin mottled and blackened around it, the white part gone to a rosy red. The other eye was wide with fear. It occurred to him that she was perhaps deranged.

"I need time," she whispered, "time . . . time to think." Her head rocked back against the seat then rolled from side to side. "Time to think," she repeated.

"You need help."

"No, no. I'm okay. Really. If you send me back, I'm done."

To Fahey's consternation, the woman began to weep. "You don't know," she told him, then lapsed into Spanish.

What little command Fahey'd once had of the language was now almost nonexistent but it seemed to him that she was talking about the devil. He heard the words *"el diablo,"* followed by some reference to the Mesa de Otay, but when he asked for a translation, she would only repeat what she had said, before slipping into some manner of unconsciousness once more.

So, Fahey thought, his first instinct had been correct. She was indeed from across the line, in hot flight from some devil in the mesa—a predicament to which he was not altogether unsympathetic. He drove on. To shelter this woman, if indeed she was illegal, was to invite calamity. Found in Fahey's custody, she would surely place him at the mercy of his enemies. Yet he was suddenly spent to the core, believing that at this precise moment he hadn't the strength to drive her much farther, even if he wanted to, certainly not as far as the hospital in San Ysidro, where he would be forced to negotiate morning traffic at the height of its mad stampede to the border. He would probably have done better in leaving her to the dunes, and still could, he supposed, indulging in ruthless speculation, but he made no move to stop or turn around. Nor did he push on with his original plan, which would have called for following his present course in an easterly direction, to a juncture with the San Diego Freeway. He turned instead upon a narrow strip of pitted asphalt marked as Hollister Drive. The road carried him away from the border and when he'd used it to cross the river he turned once more into the heart of the valley, in the direction of the sea.

He drove on dirt roads again here, and these without names, coming shortly to an opening cut among wild radishes grown ten feet tall on either side and the road itself so rutted and strewn with silt and debris one would have been hard-pressed to call it by that name. Yet he turned down it all the same, little more by now than spasm and sweat, coming at last upon the rusting chain-link fence that marked the edge of his holdings and beyond the fence, his windrows, in their narrow black lines among cast-off appliances, rusted farming gear, plows and harvesters. And beyond even that his vats of worm tea percolating in the sun and a fence made of old surfboards, tail blocks sunk into the earth and set before his trailer like the faded shields of a lost people, and finally the house itself, which seemed of late to have been taken over by a hive of ill-tempered bees—in short, everything Fahey owned in the world, circled like wagons for what could only be taken as some proverbial last stand.

Fahey stopped at the fence. He glanced once more at the woman beside him, sleeping fitfully, her hands balled into tiny fists clutched to her chest, then slid from behind the wheel to pass through the morning's heat. His own dogs were there to greet him, a pair of mongrels he'd acquired since returning to the valley, some kind of terrier mix he called Jack, and Wrinkles, an ancient hound nearly too old to stand. When he'd unlocked the gate he returned to the truck and drove inside, the terrier yapping at his tires. He parked before the ancient yellow trailer listing on blocks amid a stand of cottonwoods and poisonous oleander sown by his father before him then proceeded to sit there, astonished at what the morning had wrought, at his own reckless behavior. "My God," he said aloud, "what have I done?" His eyes were fixed on the old bumper sticker pasted to the stern of his trailer—white letters on a field of black, pitted by the years, the sun and rain. Fahey wiped at his eyes, scratched raw as though the lids were filled with sand, staring at the sticker as if seeing it for the first time, as if he himself had not been the moron who'd put it there, in another life, on a day more rosy than the present. THERE'S NOTHING, the battered letters proclaimed, A DAY OF SURFING WON'T FIX.

3

HER NAME WAS Magdalena Rivera. She came from Tijuana, Mexico. More precisely, she came from the *colonia* Cartolandia at the gates of the border. It was a place that no longer existed. The Zona del Río, the brightest and shiniest of the new Tijuana, had been built upon the bones of its inhabitants. A mother she could scarcely recall had been drowned there in the name of progress and it was for her that she'd taken up the cross. And now it had gotten her into trouble.

She watched with one good eye this man who had claimed her, saw him amid dust and a rising heat—what she could only assume to be the onslaught of fever. She watched as he opened the chain-link gate that had scared her at first but which she could now see was far too corroded with rust and grit to be anything official so maybe he was really going to help after all. He was going to help or he was like the men one read about, on the walls of post offices, an abductor of women, an ax murderer, or a rapist. In which case she would be done for, done for on the American side of the fence as surely as she would be done for in Tijuana, should they send her back, without benefit of the amparo she could only guess had been claimed by a malevolent sea.

She waited as he finished with the gate then returned to the truck, a tall, broad-shouldered man, though apparently engaged in some losing struggle with gravity. She was reminded of the homeless she passed each day, on both sides of the border, for his hair and beard were tangled and unkempt and he had about him that permanently sunburned complexion she had come to associate with denizens of the street. All things considered, she could not take comfort in the sight. Her mind tilted toward the dark side. She was too exhausted for flight. She saw him as in a dream. This was where she had come, she thought, to this place, to this man. Whatever happened next would have to be left to karma. There was nothing more to be done, the light already playing tricks with her mind, carrying her like the current that had taken her from the beach, through realms of shadow and light, as if the sun were passing among clouds, though in point of fact, the sky was blameless and cobalt blue, reminding her of the desert, the orphanage in Mexicali, the Sisters of the Benediction . . .

It had begun routinely enough—the night that had brought her to this apparent hallucination without end. She had taken a light meal on the deck of her apartment overlooking Las Playas then driven across town to the Mesa de Otay, where the residents of Colonia Vista Nueva were holding a candlelight vigil for a six-year-old child who had died of lead poisoning.

The drive had taken her through the Zona del Río, past the new cultural center, the banks, and American-style shopping centers with their fast-food franchises and decorative palms. As always, she had tried to imagine the place as it used to be, before Burger King and Ronald McDonald. The Scientologists said you had it in you to recall everything, clear to the womb if you did it right. Magdalena had spent the first two years of her life here. One might have thought she would have had more to remember now, inching her way through rush-hour traffic, caught among the absurd asphalt circles and bronze effigies that marked the Boulevard de Héroes. But as always, she came up short, which made her melancholy, filling her with nostalgia for a history beyond her reach—Cartolandia on the eve of destruction, the place of her birth.

The Americans called it Cardboardland. It had been the first thing you saw, crossing the border—a shantytown of cardboard boxes, makeshift houses, and abandoned cars. Yet Cartolandia had its own employment center, its own food cooperative and health clinic. Its history was no less colorful than its appearance, born of subversion, often violent, its first incarnation an organized invasion by veterans of the Mexican Revolution, in protest of foreign-owned land and lack of jobs.

The ensuing struggle for the Tijuana floodplain seesawed back and forth over the decades that followed. Eventually, however, a consortium of businessmen and politicians eager for development was successful in persuading the Mexican government to reclaim the land as a national resource, to label the residents as squatters, even though many had purchased their lots through the Ministry of Agriculture or paid rent to the local banks. Residents responded by staging protests, filing petitions. And then came an El Niño winter of particular ferocity and with it the rains. There were rumors in Cartolandia that the opposition was planning to open the floodgates of the Rodríguez Dam. Some residents fled, others stayed to fight. On the twenty-ninth of January, the government issued a statement denying the rumors. On the thirtieth of January, the floodgates were opened. A hundred people drowned that night, Magdalena's mother and grandmother among them. Magdalena was found at dawn, on a set of box springs with the family dog, and raised by the Sisters of the Benediction in Mexicali. She was lucky. The orphanage was a good one. The mother superior took a special interest in her, arranging for her to attend the Catholic grammar School in Calexico, orchestrating transportation, providing her with the gift of English, and yet a price had been exacted. For six years she'd been driven back and forth, across the border. There had been little chance for friendships with her classmates outside of the school. She came from another country in the company of nuns, and these made of her a curiosity, a child set apart. By the time she entered junior high school in Mexicali she'd been more proficient in English than in Spanish. By time she finished high school she was accomplished in both, a marketable skill. It made the other things possible. She now worked for an attorney in Tijuana while going to school part time, taking night classes in environmental law at the Universidad Autónoma de Baja California, situated on the Mesa de Otay, within sight of the banks and shopping centers of the Zona del Río, the new Tijuana. It was what she had wanted. Each day was a reminder here, each commute a trip in time, a consorting with ghosts.

The sky had begun to color by the time she reached the mesas. The factories were changing shifts and she fell in behind a convoy of buses, which were ubiquitous. Day and night they chugged in and out of the mesas like so many gigantic blue insects with their loads of workers, from the *colonias* to the factories and back again. She sometimes thought of the foreign-owned factories as the parts of some monstrous organism dropped from the heavens, settling its tentacles into the arid ground, reaching deep into the heart of her country. With the advent of NAFTA, the monster had grown stronger and fatter, with more factories, more pollution, greater abuse of the workers—the very things she had come to fight, in her mother's name, in the name of the planet. She thumped the steering wheel with the butt of her hand, blowing her horn. The buses made no attempt to let her by. They lumbered on. Magdalena looked at her watch. She honked a few more times just for the hell of it then settled back, resigned, inhaling exhaust. It was all too perfect. While the buses fouled the road in their efforts to feed the monster, she rushed to join the residents of Vista Nueva in mourning what the monster had wrought.

The community in question occupied a tract of land at the foot of the mesa. Above it hunkered the remains of Reciclaje Integral, a deserted smelting and battery recycling plant. For years the residents of Vista Nueva had reported skin ulcers, respiratory ailments, birth defects. A number of children had died. Magdalena was proud to have had a part in getting the factory shut down. It was her first year at the university and the attorney she worked for was handling the case. And the case was going well.

When it became apparent that charges would be brought against him in a Mexican court, however, the owner, an American, simply filed for bankruptcy in Mexico, left the factory as it stood, and withdrew across the border, where he continued to prosper. Magdalena had never seen him face-to-face, only in pictures—a middle-aged man with silver hair. His name was Conrad Hunter. He lived in a million-dollar house somewhere in San Diego County while his deserted plant continued to poison the residents of Vista Nueva. And of course the government of her own country, always a friend of business, did not think it their job to pursue the culprit, or to clean up the mess he had left behind.

In tears, she had gone to the attorney she worked for, a woman by the name of Carlotta. They had taken coffee on the little patio behind the office, sitting together in wrought-iron chairs as the sun crossed a corner of sky.

"There's a story to make you crazy in every quarter of the city," Carlotta had told her, "on every block."

"Right," Magdalena had said. "But what about this guy Hunter? We're just going to sit here?"

"We are appealing to the CEC."

The CEC was a secretariat of NAFTA: the Commission for Environmental Cooperation. The point of the appeal, as Magdalena understood it, was to expose the CEC as little more than a toothless lion. It was an exercise. She said as much to Carlotta.

"A necessary exercise," Carlotta said.

"But still an exercise."

Carlotta had arranged her fingers like the peaked roof of a tiny church then looked at Magdalena across their tips. "There is a point of American law," she said. "It's called Minimum Contact. It goes something like this: If we could establish a connection between this guy in San Diego and some other business here, in Mexico, it might be possible to go after him over there, bring charges against him in the States."

"Then why . . ."

"Because it's a difficult thing to prove. It's time consuming. You need some kind of paper trail that will stand up in court."

Magdalena had asked for the job.

"You got it," Carlotta told her. "If you can build a case against Mr. Hunter, great. If you can't, remember this: Reciclaje Integral is not the only game in town. So look around. Find me a case. Any case. If we can prosecute just one of these people, we've got a precedent to go after more."

And that was the beginning of Magdalena's files. She called them the Dolores Rivera files, in honor of her mother. The project became her obsession. There were a dozen sites like Reciclaje Integral just along the highway that led from Tijuana to Tecate—foreign-owned, toxic, and abandoned, and God knew how many more scattered throughout the country. She began with the collection of factual reports, one for each of the sites. She made lists of the sites' owners then set about searching for any ties to Mexico, any at all. The process was both time consuming and expensive, expensive because any search done through a public agency, such as the Registry for Property and Commerce, had to be paid for and this she did from her own pocket. She also collected old case files, curious about repeat offenders, and on occasion, original inspection reports. She took some pride in the acquisition of the original reports, as each could only be gotten from the person who'd written it. The reports were simple and to the point. They named names. Once a case was filed and put into the system, the reports were copied, and there was always the chance that they might be compromised. If the complaint for which the report had been written never made it into the system, the reports were often discarded, or otherwise lost. This made of the originals an invaluable source from which to acquire the names of offenders, so that these in turn might be compared to other names from other sources, both now and in the future. And so it went. Her files grew to fill an entire room, in offices already pressed for space. After eighteen months, the files represented as complete a picture of environmental and labor abuses along the Mexico-California border as one was likely to find. By sheer volume they were unique. In their assemblage of original inspection reports they were irreplaceable. Taken altogether they were an exceptional resource. Everyone said so. Yet the children of Vista Nueva continued to suffer.

Then something happened. Someone had broken into Carlotta's offices, destroying computers, ransacking files. An attempt had been made to burn them out. The fire department had been quick. Still, much had been lost. Magdalena had taken her remaining files and moved them into hiding. Every case Carlotta handled was potentially dangerous. Any case involving environmental wrongdoing in Mexico would by its nature involve governmental corruption. The laws were on the books. People were simply paid to look the other way. Everyone had an agenda. Every case generated new enemies, potential suspects. They would both, Carlotta warned her, have to be very careful. The older woman was worried. Magdalena had seen it in her face. Magdalena was ecstatic, caught on the wave of some adrenaline high. She was convinced that whoever had broken into the offices had been after something in her files. Word of their existence had gotten out. The enemy had been engaged. It was her reason for being, the reason she had come home, back to Tijuana, the scene of her mother's murder.

It was dark when she finally reached the old factory and her thoughts shifted from the case against Reciclaje Integral to other events that had transpired here during the past weeks: Three young women, all factory workers, had been murdered on the dirt pathways that led from the factories to the *colonias* below. The women had been raped, strangled, and mutilated, then left among the weeds and refuse that cluttered the hillsides—a common-enough crime along the Mexican border, where the women worked in the factories and the men loitered, unemployed, and the gangs ruled the streets. In this case however, Magdalena had known one of the victims. She had interviewed the woman when they'd first begun the case against the plant, had known her as a sister in arms, and now felt both violated and diminished by her passing. She supposed it was how one ought to feel, about any such crime. And yet the world was so full of death. If one were to feel violated and diminished by each there were be little of oneself left to go around. She judged it a risk of her chosen profession, in a land where the murdered factory girl and the dead boy whose vigil she'd come to attend were but two sides of the same coin—the price her country seemed more than happy to pay in its slow ascension to the lights.

She parked in front of the old smelting plant then sat for a moment to observe her surroundings—a precaution she would not have taken a month before. But the shifts were still changing in a nearby factory and there was activity in the street, food vendors and buses, workers, predominantly women in blue smocks and hairnets, conversing in groups, sharing cigarettes, some dancing to the music that spilled from their plastic ghetto blasters. As Magdalena got out of her car, she was recognized by one of the women, who waved a greeting. Magdalena waved back, taking in the smells of sizzling tacos, the exhaust of the buses, the reek of chemicals and burning rubber. She smiled in spite of herself. Welcome to the Mesa de Otay, she thought, the soiled heart of the monster.

Upon her return to Tijuana, Magdalena had spent time at a women's center known as Casa de la Mujer. Established to aid the young women streaming north to work in the factories, it had grown into an all-purpose facility where Magdalena had done everything from teaching classes in personal hygiene to facing down drunken husbands. The work was strictly voluntary and of late she'd not had time for it, but she was glad to have done it for it had put her in touch with women throughout the city, some of them activists and some in need. She supposed the woman who waved had been one of the latter. Under other circumstances she might have walked over to find out, to see how things were going. On the evening in question she waved and went on, thinking that when her workload had lightened she would have to spend more time with the women of Casa de la Mujer. It was frontline work, similar in spirit to her work with Carlotta, but taken to the street, where the game was faster, the victories more tangible, if not, perhaps, as thoroughgoing as what might be won in the halls of justice amid paper trails and writs.

She walked back across the front of the condemned building, its doors and windows sealed, the plywood that prevented entrance decorated with spray-painted warnings of PELIGRO and CONTAMI-NACIÓN together with skulls and crossbones. She noted too a smattering of gang graffiti, together with a crudely painted devil, replete with horns and forked tail, the artists apparently blind to the contaminants already leaching in ugly, colored stains through the cinderblock walls. She seemed to recall hearing there was even a homeless person, evidently deranged, rumored to have taken up residence there—yet one more reason to be rid of the place. The thought of someone actually trying to camp amid those ruins made her shudder and she turned onto the dirt path that led between Reciclaje Integral and its nearest neighbor, a sprawling auto shop surrounded by corrugated tin and barbed wire. It was the kind of path from which the women of the past weeks had been abducted. Soon, however, she was within sight of the mourners on the bluffs at the rear of the factory, the lights of Vista Nueva at their feet.

Most of those in attendance were women from the community below and Magdalena knew them well. She was greeted with hugs and kisses, then provided with a candle and a paper party cup. The cup had a little hole punched in the bottom to make way for the candle and was meant to protect the flame. When lit from within the cups appeared as tiny inverted lamps hung upon the night air. But it was unusually cold and breezy atop the mesa and the delicate lights were difficult to maintain.

A small group of students from the university had come with guitars. They had taken to the high ground—a broad mound of dirt where they sat strumming inspirational songs and at whose base were the scattered remains of an old refrigerator, gleaming like the bones of some dismembered animal in the scant light. A trio of documentary filmmakers had come as well. The filmmakers were from Seattle. They were making a movie about the maquiladoras and had been told about the vigil. They had a single handheld camera and a powerful spotlight with which they periodically washed the walls of the old factory and blinded the mourners. Magdalena was introduced to the film's director, a young woman with high-topped black sneakers and a pierced nostril. The director was interested in interviewing Magdalena for her film and wanted to do so in her Spanish, which was limited. "It's okay," Magdalena told her. "We can use English." The director persisted in her poor Spanish. But then the questions were simple and inevitable. Who is responsible? Why hasn't the Mexican government acted by now? Why is the man allowed to do business in the United States when his factory is still killing people in Mexico? Magdalena answered by rote then disengaged to circulate among her friends.

The women of Vista Nueva were understandably obsessed with the recent murders and not quite able to leave it alone, even here, at the vigil for the young boy. Theories were advanced. Two of the girls who had died had been moonlighting as taxi dancers in the old red-light district, where a certain amount of credence was being given to a folktale in which a handsome, blue-eyed stranger stalks the floors of the brothels and dance halls. According to the legend, the stranger is the devil himself, come to carry away Tijuana's fallen angels. Apparently one of the recent victims had been seen talking to a flashy young cowboy in a red convertible shortly before her death. The man had come to visit her during a break at the factory but she'd told her friends of meeting him on the dance floor at one of the clubs. The story was repeated here in hushed tones amid gusting winds as the students sang, as the spotlight swept the walls . . . Other theories were advanced as well, without recourse to the supernatural. For Magdalena, however, the talk only added to the gloom of the event and when she had made her rounds and her candle had gone out for about the fifteenth time, she said her good-byes and made her exit.

The truth was, she was not feeling altogether well. She had been putting in long days of late, cramming for exams, working for Carlotta then sitting up till nearly first light, alone with her files, searching for clues as to who might have invaded the offices. The pace was beginning to take its toll, accounting perhaps for the creeping depression she had experienced upon the bluff. That a number of local officials had been invited and failed to show was hardly surprising. But on the evening in question their absence seemed only to fuel her depression, as did the film director, with her poor Spanish and simple questions. Ditto for the nervous twittering of the young women from the *colonia*, reminding her yet again of how naive and uneducated so many of these people were— her people after all—that they should entertain folktales of handsome strangers with cloven hoofs while the real Devil, such as he was, was made manifest all around them, his form as shifting as the vapors that seeped from the factories to cover the old border town like a dirty blanket, and she had been hard-pressed to refrain from saying so. But the night was for mourning and not for lectures. What was called for, she concluded, was a hot bath, a night's sleep, maybe even a day or two back at Casa de la Mujer, where she could lead a strike, demonstrate the use of condoms, and face down a drunken boyfriend or two, all in the space of forty-eight hours—a little something to raise the blood, and so thinking she slipped out the way she had come, on the narrow footpath between the factory and the body shop with its pack of scrawny watchdogs barking at her in the dark.

At one point along the path, she thought she heard something move behind the block wall of the factory—something too large to be a rodent—and she quickened her step. She reached the car without incident, got quickly inside, and drove away.

◆　◆　◆

She took a different route going home, skirting Cerro Colorado, through La Florita, the district of the flowers, then picking up Mex One as it swept down from the mesa, on its way to the sea. It was here that she realized the car was not handling well. This was not without precedent. She drove a 1989 Ford Taurus with bald tires, a torn headliner, and somewhere over two hundred thousand miles. But who was counting? One thing about Mexico, its mechanics were the best; you kept them in spare parts, they could keep anything running. And the country was made of spare parts.

The lights of Las Playas danced below her. She would be home soon. Tomorrow she would call the garage. But as she started into a long right-hand curve there was a loud cracking sound from the front end of her car. The steering wheel jerked beneath her hands and suddenly she was unable to steer. She hit the brakes. The car began to slide. It was unimaginable. She had seen the lights of home, yet here she was, trapped inside a metal projectile, unable to maneuver, hurtling down a hillside at sixty miles an hour, and it had happened just like that, in the wink of an eye.

She clung to the wheel with both hands, trying by force of will if necessary to turn away from the skid, to hold the car on her side of the road, then watched as the double yellow line passed beneath her, as the inevitable headlights made their appearance, as the night filled with the thundering blast of an air horn . . . She shut her eyes, anticipating impact, the plastic wheel rushing to crush the bones of her chest. Yet somehow the truck missed her. The car rocked in the wake of its passing—a no doubt momentary respite. Magdalena screamed. She screamed for the car to stop. She screamed in the face of what she saw—her own death—a smear of gore upon the highway. A rocky shoulder appeared before her, and beyond that, the side of the mountain from which the road had been cut. She shut her eyes once more. The car slammed broadside into the mountain. The impact bounced her head off the driver's side window. And still the car continued to move, its interior filling with dust, choking her screams, grinding away toward some final resting place above the lights of Las Playas, wed to the flank of the old mountain as surely as if God had intended it.

And that was where she sat, in the dampness of bodily fluids, confounded by her own survival. She seemed reluctant to give up the wheel, but sat still gripping it amid clouds of dust, the reek of gasoline, as rocks of various sizes continued to rain from the mountainside. One came through the windshield, striking the dash. The event suggested an imminent death. In time, however, even the sporadic landslides seemed to pass and she was alone with the hissing of a dead engine, the popping of hot metal, cooling in the night, and finally, as from a great distance, the sound of footsteps on the highway. Her eyes ticked to the rearview mirror. She saw a moving shadow in dim light. Still, she was ready to be helped and she reached to undo her seat belt even as someone began to tug on the passenger side door. The door no longer opened smoothly. The car rocked. The door released with a loud pop then swung back, groaning upon its hinges. Magdalena put her head against the headrest and closed her eyes, awaiting a voice, a helping hand. What she got was silence, the sound of surf from the far side of the road—which struck her as odd. Even in her condition she was capable of this observation, that there was something wrong with the silence, the muffled pounding of surf, and she turned to look.

At first there was only the night sky, a few faint stars scattered above the sea, and then a man, bending to peer into her car. The man was ragged and unwashed, missing teeth. He wore a leather jacket over a naked torso, a large Aztec sun tattooed upon his abdomen. She knew about the missing teeth because the man was grinning like a hyena, which, under the circumstances, she was willing to take as a bad sign.

A kind of sickness swept over her then—a dark thing that cut to the bone. There was no way out on her side of the car. The man reached inside and began to pull at her arm. She hardly knew how it happened. One second she was frozen behind the wheel, the next she was outside, the wind on her face, her back against the ruined car. And still, no words had been spoken.

The men were two in number. She could see them clearly now. The man with the missing teeth continued to hold her by the arm. His grip was strong and cold. "Check it out," he said. The missing teeth gave him a lisp. "The bitch is still alive."

The other man was standing a few feet away, in the middle of the road, looking back in the direction from which they had come, a shadowy figure, yet close enough for her to see an eyeball tattooed in the bald spot at the back of his head.

The man who held her appeared to be waiting for the other to give instructions. "Maybe we should take her to the beach," he said.

Magdalena waited with him, staring into the tattooed eye. It had no lids but floated there as a perfect orb, trailing gore, as though recently plucked from another's skull. The effect was both dispiriting yet oddly mesmerizing as quite suddenly the entire scene went up in lights and one more truck, like the one that had narrowly missed killing her, came barreling down upon them.

The truck seemed to fill the entire road and as the man farthest from the car danced to avoid being struck, Magdalena managed to free a hand and began to wave. The toothless man cursed in her face, reclaiming her arm then bending it behind her back. He put his weight against her, pinning her to the wrecked car. She slammed her forehead into his nose. Cartilage cracked against her skull. Blood sprayed her skin. The man's hand flew to his face and Magdalena broke free, directly into the path of the coming truck.

What followed was a cacophony of horns and brakes, a storm of dancing lights and burning rubber. Magdalena ran toward the far side of the road, the huge truck jackknifing behind her, sliding into what was left of her car. Given the immense weight of the truck, the sound that accompanied this collision was like a heavily booted foot crushing an empty aluminum can. Magdalena did not look back. At her feet was a long sloping shoulder that dropped to a dirt road. The road ran to the border, skirting the last of the Tijuana beaches. There was little time to think. She launched herself from the shoulder, half running, half falling. She covered the last few yards on her ass, in a landslide of dirt and gravel. She could hear them above her. She heard voices raised in anger and then a gunshot. And she began to run once more. She ran for the steel fence and the lights of the border patrol. She chanced a look over one shoulder and saw them coming—little more than shadows, the dust of their descent hanging above the highway where the lights of the truck continued to burn.

Magdalena ran on. Surely, she thought, the border police would have to see; they would have to come . . . But the dirt road stretched out empty before her and she could not risk a foot race to the fence. She cut instead between a pair of tiny wooden shacks that sold colored ice to the children, locked and boarded for the night, then stumbled into the sand. Unfortunately the move was not enough to elude the men. Where, she wondered, was the goddamn patrol? She ran toward the border—not fifty yards away, yet the men were still behind her. She went directly toward the fence, waving her arms, calling for help. A spotlight swept the beach from the U.S. side. She ran to that place where the light pooled in the sand. A shot rang out at her back. The sand jumped not a yard in front of her. My God, she thought, they will stop at nothing. And she made for the water, where it was only after she had lost her footing on the uneven bottom and felt the cold, that the rashness of this act became clear to her. It was only then, unable to stand, that she remembered the terror of Las Playas.

The current took her at once, stronger than any man. She was carried north, fighting to breathe, to call for help. The huge fence loomed above her, repository of crosses, the names of the dead—the infamous fence. In Las Playas they died among its narrow pilings on a regular basis, pinned there like so many exotic insects by the powerful currents that swept the beach, the currents she had failed to consider. And she had seen how it would be, drowned at the border like one more clueless pilgrim, within shouting distance of the river that had taken her mother. The irony drove her to renewed efforts. She struck out with her arms, pulling for the beach, but already the fence was upon her. She slipped beneath the surface, striking a post with her shoulder. Incredibly, however, the terrible fence seemed to give way beneath her. She clutched at something in the darkness—ragged metal that cut her hands then crumbled in her grasp as suddenly she was through. For an instant her head broke the surface and she saw the big fence one more time, sliding away from her now, moving south as the currents swept her north. She would drown, she concluded, in the land of the free. Whereupon a big wave broke directly on top of her, taking her wind, driving her down. She thrashed in the darkness, in the terrible creeping cold, till death was something she could taste, and in the end she gave herself to it . . .

Later, in the days that would follow, amid delirium and fever, she would remember that she had given up—she who had always been so proud of her resolve, a believer in the strength of will. She had quit on life. But a strong arm had taken her. At least this was how it had seemed, that in the absence of hope, a strong arm had found her, and pulled her—it could not have been more than a few yards—to that place where her feet touched bottom so that in the end she actually staggered from the sea beneath her own power to lie half dead and gasping on a broad beach, sky above, earth below, and no sign at all of anyone or anything that might have helped her, though once, gaining her knees, blinking the salt from her eyes, she believed that she had seen something—a spectral figure, half clothed, hovering at the edge of a dune. But the image seemed to fade before her eyes, dissolving like ectoplasm into the gray predawn light as if the light itself had begotten it, so that when it was gone and she was alone on the beach she could not be sure if what she had seen was a thing that truly existed or only some trick of the morning—an image brought forth out of water and air. She had called out anyway, her voice thin and wavering, every bit as ethereal as whatever it was she had called out to. There had been no answer. No voice on the beach save her own. And yet this was the story she had to tell. Had it happened on the Mexican side of the fence they would have brought flowers, there would have been a shrine, a visit by a priest. Pilgrims would have thrown themselves to the waves, to Our Lady of Las Playas.

On the U.S. side of the fence, there was only this Fahey, the man who had followed her into the dunes, who had killed the dogs, and so she told him. She told him of the wraithlike presence, of the currents and the men on the road, of the fence that had broken beneath her, and of the names of the dead . . .

The words came in torrents. The man listened, or so it seemed. Her surroundings were unclear. They came and went. Once she opened her eyes to find the man bending over her. He appeared to be wearing a T-shirt with a picture of a worm on the front. The worm was brilliant green with a yellow stomach. It wore sunglasses and a cowboy hat. A bubble above the worm's head contained the words "Worm Farming Can Be Fun." She thought that perhaps she had begun to hallucinate. At her side was a table lamp in the shape of a hula girl with a shade beaded by dusty fringe while above the man's head there was what she took to be a surfboard suspended by canvas straps. She watched as the surfboard multiplied and began to rotate, at first like the blades of a fan, then morphing into a kind of pinwheel and spinning points of light. In a moment of lucidity she concluded that it was the cuts, the bad water. She felt the onset of chills, a deep pain snaking through her lower abdomen. The wheel of lights spun faster. She saw the man once more—a weathered face framed by beard and matted hair. He seemed to be bending over her, eyes so bloodshot as to appear both blue and red. The colors of his flag, she thought. She felt his breath upon her skin. A wave of fear swept through her. "I'm going to be sick," she told him.

4

THE COWBOYS were putting a burro into a horse trailer when they caught sight of Fahey's truck raising dust on the Dairy Mart Road. It was early and the dust was nearly indistinguishable from the pale rags of fog still drifting above the marsh grass of the estuary.

The cowboys, as Fahey liked to call them, were employed by the California Department of Parks and Recreation. Each carried a business card designating them as "workers" for the Tijuana River National Estuarine Research Reserve. Their names were Jack Nance and Deek Waltzer and they drew modest salaries for maintaining Border Field State Park, where as part of their duties they cleared trail and mended fences. Their preferred mode of transportation for this work was horseback—in part because there were horse trails across the valley, from the freeway to the beach, and people willing to ride there, particularly in the summer months when the valley was deemed to be less toxic, and in part because they loved horses and all things connected to them. They were frequenters of the rodeo, especially the illegal Mexican rodeos staged by the Oaxacan Indians in a section of the valley known as Garage Door Tijuana—a labyrinth of corrals, stables, and ramshackle housing screened from public view by scores of cast-off garage doors strung together in a crazy quilt of makeshift fences and behind which the Oaxacans were more or less free to carry on as they pleased. The San Diego sheriff's department held jurisdiction there, as throughout the valley, but unless someone was murdered in broad daylight, they seemed content to leave the Tijuana River Valley to the park rangers and border patrol, to the assorted cowboys, truck farmers, Indians, environmentalists, drug runners, bandidos, and burro eaters who either made the place their home or at least the source of some meager income.

Deek had lived in the valley for nearly thirty years and liked to say that it was neither America nor Mexico, but rather a country unto itself and that was what he loved about it. Jack compared the valley to the forbidden zone in *Planet of the Apes,* a vast wasteland caught between the gates of two cities, a repository of fringe dwellers and secret histories. Jack had lived in his car till he was thirty-five, when a woman had gotten him out, but she was long gone and he lived now on the Otay Mesa in the back of a pickup where his family had left him some land and where he could ride his horse to work each day in the valley below. Deek lived in Garage Door Tijuana with the Oaxacan Indians in a thirty-foot travel trailer. He'd come to the valley so far down on his luck that the first job he'd taken was driving for Blue Line Cabs, a taxi company notorious for running illegals across the border in the seventies and eighties. In short, the cowboys, like Fahey himself, were representative of what the valley attracted, and one could not quite imagine things working out for them anywhere else.

Jack Nance, who now was forty-two years old and still rode the occasional wave, when he could find one small enough, on a long board off the beaches just north of San Diego, remembered Fahey from his days of drug running for the Island Express. And once at daybreak, on a huge winter swell now some twenty years past, he'd parked atop Spooner's Mesa with a handful of friends and a bag of dope to watch the waves beyond the mouth of the Tijuana River—like rolling mountains of water, their peaks lost to the fog, somewhere out past Third Notch, and had seen both Hoddy Younger and his protégé, Sam the Gull Fahey, ride what just might have been the Mystic Peak.

Deek Waltzer, thirty years older than Jack Nance, and not a surfer, knew Fahey only as a recluse and convicted felon, the proprietor of the Fahey Worm Farm, an establishment of such dubious reputation it was known even among the migrants he'd driven from the border, back in the day, and he missed no opportunity to disparage the man's character.

"That was the old man," Nance would tell him. "Back in the day. Fahey's different."

To which Deek would only shake his head, stating with dead certainty that to this day the name of Fahey was still maligned among the Indians and the farm measured as a place to avoid, if only to escape its restless spirits.

But Jack was willing to dismiss such judgments with a wave of the hand. "Sam Fahey was a surfer, still is, if you ask me. There's nothing out there to be afraid of now."

"Probably still a drug runner too, if he's anything at all," Deek might respond, at times going so far as to challenge Jack's story at its very core. "Maybe it wasn't even him you saw out there that day," he'd say. "You ever think of that? Maybe that was someone else and Fahey just took credit for it because he's a liar and a thief like his old man. And you were looking at those waves from a long way off. You've said so yourself."

But Jack would only offer up a sad smile and say that he knew quite well what he had seen. "It was him, you stubborn son of a bitch. It was the Gull and Younger. They rode the Mystic Peak and as far as I know no one's done it since."

"Yeah, well, they're not likely to either, now that the water's all fucked up."

"They're not likely to 'cause the guys that ride waves like that are all over in the Islands, or off in Tahiti, or up in Northern California, pulling each other into them on a bunch of fucking Jet Skis. It's not like it was."

To which Deek was apt to reply that nothing was like it was and this would give both men pause, after which Deek would go on, "And I guess you're going to tell me he's not like he was either."

"No," Jack would say, "he's not."

"And what do you suppose happened?"

It was the question many such conversations came to in the end and Jack had yet to answer it. "There's some guys," he would say, "they get all the gifts, and they piss it all away."

And that was about the best Jack could do and the older man knew it. "Yeah," he said. "And some are just born bad." It was generally his final word on the subject.

"Some are born to sweet delight. Some are born to endless night." And those were often Jack's last words, the only lines of poetry he'd ever committed to memory, and these not taken from any book but from a movie in which they were so quoted but which, regardless of their source, seemed to have some particular application to the life of Sam the Gull Fahey, which Jack Nance was apt to see as both a profound mystery and cautionary tale.

The cowboys watched as Fahey parked his truck and walked over to where they stood with the burro. He was wearing a filthy pair of jeans and a sweatshirt with an absurd-looking worm airbrushed across the front. His hair fell to his shoulders, sun-streaked and tangled. In general, he appeared wild and unkempt. His eyes were tucked away behind dark glasses, the lenses black as two chunks of coal, the frames held together with silver duct tape.

"Where'd you get the zebra?" Fahey asked them.

The burro had been tricked out with black and white stripes, spray-painted as though it was the product of industry and not a living thing. The street vendors of Tijuana seemed to think it pleased the tourists.

"Found him on the beach," Deek said. "What brings you over here? One of your worms get away?"

Fahey was still looking at the burro. "What part of the beach?" he asked.

"He was up by Border Field," Jack told him. "You remember that old storm drain used to run down out of Las Playas? Well, somebody's dug it out again. Fucking thing runs right under the fence. Been wide open for three weeks. You'd think the border patrol would've found it by now."

"I guess you could always tell them."

Jack just smiled. "Let 'em find it on their own," he said. "Keeps things interesting."

Fahey knew all about the old storm channel, that and every other route of passage between the valley and Mexico. The truth was, he was sorry to hear someone had opened it back up, but he saw no reason to say so. He was thinking about the woman he'd left sleeping in his bed, and for a short time all three men stood there in silence. Fahey looked at the burro. The animal was staring back at him from the side of the trailer, its long ears rotating in the slatted light. "What will you do with it?" Fahey asked.

"Wash him up, drive him out to the adoption center on the way to Trona."

"His good luck then."

"No shit. Fish and Game said they put you onto those dogs."

"I've got three of them in the truck."

The men walked over to have a look.

"Damn," Deek said. "You got right on top of them."

"Actually, it was the other way around."

With the woman sleeping, Fahey had risen early and gone to get the dogs. He would stop in at Fish and Game for the bounty, then on to the animal shelter in San Ysidro where the dogs' bodies could be disposed of. After that he would try to find some medicine for the woman.

"If someone got sick from the water, what would you give them?" Fahey asked. He waved toward the ocean, a silver strip of which might be seen catching sunlight above the greenery of the valley.

The cowboys traded looks. "Drinking it or swimming in it?" Deek asked him.

"Swimming. But there were cuts."

Deek looked him over to see if he was talking about himself.

Fahey waited in the rising heat.

"Wash the cuts with Betadine," Jack told him. "Get some Cipro, probably five hundred milligrams twice a day. Bill Daniels told me there were four dogs."

"There were these and a border collie. The collie got away."

"What happened?" Jack asked him.

"I shot and missed."

The cowboys just looked at him.

"Okay," he said at length. "Betadine and Cipro . . . Thanks for the tip."

He went to the cab of his truck and got inside.

Jack Nance waited a moment then walked over to the open window. "Good south swell running," he said.

Fahey looked out over the valley, toward Mexico, just long enough to suggest he might actually be giving the matter of the swell some thought. "Yeah," he said. "I noticed." Fahey started the truck.

"They say we've got an El Niño in the works. Suppose to come early."

Fahey nodded.

"I've had my eye on this typhoon's been brewing off the Philippines. You get that thing bumping into a good storm out of Siberia, who knows . . . We could get something down here." He gave it a moment to see if Fahey would respond. "You ever look at that site I showed you?"

When Jack Nance heard Fahey had gotten online to sell his worms, he'd provided him with the link to a surfer's website that tracked storms and predicted swells. Fahey had looked at it a couple of times before deciding it was a waste of time. He wasn't going anywhere. There would be waves or there wouldn't be. He would ride them or he wouldn't and there was nothing the site could tell him about that.

"Listen," Jack said. "I was wondering . . . you still set up to shape boards out there?"

Fahey just looked at him.

Jack fidgeted at the window. Fahey's look made him nervous, for reasons that would have been difficult to explain.

At length Fahey nodded.

"I was wondering if maybe you'd shape me one."

"What for? You going to ride the Mystic Peak?"

"Never in a million years. But I was thinking, it might be cool to have, you know, one of those guns like you and Younger used to shape . . ."

Fahey watched heat waves rippling at the foot of the mesas. "I guess you could come out some time. We could talk about it. Bring your checkbook."

Jack smiled. "And a case of beer."

Fahey put the truck in gear. He started to drive away then hit his brakes. The dust swirled around his open window. He leaned out and called back, "That Betadine . . . how do you use it, exactly?"

"You mix it with some distilled water, maybe half and half, take a cotton ball and wash out the cuts."

Fahey nodded. He pulled himself back into his truck and drove away.

The cowboys watched him go.

"Strange son of a bitch," Deek said. He took a can of Skoal from the pocket of his shirt and put a pinch between his cheek and gum.

Jack nodded. "We used to call him the Electric Gull."

"I know," Deek said. "You told me."

"He had this way of holding his arms when he surfed, like a gull swooping across the face of the wave. Kind of cool, though. Then he started eating a lot of acid so we called him the Electric Gull. But that's how I know it was him I saw that day, Outside the Bullring."

"The acid part I'll believe." Deek's clearest memory of the Electric Gull was that of Fahey stoned out of his gourd, staggering around in the middle of Ocean Boulevard at the foot of the pier, throwing empty beer bottles and yelling, "See the drunken Indian eat glass." The story did not pale in the retelling. In truth, Deek had been just a little bit frightened by Sam Fahey that night and found that he still could be, on occasion. The man had a way of filling up space Deek was not especially comfortable with, though he would probably never have come right out and said so. "I wouldn't go near him with a pole," was about as close to such feelings as the old cowboy was likely to get.

But Jack had heard it all before. "That was the night they unveiled the Surfhenge monument downtown. I believe the Gull was upset about something."

"Fucked up is what he was." Deek nodded after the departing truck. "What were you talking to him about before he left?"

"I was asking him about shaping me a board."

"Wha'd he say?"

"He said to bring my checkbook."

"Yeah, well . . . I wouldn't pay him till he was done."

"Hoddy Younger used to shape these big wave surfboards, back in the day. He shaped them for the straits. But people like Hap Baker, Buzzy Cline . . . they used to come down here and buy them from him on their way to the Islands. Younger taught the Gull how to shape. There's a kind of lineage there, you know. It would be a cool thing to get . . ." Jack's voice trailed away.

"While he's still alive, you mean."

Jack shrugged.

They watched the last of Fahey's dust, thinning before the sky.

"Betadine and Cipro. What do you suppose he's up to out there on the farm?"

Jack shrugged once more. "Who knows?"

Deek put a line of tobacco juice into the dirt, then stuffed his hands into the hip pockets of his jeans. "No good, most likely."

5

FAHEY DID AS the cowboys had suggested. He parked on the American side then walked across. Tijuana produced Betadine and Cipro. As a prudent measure he added Valium, Vicodin, and Percocet, and these for himself. He walked out of the pharmacy as broke as he'd entered Fish and Game to collect his bounty.

Panic attacks started amid the blue steel piping of the great cattle chute by which pedestrians were funneled back across the border, where apparently even the foot traffic had gotten bad since 9/11, sweating it out for an hour and a half amid the reek of humanity, the exhaust of passing cars. At his back an obese woman had fainted. Two men ahead of him were busted by border police and hauled away. It happened in utter silence, a scene from *The Twilight Zone*. Imagining intrigue beyond his wit, Fahey inched forward, broke cold sweats, crossed the border trailing water.

◆ ◆ ◆

For the next forty-eight hours she was sick as a dog. Fahey carried her from the bed to the bathroom and back again. He opened and closed windows. He bathed her cuts in the solution the cowboys had prescribed. He fixed ice chips in a bowl and heated cans of low-fat chicken broth that she would not touch till the evening of the third day, after which she slept through the night. By morning she was feeling well enough to thank him for his troubles.

"You've been very kind," she said. She was sitting up in his bed. Her hair was tousled and fell to her shoulders, black before the pale walls of his old trailer. It occurred to him that she had about her some aspect of a beautiful child wakened from a bad dream. He had given her a T-shirt and a pair of sweatpants to wear and the shirt hung from her slight frame, settling about her waist like the folds of a tent. Blankets covered her legs. So wrapped she might have been made of sticks but Fahey had just spent the better part of three days caring for her and though he'd done his best to give her as much privacy as he could he had noted in spite of himself that she was a long way from skin and bones—long-limbed in spite of her height, delicate and yet sinewy beneath a rather startling expanse of copper-colored skin. In truth he found her rather exotic though it might also be noted that he harbored a weakness for things injured, for the bird with the broken wing, for wild things found hurt in the valley. It had always been so. And yet he had not always been successful in saving such things and there had been a time, with this woman, with her face on fire beneath his palm, her long lashes fluttering upon the flushed skin of her cheek, when he had wondered if he had not made a mistake in agreeing to care for her, though now that her fever had broken he was beginning to feel like maybe it had been okay, that he was off the hook, and he told her of his fears. "I was beginning to wonder if I'd made a mistake," he said, "in not taking you to the hospital."

"You did the right thing," she told him. "Believe me. You did." She turned to the window at her side, its louvered panes thick with dust, patched in duct tape. The window looked out on a small, ragged garden—yellow chrysanthemums, waist-high above a stand of weeds.

"How long?" she asked.

Fahey told her, then watched her hand tighten on a corner of the blanket.

"And I'm behind in my work," he added.

"I'm sorry," she said. "It must be my fault."

"I don't need much of an excuse. But today? The buck stops here . . . as they say," Fahey's idea of banter. Christ, he thought. Christ almighty. But then it had been a long time since there had been a woman in his bed and there followed a moment of awkward silence. "Listen," Fahey said finally. "Maybe you'd like to come out to the porch. I could fix you a chair."

He watched her smile for the first time.

"That would be nice," she said.

Fahey carried pillows to one of the old redwood loungers he kept in the little room he'd built along one side of the trailer. The room had begun as a deck. Over time he'd added plywood walls with large, screened windows and a tin roof. He helped her to the chair, fixed a pillow for her head, and put a blanket over her feet.

"You can watch me bring in the herd," he told her.

She narrowed her eyes against the glare, looking out across Fahey's land. "What herd?" she asked.

Fahey went to one of the white boxes stacked beneath a screen just outside the room. He came back with a handful of black, moist soil in which a number of reddish worms could be seen wriggling in his palm. "These guys," he told her.

Magdalena looked at the worms. "I see," she said.

There followed several hours of hard work: Fahey on the farm, the Gull's three acres, shoveling red worms into the motorized harvester he'd bought used from a woman in Perris.

The harvester was six feet long, cylindrical in shape, and reminded Fahey of an amusement park ride—some small version of the hammers and loop-the-loops he'd ridden in supermarket parking lots as a boy, a noisy, rotating amalgamation of metal and mesh. It was comprised of three separated compartments. Into one he shoveled the contents of a windrow. The windrows, now three feet high and looking like no more than long lines of black dirt, had begun as shallow rows of cow manure into which the worms had been planted. As the worms fed, reproduced, and defecated the windrows had grown. The worm shit was known as castings. The worms were referred to as a herd. The roundup consisted of separating the castings from the herd. The harvester did its thing—sifting the contents through screens that would leave castings in one compartment and worms in another. Each could then be sold. The castings went principally to nurseries. The worms went mainly to individuals. Some owned bait shops. Some wanted to begin worm farms for themselves, others wanted to populate a garden. Fahey operated his own website. People ordered through it. The castings went into bags. The worms went into white, wooden boxes, along with a certain amount of soil. Fahey produced a third product as well—a substance known as worm tea, a mixture of water and castings allowed to simmer in the sun in large metal canisters the size of beer kegs. The worm tea could be placed into plastic bottles and sprayed over gardens or lawns. Fahey had explained these things to Magdalena. He had gone so far as to draw her a diagram of the harvester on a pad of ruled paper so she would know what went where. He had imagined that if she could follow what was going on, it might prove therapeutic. She could take a break from her devil in the mesa. Fahey had devils of his own to contend with. He knew about diversionary tactics.

Fahey drank as he worked. Beer. He kept a case on ice in a plastic trash container next to the vats of worm tea. The sun rose above Mexico, and came on, the heat with it. Fahey removed his shirt. He drank steadily. When one can was empty he would toss it into a container next to the one that held the beer and take another from the ice. The beer both invited speculation and dulled thought. It evoked memories yet held them at bay, enabling Fahey to observe them as one might observe a parade of tall ships passing through a fog.

Fahey's father had come to the river valley at the close of the 1960s, trailing creditors the way a dying animal trails buzzards, the last of his savings in hand, looking for an out and believing he'd found one, for by that time the Mexicans were not the only ones who wanted to develop the Tijuana River Valley. On the U.S. side, too, there were businessmen eager for development. There were also longtime residents, truck farmers and small-time ranchers in clapboard shacks and travel trailers set to blocks, who needed to be displaced before it could happen. In San Diego, the city fathers had requested federal funds to study the problem. They brought in the Army Corps of Engineers to recommend the channelization of the Tijuana River. Claiming an increase in land value, the city began to raise taxes on valley farmers, forcing many to sell. They sold to speculators banking on development. They sold to men like Lucian Fahey.

As in Mexico, this development did not go unopposed. Unlike their Mexican counterparts, however, the U.S. protesters eventually succeeded in demonstrating that the Tijuana Flood Control Project was in essence a thirty-million-dollar public subsidy for land speculators who stood to earn over one hundred million in profit. It was also deemed to be an ecological disaster, the valley being home to dozens of migratory birds and the last great saltwater estuary on the California coast. In the end, the project was stopped in its tracks. The large-scale color relief maps faded with time. Architectural drawings of marinas and hotels and oceanfront condos cracked and yellowed, turned nicotine-stained edges in drawers and dusty bins while the valley itself, empty now of its old inhabitants, their trailers gone, their shacks dozed or abandoned, went to mud and marsh and sandbar willow, tamarisk and wild radishes and marsh grass, sage, poppies, and yellow sumac. In summer it blistered, bone dry beneath the Mexican mesas. In winter the same mesas, home now to Mexico's burgeoning maquiladora industry, flowed with rain and toxic waste. These in turn mingled with the sewage and mud running down from the canyons, from the countless clapboard *colonias* erected overnight to house the peasants streaming north to work in the factories. It came by the ton, swamping the old Mexican treatment facility, joining itself to the Río de Tijuana, on its way to the sea, on the American side of the fence, so that after a few good rains the valley filled with mud and waste and was, for at least a portion of every year, an ecological disaster, though not of the type imagined by the people who had once battled the developers on its behalf.

The border patrol asked for high-risk pay. The Navy SEALs out of Coronado forsook the mud and empty beaches in favor of new training grounds, having lost too many of their number to a variety of exotic, flesh-eating bacteria. The migratory birds on the other hand seemed not to mind and the polluted ocean teemed with life. And of course there were still the immigrants who would stop at nothing, and the drug runners and bandidos, the handful of small-time farmers still clinging to their land, the cowboys, and assorted derelicts . . . And finally, there was Lucian Fahey, right down there among them, one of the people, having leveraged himself silly to all but steal the land from beneath some aging worm farmer, and just in time to see the whole scheme go belly up and who in the aftermath of this calamity was left with nothing to show for himself but more bad debt, an absentee wife, and a scrawny, towheaded kid he would just as soon have fed to the fishes, or the worms, or the beaner wetbacks and burro eaters. In short, he never took it well. Unlike that old miner in *The Treasure of the Sierra Madre*, when the gold dust blew to the four winds, Lucian Fahey wasn't laughing. He was deep in Chapter 11, sitting on a worthless worm farm in the goddamn toilet of the Western world.

His back to the wall, Lucian Fahey elected to work the land. He read a mail-order pamphlet on vermiculture as the road to riches then spent what little money he had left trying to rebuild his stolen worm farm. As was usual for the old man and as would prove true for his only son as well, his timing was impeccable, if, that is, one took into account its appeal to the grotesque. Those were especially hard years for would-be worm farmers, the business teeming with miscreants and scam artists. An especially popular form of subterfuge in those days was the buy-back scam in which a grower, promising to buy back the offspring, sold worms to a mark. When the appointed time for this transaction arrived, however, the grower was generally somewhere in Mexico or Chapter 11 and the mark was left without buyers, alone with a herd too small to attract the attention of more serious clients. Appalled at once again finding himself the object of such humiliations, Lucian Fahey made yet one more disastrous decision. He decided to build the size of his herd, possibly hoping to engage in a buy-back scam of his own. He did it on the cheap, of course. He brought in garden-variety yard clippings and other forms of green waste because they were less costly than manure, piled it on too thick, and caused his windrows to combust. The image that followed was a haunting one and Sam Fahey to this day could still see the gaunt figure of his father set before a patch of night sky turned to crimson by the flames of sizzling red worms and European night crawlers cowering amid the pall of his smoking windrows and bawling like a baby.

Fahey took it as a comment on the nature of life that he should only now find himself moved by the image of that broken old man. On the night in question he had been able to summon nothing but contempt. On the night in question, Fahey had been more interested in the direction of the wind than in his father's most recent calamity. On the night in question, the wind had been hot and dry, blowing down out of the canyons and the deserts beyond, promising clear skies and long, clean lines of surf. For Fahey was a surfer then. It was the act by which he defined himself and already he had begun to distance himself from the bitter and abusive old man whose calamities came so quickly, one upon the heels of the other, that Fahey had begun to suspect the two of them were not actually related. His mother must have been fucking the milkman, or the postman, or the guy in the ice-cream truck, or any bum on the street . . . anyone at all, save this scarecrow now howling at the edge of the great worm cookout. In the best of his fantasies, she had of course been fucking Hoddy the Dog Younger, the first and greatest in a long line of watermen who would come to challenge the big waves at the mouth of the Tijuana River.

A lanky cowboy out of the Dakota Badlands, one quarter Lakota Sioux, Hoddy Younger first rode the place in 1937 and never left. It was that kind of wave. He dubbed the spot Tijuana Straits and so it would be known, though principally among those watermen who, in time, would make of its liquid giants the stuff of myth and legend, much like the man who had authored the name.

Younger could have been any boy's hero, cowboy handsome and

cowboy tough. Hoddy could paddle a hundred-pound redwood surfboard a mile out to sea through lines of churning white water, lose it to a wipeout in thirty-foot waves, swim to shore in Mexico, walk back across the invisible line that then separated the two countries, retrieve his board from the beach, paddle back out and do it all over again, in the dead of winter, with nothing to keep him warm but an old-fashioned woolen bathing suit. As time passed, he came to ride the waves Island-style, always in trim, always in the fastest part of the wave, at one with the sea. A man of enormous physical power and charisma, he had many admirers but few close friends for he was also a strange and often silent man. If he liked you he would give you the shirt off his back. If he didn't, he wouldn't piss on you to put out the fire. For Sam the Gull Fahey, in the summer of his fifteenth year, Hoddy Younger did the unthinkable, he showed Fahey the lineups he used to surf the straits. He drew them in the wet sand with a stick—Goat Canyon, Smuggler's Gulch, Spooner's Mesa . . . He showed him how to find these landmarks from the water and how to line them up with the old Tijuana lighthouse at the edge of the bullring so that he could wait for the waves in the spots from which he would be able to catch and ride them. And it was Hoddy who pointed out to him that it was a mistake to call the fourth peak the Mystic Peak. Better, Hoddy said, to simply call it Outside the Bullring because that far out, the lineups didn't work anymore and one needed to be in tune to other, more subtle hints of seismic activity—like the eerie whistling sounds that seemed at times to emanate from among the great stones washed for a thousand years from the mouth of the river to create the broad alluvial fan that lay now beneath the surface of the sea, to form there the contours and configurations that allowed for the spot's thick, open ocean waves with their long, peeling shapes. This, or the sudden disappearance of the Coronado Islands, at which time one would do well to hit the deck of one's board and paddle for one's life in the general direction of the Baja Peninsula. In short, Hoddy taught him all he knew, and for a time there it really did seem that he had become the son Hoddy never had, and Hoddy the father of which any boy might have been proud, and in fact Hoddy renamed him as well, for it was Hoddy who dubbed him the Gull.

For many years, Hoddy never owned a house. He lived in a hut made from driftwood and whalebone tucked behind the dunes at the edge of the valley and he taught the Gull about more than the waves. He taught him how to run traps and lobster cages, where the wild squash and tomatoes grew, how to trade with the Mexicans in Tijuana before the coming of the fence. A man could live in the valley then, live off the land and the sea, for Hoddy was more than a surfer. He was a waterman and that, to the mind of the young Fahey, was not so much about practicality as it was about following a path. It was like finding religion, the Gull, his benediction.

Eventually, when the city of Imperial Beach, at that time little more than some vestige of the wild western towns that had once preceded it, decided it needed a lifeguard—which in turn was akin to the town of Tombstone deciding it needed a sheriff—they sent for Hoddy Younger. So that for a while the old surfer moved into a big wooden framed house right down on the sand at the edge of town and filled it up with aspiring surfers and gave them jobs as lifeguards because Hoddy believed, as the city fathers had believed before him, that any man who could handle himself in the straits could lifeguard for the city and this went for the Gull as well. Fahey was sixteen at the time, and those were the golden years, the days he went to now in his mind, days of offshore winds and evening glass-offs, of rides so long one's thighs burned at their ends. Then came the first in a series of El Niño winters and with it the waves—one great swell after another, sweeping down from the Gulf of Alaska. In Hawaii, at the All World Wave Masters Surfing Contest,

Jason Duane earned fifty thousand dollars and got his picture on the cover of half a dozen surfing magazines. In California, a stone's throw from the Mexican border, at the mouth of the Tijuana River, the Gull and Hoddy had ridden waves every bit as awesome, perhaps more so when one took into account the colder water, the longer swim, the absence of helicopters or other emergency vehicles. Yet the feat was witnessed by none save a carload of stoned locals, and even they lost much of it to the fog that had hovered upon the horizon all that day, so that in the end it was the Gull alone, caught inside, awaiting obliteration, who'd seen Younger on what just might have been one of the largest mountains of water ever ridden. It was not much more than a peek, really, for in a moment the very same wave that Hoddy was riding would send him diving for deep water, holding to the eel grass that grew among the stones to save himself from being pulled back up into the maelstrom above—another of Hoddy's tricks. And afterward there was the swim, rolling sets . . . Christ, he must have made land halfway to Rosarito, then walked home, frozen to the bone . . . Tacos and *cerveza* from the Mexicans who knew . . . And finally, Hoddy himself, waiting at the border, to shake his hand, for after all, Sam the Gull Fahey had ridden the Mystic Peak. He'd gotten a single wave of his own before Hoddy's monster had gotten him. And yet he had glimpsed something more. He had seen his mentor, dwarfed by the mountain he had ridden, the wave face turned to silver in a misty light—a vision by which to steer—and it had seemed to him on that morning, shivering on the beaches of his own home break, there was no end to what he might accomplish.

In the course of the next few winters, he and Hoddy had surfed Outside the Bullring twice more, neither so glorious as the first, yet with none but themselves for company . . . and such were the gleaming paths he trod now in waking dreams, shoveling his earth and worms—one thousand to the pound, sweating out the beer in the noonday sun, hosing down the boxes to keep them wet. On a good day he could find a groove, a crease in time that was neither quite here nor quite there. On a good day he could still imagine himself on a wave like Hoddy's. He could still mind surf Outside the Bullring, body English turning his shovel, hips swiveling in the direction of the turn. On bad days, his rhythm was off and the groove eluded him. Money worries and the advance of years dogged his heels . . . Images of Hoddy in pee-stained khakis, when the city was done with him and the house gone, his beloved beaches lost to pollution, wandering the valley. Or how about the time the staph infection almost took his leg, pumped it up like some African boy with elephantiasis, putting him flat on his back for the better part of a summer—all heat and fever and memories like the living dead? And when he got down to shit like that and the Island Express it was time to add the pills because the beer wasn't cutting it.

But he was hoping it wouldn't come to that, at least not today, what with the first female companionship he'd experienced in more years than he cared to remember watching from the porch as he stacked up the last of the boxes then hosed them down and himself too, then hosed down the windrows as well, water pulling rainbows from a blaze of sky, and the feeling came to him that on this particular day, it would all be okay. And when he'd gotten a towel out of the truck and wiped his face with it he went up onto the porch at the side of the trailer and found that she was fast asleep.

The ruled paper with its drawing of the harvester had fallen to the floor by her side and Fahey picked it up. He saw that she had turned a page and done some writing of her own. The writing was in Spanish and might just as well have been Sanskrit for all Fahey could make of it. On another page, however, he saw what appeared to be a list of names together with accompanying dates. And finally,

in the center of a third page, a drawing. It was a rather crude drawing of what Fahey took to be a disembodied eyeball. It struck him
as the sort of thing with which schoolboys might decorate their
sweatshirts and he looked once more at the sleeping woman, her
mouth open just enough to show the tips of her teeth, her eyes
clamped shut, their lashes like crescent moons. He supposed his
enactment of the roundup had not proven as therapeutic as he had
hoped and he considered once more the childish drawing in his
hands. In fact, he did not seem quite able to put it down. This both-
ered him. You would, he thought, really have to be losing it, to find
it spooky.

6

MUNICIPAL POLICE had investigated the fire in Carlotta's offices, with predictable results. *Nada.* Still, the lead officer turned out to be a young man Magdalena had gone to high school with in Mexicali. Like Magdalena he had been born in Tijuana, and like Magdalena, he had come home. His name was Raúl Ramírez, and a day or two into the investigation she had agreed to meet him for lunch in Las Playas. The restaurant was situated atop one of the mesas overlooking the Tijuana River Valley, with a view of its beaches and the sea beyond. They made the requisite small talk. They spoke of people they remembered from school and what had become of them. They spoke about their hometown and what was becoming of it.

"See that river," Magdalena told him. She was looking toward the marsh grass and willows that marked the river's path to the sea on the American side of the fence, for with talk of Tijuana and its future, the conversation had turned to Magdalena's crusade. "When the rains begin, it will be little more than raw sewage and toxic runoff."

Raúl nodded; he'd been watching her and not the river. "This is all true," he said. "But there is some good news." And he checked off a rather impressive list of clubs and bands, a number of movies he had seen in the new cinema complex in the Zona del Río near the cultural center. "Maybe you should get out more," he told her. He was smiling when he said it and she did not find him unattractive. She told him about the children of Vista Nueva. Raúl fell silent. He had nothing to say about the children of Vista Nueva and in time Magdalena fell silent herself. She watched pelicans diving for fish near the mouth of the river and wondered if it was him or her. Was he simply insensitive or had she become humorless and strident, an aging curmudgeon before her time? She tried to remember the last time she had gone out, to dance, or hear music. She went so far as to calculate how long it had been since she'd slept with a lover. She was twenty-three years old for God's sake. Maybe he was right. Maybe she should get out more. She thought about going out with Raúl and wondered if that was why he had asked her to lunch. But the plight of the children, together with Magdalena's concerns, her view of the maquiladora industry in particular, had clearly put a damper on the occasion from which it was unable to recover and they finished the meal with more small talk, as though the lunch had suddenly become just one more thing to be gotten through.

When it was over, he had walked her to her car, the ratty Ford. Christ, you could see the torn headliner half a block away.

"I think," Raúl said, "that you might want to consider getting an amparo."

Magdalena felt it in her gut—the reason he had asked her here, to talk. "Really?" she asked. "Why is that?" She turned to face him.

Raúl looked away. "You believe in your cause," he said. "I under-stand that. I respect you for it . . ." His voice grew faint. "But you make enemies. This is obvious."

"Do you know something about who set the fire?"

His eyes were dark and sad, sadder than they had appeared in the restaurant. As if suddenly becoming aware of this fact he now took steps to hide them, behind a pair of expensive-looking dark glasses. "Just get one," he told her. "It's all I can really say. It would be a good thing to have."

They shook hands at the side of her car. He opened the door for her. She got in then sat watching him in her rearview mirror. She watched until he was lost amid the rush of traffic, the glare of mid-day sun.

An amparo was a document by which one might protect oneself from the local police. It was issued by a district court. The district courts had more power than local or municipal courts. They were also deemed to be somewhat less corrupt. In any country more sen-sible, such a document would have been wholly unnecessary. An amparo said, "Cut the crap. You want to make a charge stick, then present it in a district court, before a district judge." Without it one was at the mercy of whatever muck lay at the bottom of the judicial system, where every street cop, drug cop, border cop, or *federal* was on someone's payroll. What her friend the street cop had been telling her was that whoever was behind the burning of the offices had at least some degree of pull. He was telling her that someone important was out to get her. Or at least this is what she believed he was telling her, before he put on his expensive shades and walked away. By evening, he would no doubt be at one of his clubs, listen-ing to music, or perhaps taking in a film at the new cultural center in the Zona del Río. Magdalena would be alone in her apartment, staring into a computer screen.

But she had gone to Carlotta. They had procured the documents, one for each of them. And she had increased her vigilance. She had been on guard. And they had gotten her anyway. Little good her official document had done her on the side of the road, on the sand of Las Playas. And now it was lost to the sea. Certainly she could not go back without it. Nor could she return to Tijuana before putting a face to her enemy.

Hence the list on Fahey's pad. She had begun by trying to reconstruct the accident, to remember how she had gotten from the car to the Tijuana River Valley because this part was very hazy to her now. Something had snapped in the steering column. She could remember that much, or perhaps in the linkage at the front of her car. There was sensory recall. She could feel the jolting of the wheel in the palms of her hands. When she closed her eyes, she heard the voices of men. Further details slipped away even as she tried to reclaim them. She went on to names and dates—an attempt to reconstruct some of what she had been working on in her files. That was where the answer lay. It had to be. She was on to something and yet somehow she had shown her hand. Word had gotten out, clear to the street, to the ear of Raúl, who had taken her to lunch to warn her. Or perhaps he had taken her to find out if she could be dissuaded. The accident had occurred later, when he found that she could not. She returned to her list, wondering where to put his name, then realized there would be no end of it. Nothing like a threat on one's life to induce paranoia. By this time, however, her head had begun to ache and she had turned to doodling, an image from waking dreams—the disembodied eye: Primitive juvenilia, yet linked somehow to the events that had brought her here. She looked back over what she had written then dozed fitfully to the drone of Fahey's mechanical harvester. From time to time she would open an eye to find him still at work, his broad back gleaming in sweat as he bent to shovel the dirt containing the worms into the absurd device he had drawn her a picture of, an apparently interminable procedure, before letting go altogether, falling at last into a deep and troubled sleep.

She awoke hours later, drenched in sweat. For a moment or two she could not quite place where she was or how she had gotten there. She believed that there was even a split second when she did not know who she was—just some bit of consciousness which, had she been more of a mystic, she might have taken as evidence of the illusory nature of the self but which in her present condition she took only as evidence of further deterioration, the possible results of internal injuries as yet undiagnosed.

But she saw the surfboard in its canvas straps, hanging above her in the old trailer and it all came back, most of it anyway. It was dark outside, pitch black beneath the trees. She got out of bed—the first time she had done so under her own power. She felt an overpowering need for night air and went out onto the porch, then through it to stand on the hard-packed dirt in her bare feet. It was cooler here. She could hear the distant pounding of the surf that had nearly claimed her life, the very waves she had watched only days before from the safety of the restaurant, dining with Raúl overlooking the valley.

As her eyes grew accustomed to the darkness she noted a few faint stars scattered among the branches of the trees and off in the distance, in those few places where some break in the foliage permitted it, a pale frosting in the southern sky she took for the lights of Tijuana, so near and yet so far. And she thought of Carlotta. The name landed upon her like a stone. She could scarcely believe that even in her dementia this had not occurred to her from the very beginning. My God, she thought, if someone tried to kill her, then why not the woman she worked for? Her next thought was both horrific and inevitable: a broken Carlotta, dead by the side of the road.

She returned to the trailer, in search of a phone. The vehicle was comprised of little more than two rooms, a living room at one end, a bedroom at the other. In between were a tiny kitchen and an even tinier bathroom. She went quickly from one room to the next, pacing the narrow floor with more sense of purpose than she had experienced in some time. In fact, now that she realized there was something to be done, all manner of ideas began to take hold. She went so far as to entertain the notion that even all of this, everything that had occurred, was in some way okay—assuming of course that Carlotta was still alive. Her work was bearing fruit and she was the proof of it. She might have tipped her hand but an enemy had tipped his as well. He had also provided her with evidence. She had after all survived a murder attempt. It was not just the accident. There had been men on the road. And men might be traced. They might be induced to talk. One thought tumbled after another. She was still alive, yet her enemy probably believed her dead. Certainly this could work to her advantage. The thing to do was not only to warn Carlotta but also to get her out of Tijuana—Carlotta and the files. Why not? What if she had access to both of them? Together they might figure it out. They might prepare a case. And why not do it right here, within sight of home, yet tucked away in a corner of the world where no one would think to look? It would require a certain amount of planning. She would definitely need the aid of this man who had saved her from the dogs, this Fahey.

Her enthusiasm gave way to fantasy. She imagined them all in some high court, the owner of Reciclaje Integral having been extradited on charges of attempted murder, in this case her own, standing before a judge. She imagined the look on his face as he was led away. She imagined his reception in the prison at La Paz. She knew it was a reach, but what the hell . . . days of despair and now this.

She looked at a photograph on the wall—a lone surfer on a huge wave, arms spread rather, she thought, like a gull in flight. She had seen the picture many times during the past few days, but it suddenly occurred to her that it was a picture of Fahey. Perhaps there had been something about watching him at work, some way he had of holding himself. She took the picture from the wall and studied it closely by the yellow light of a lamp. There was no doubt about it. The photograph was of Fahey, the worm farmer. He was younger, to be sure, younger and leaner, a thick mane of blond hair flowing in the wind as he carved a turn from the base of a towering indigo wall, but still Fahey.

It did not occur to her just then to wonder what had gone wrong. For the moment, the photograph seemed only to add to her burgeoning confidence. It was, after all, one big wave. And anyone who could do that . . . Surely, she thought, he was her man. Nor did she really need that much. One could say he had done as much already, and more . . . He had killed the dogs. He had gone to Tijuana and come home with the meds. All she needed now was his forbearance, a little time, a little space, possibly a trip across the border to help Carlotta with the files . . .

Magdalena went once more from one end of the trailer to the other, the photograph still clutched in her hands. She would tell him everything, she decided. She would enlist his aid in her struggle against the monster. She would make of him a soldier of Christ, thereby saving his immortal soul in the bargain, as the Sisters of the Benediction would have it, though she was no longer always so sure what she believed with respect to immortal souls. The thing that had come to her of late was that the fight went on, with immortal souls, or without them. The fight was the thing and to give up on it was to surrender one's soul—right here, in the here and now. The hereafter would be what it would be. The struggle itself was the act by which one gave meaning to the world.

Suddenly, however, she felt dizzy and stopped to sit on the edge of the bed. She placed a hand on the back of her neck and found that she was damp with sweat. She supposed she was overdoing it. That Carlotta should be warned, however, was obvious and unequivocal. She found herself staring into the small, chipped face of Fahey's plaster hula girl, the tiny dancer bathed in the light of her own sixty-watt sun, her grass skirt brittle with time. She was several seconds in observation of this sorry statuary, remarkable if for no other reason than its lack of duct tape, before realizing she had yet to uncover a phone. Perhaps, she thought, he carried one with him, but quickly realized she had no idea where he was. During the course of her illness, when she had kept to the bed, too weak to move, Fahey seemed always nearby. Later, as some of her strength returned and she was able to sit up, she would get the occasional glimpse—Fahey sitting or asleep, on the little couch at the far end of the trailer. During the last couple of days he seemed to be less visible. She had taken it as one more token of his generosity. He was allowing her more space, and more privacy to go with it. And so it was that she was alone just now.

She had been here for the better part of a week yet scarcely knew what else was on the land. There was an old outbuilding at the edge of the property, that and the farmhouse, both of which could be seen from the trailer, though she seemed to remember his saying that the outbuilding was unused and that the house had been commandeered by bees, possibly killer bees out of Africa by way of Mexico. Still, she had no other idea about where to look and when she went to the door she saw that there was indeed a yellow light burning in a small room at one end of the old house. It quickly occurred to her that she had seen this light before, from the louvered windows at her bedside, that it had burned there each night, all night, and was there in the morning and daytime too for she had seen it even in the afternoon in the shade of the cotton-woods.

She slipped easily into the sandals Fahey had provided and went outside once more, still a bit woozy, crossing the intervening fifty feet or so of weed and rock till she had come within reach of the yellow light and the structure that contained it, little more than a crude afterthought to the rest of the house—an old porch, perhaps, tin-roofed, enclosed in plywood that might have been salvaged from the valley itself—all of it, roof and siding alike, painted in the same drab shade of olive green to which the entire dwelling had been made subject, as though the U.S. military had taken some hand in it. Holes had been cut from the side of this shanty into which a pair of cheap aluminum-framed windows were fitted at angles not quite square to the line of the roof, their glass clouded with dust and time. She came close enough to feel the coolness off one such mottled pane upon the skin of her brow, and peering through it, found the room beyond pressed into service as a kind of workshop. At the room's center was what she took for a surfboard in progress—a large chunk of foam cut to a rough shape resting on a pair of sawhorses and all around it walls papered with surfing photographs which, judging from their condition, had been there for some time, as many were torn, their edges frayed and peeling, their colors bleached by the sun. Tools hung suspended from metal hooks. Others lay scattered across a high table. She looked in upon all of this for several seconds before some movement beneath the surfboard in progress drew her eye to the remnants of foam heaped upon the floor and she saw that Fahey was contained there as well.

He could have been easily overlooked, in the midst of sawdust and shavings, but there he was, her benefactor, swathed in a ratty sleeping bag, in the fetal position, a six-pack of beer and a small plastic pill bottle situated near his head. It had not been her intention to spy, yet she continued to stand at the window, transfixed, as he twitched one way and then the other, suddenly shouting in his sleep and flailing about. A hand scuttled across the floor, crablike, in search of something it could not find before retreating into the folds of the bag. She could hear the occasional burst of snoring, rattling through the thin panes of glass, then stood there another ten seconds before putting it all together . . . the lights she had seen through the trailer window, no matter the hour, the figure supine before her . . . "My God," she said, half aloud, surprising herself with the sound of her own voice. "He sleeps with the lights on."

7

FAHEY'S FINEST hours were, in retrospect, rather short lived. In the years that followed he would mark their passing by a single incident. In Tijuana, Fahey had become friends with a family who wanted to emigrate, albeit illegally, to the United States and he had offered to help. The farm was still his home, though he was rarely there. He often slept on the beach in those days, rising early to catch the morning glass, going to school, or not, as the spirit moved him. No one seemed to mind, certainly not his father. Weekends were spent lifeguarding in Rosarito, where Hoddy had contrived to establish a training program for Mexican lifeguards, and that was how Fahey met the family in question, dragging their dog from the shore break on a Sunday afternoon as a big south swell swept the beaches at a dangerous clip. The plan was hatched later in the day, amid beers and tacos in the People's Park overlooking the river valley.

The family would have to make its own way out of Tijuana but once in the valley, Fahey could offer the farm as safe haven. Later, he would help them to move farther north. He cleared the plan with the old man, who claimed not to give a rat's ass, joking that all he wanted for his hospitality was a bottle of good tequila, meaning some particularly objectionable brand of rot-gut, chocolate-flavored shit most likely banned in the States but sold in Tijuana to anyone foolish enough to buy it and for which, in the midst of his decomposition, the old man had developed a taste. Fahey had gotten it for him himself, of course, given it to the family to bring with and was up at midnight one week hence to meet them in the old avocado grove at the mouth of Smuggler's Gulch. He could, to this day, still see them there, beneath those darkened limbs—mother, father, assorted offspring and relatives, all smiles and open arms, the tequila in a brown paper bag, walking to America, emerging from the ground fog like the ghosts they were soon to become, because in America, Lucian Fahey was waiting.

Drinking heavily and down so long it was beginning to look like up, the old man had conspired with thugs to betray them all. And just as Fahey could still see the family, an even dozen altogether, not counting the pet he had hauled from the currents, he could see his father as well—a wizened figure, gaunt and unshaven, white hair falling to his shoulders in the moonlight, flanked by men with guns and trucks and not a thing for Fahey to do but shower the old man with the slings and arrows of a righteous indignation, receiving for his troubles a butt stroke to the jaw. The resulting injury had left him taking meals through a straw for the next six weeks. The last he had seen of the family were their bent shapes in the beds of the pickup trucks, vanishing into the darkness from which they had come.

It takes some men longer than others to find themselves. For Lucian Fahey it took some fifty-odd years but once he'd come into his own, he did so with a reckless abandon, cutting deals with street punks and coyotes alike to do what his own son had done for free, lure pilgrims into his web. It was hard to know now just how many there were over the years. On the night in question Fahey had taken his unhinged jaw together with what possessions he could carry and left for good. Threats of death and dismemberment had followed him into the night. He had believed every one.

Hoddy had taken him to get his jaw wired and for a while he'd tried living with his surrogate father. It was at about this same time however that a new city council had deemed the aging surfer too old to continue as captain of the guard. The charge was strictly bull-shit. Hoddy could still have outswum, outsurfed, or outfought any man in town. It was the old Badlander's rough and rowdy ways the city fathers had reason to find objectionable—visions of gentrifica-tion and increased land value in the wake of a recent California real estate boom dancing in their heads. Still, Hoddy lost his one and only job, together with the house that had accompanied it. Vandals had long since destroyed his shack on the beach and the valley had grown more dangerous. Hoddy took up residence in a fellow surfer's converted garage—one room and a hot plate. He did his dishes in the bathroom sink. It marked the beginning of a long decline. Fahey spent a couple of strange and uncomfortable weeks on the old man's floor, then struck out on his own.

In the end, the home Fahey found for himself was with the Island Express—an aspiring group of drug runners headed up by a math teacher from a local high school. The Express's drug of choice was marijuana, and before they were done they'd moved it by the ton. They packed it on foot, through the valley and along the beaches. On big south swells they paddled hollow-bodied boards out of Rosarito and rode the currents north, sometimes off-loading in broad daylight at the Imperial Beach pier. The money rolled in. Fahey bought a modest condominium near the sand. He never knew for certain what had become of the family he had tried to help. He drove out to the farm one night, by now little more than a garbage dump, with the intention of learning the truth. He would beat it out of the old man if it came to that, which it did. But then it wasn't much of a fight and the old man lost consciousness before he could do more than issue threats, which in fact he made good on by the following week, sending thugs to Fahey's apartment to break a kneecap. Neither could go to the cops of course. If one went up, the other was bound to follow.

In time the Island Express turned to cocaine and crack. Fahey sampled his wares. He said it was the knee that kept him out of the water. Some said he might have turned pro. Hoddy had driven him to a contest once, in Huntington Beach. Fahey had entered unseeded, won the trials, then advanced to the final heats, where he had finished in the top three, among the pros. Cutting his teeth at the straits made most of what California had to offer seem easy. Still, in comparison to what he could make with the Island Express, competitive surfing was a slow way to earn a buck. Hoddy tried to talk to him. Coked to the gills, Fahey told the old man to go fuck himself. Hoddy believed in a lifestyle already gone. Fahey could see it even if the old surfer could not. He developed a taste for speed. The Island Express facilitated his appetite. Hoddy wanted an heir. Fahey wanted to forget the life he had turned his back on, the family he had betrayed. Drugs made it happen.

Not long after that the Mystic Peak broke once more. Hoddy came to his house that night. It was the last time they would see each other. They stood in silence on a wooden deck, listening to the thunder of huge waves. The old man had brought a gift. It was the ten-foot rhino chaser Hoddy had shaped himself then ridden, Outside the Bullring, on the day of the epic wave. He left it on Fahey's porch and never said a word. The Gull lay awake for the rest of the night, listening to the waves. By dawn he was expected on the beach at Rosarito, the math teacher having arranged to move a load of hash in a two-man submarine hijacked from the Scripps Institute of Oceanography by some physics professor with aspirations to the high life. It was a troubling scenario, Island Express outings becoming more outlandish by the day. Fahey should have known. He should have listened to Hoddy. He should have followed his heart. Dawn found him on the beach at Rosarito. The submarine foundered in ten feet of water. The math teacher ratted out everyone with whom he'd ever done business. It was a federal bust, on the word of a snitch. Fahey lost everything he owned, did four calendars at Safford, Arizona, and got out with nothing. Too old now for the contests he'd once eschewed, still cocky after four years in minimum security, he waited out a year of parole then tried to get back into the game. But with the passing of the Island Express things had changed and before it was over he'd sunk to cooking meth on the Mesa de Otay, where he finally learned everything there was to know about the sins of the father, learned about the men robbed and murdered, the women sold into slavery. Because this was where it had all gone down, for the family he had befriended, for the countless others who had followed. And they said you couldn't go home again. An old Mex meth chef even showed him the bones in the ground and he saw for the first time the enormity of what he had begun. He saw iniquities without end, as a procession of days, and to these he had added other and greater iniquities in which his father had played no part and of which he would not speak, neither then nor now, yet he knew himself for what he was, his father's son, and he vowed to finish what he had started the night he'd gone to beat the truth out of the old man, if only to rid the planet of them both, for in this crime he had no concern with perfection. He sold a few rocks to a guy he'd done time with before it could happen. It was strictly from charity and the goodness of his heart. Unhappily, the man's parole officer caught him with the needle still in his arm. He had to give up somebody.

They nailed Fahey within twenty-four hours, smoking his own shit. The news was not all bad. So fucked up had he become and so far had he strayed from the old Mexican's recipe, the stuff he had cooking in the sink could not rightly be identified as meth, or anything else for that matter. He told them he was making a sealer for the roof of his trailer. This time around it was a state bust, and in the end all they had him on was possession. The bad news was that the DA took a personal interest in the case. The man was so pissed about not getting more mileage out of a second offense that he kept Fahey in a county lockup for six months awaiting transfer and another six in what they euphemistically called bus therapy—that is, in constant motion, from one facility to another, all the way to Leavenworth and back again. He finished at Lompoc. In the end, he had done twenty-seven and change—a little over two years.

He still might have killed the old man, in spite of everything. It was a possibility. But pills and booze had pretty much done the trick by the time they let him out—diapers and a straw in the old folks' home in Escondido. Within the week Lucian Fahey had drowned in his Gerber's when a Filipino orderly high on smack ran the feeding tube into his remaining lung instead of his stomach. Samuel Fahey got the farm. He could not say he hadn't anticipated the inheritance. He could not say he didn't want it. The time in county had done what four years in Safford could not, left him feeling old and scared and ready to be good.

He tried to find Hoddy. They told him Hoddy was down with the Alzheimer's, wandering the valley in pee-stained khakis. He thought he saw him once. He'd taken the job for Fish and Game, was trailing some feral cats at the edge of Border Field, and caught sight of a shadowy figure, dressed in rags—had called out to no response, followed a few faint tracks to a hole in the fence at the bottom of Yogurt Canyon, written it off to some derelict from the other side . . . This before the tracking job became federal, ruling out known drug runners and convicted felons. Dark days followed. Panic attacks in the unemployment lines in downtown San Diego. In the end he settled on worm farming like the old man before him and two years of any shit job anyone was willing to give, staying alive while he cleaned up the farm, reading everything he could find on vermiculture, the road to riches. And over time . . . a windrow here, a harvester there . . . Add a website . . . Observe the Nike ad: Just do it . . . So he keeps on reading. He visits a worm farm in Perris, California, to see how it's really done. The years click by. And now look . . . One more year and Sam the Gull Fahey may just break into the black, on a legal enterprise for the first time in his life. God knows what then. He can't see that far. His last parole officer, a certain Mitchell Bovie, a decent man with whom he has kept in touch, says one foot in front of the other. "Inch by inch," Mitch proclaims, from an office no bigger than a coffin, feet propped on a desktop littered with doughnut crumbs, rolls of Tums, and dirty Styrofoam cups. Fahey follows Mitchell's advice. He takes it a day at a time. Sometimes he climbs to Spooner's Mesa to smoke dope and watch the waves. In the absence of rains, when the water is cleaner, he takes the old ten-foot rhino chaser from the straps in his living room. It is the same board Hoddy left on his porch all those years ago, and he paddles the length of the straits by moonlight in the absence of any swell just to see what it feels like, to keep his paddling muscles from disappearing altogether. He might do six miles a night in the summer. Once in a while he will go to the surfer's website Jack Nance has taught him to use, tracking the storms that will generate waves in distant parts of the globe that he will not ride. And now he hears talk of another El Niño forming in a distant quadrant of the sea and wonders if he will see the Mystic Peak break again and wonders what it will be like if he does, and what he will do, if he is still young enough to do anything at all. He reads the magazines, chroniclers of a sport in which he might have been somebody, if this, if that, if only . . . He thinks about the life Hoddy once had here. He thinks about what might have been, and of what is. Age adds a new wrinkle: He leaves the valley and he gets dizzy. His heart palpitates. What in God's name is that all about? Jack Nance invites him longboarding, but he thinks surfing is something you earn. He thinks he has blown his chance. Pills and beer hold the memories at bay. He sleeps with the lights on. The last thing he needs is trouble.

PART TWO

8

BEFORE THERE was a third eye tattooed in the bald spot at the back of his skull, indeed, long before there even was a bald spot, before the factories of Tijuana, before the hospital in Reynosa or the shallow graves at the edge of La Mesa de Otay, Armando Santoya had dreamed of becoming a fighter. It began at the age of fifteen, in Mexico City, seated on an overturned oil drum in a tarpaper shack belonging to his mother's sister, where he saw his first and only movie. The story featured, among other things, a handsome fighter in love with a beautiful prostitute. Later, on a street in the city, some boys had taken him to a gym where, through cracks in a wooden fence, he'd watched two men gliding about a ring. The men were kickboxers and used both their hands and their feet. Their bodies were corded with muscle, streaked with sweat. Armando, still under the influence of his first and only movie, could imagine nothing finer.

It was a somewhat unusual dream for a boy from Tierra Blanca, where the *corridos* that spilled from the cheap plastic ghetto blasters and funky dives sang the praises of *mota* and the principal shrine was that of Jesús Malverde, the patron saint of *narcotraficantes*. Still, Armando began. He soaked his face in brine and hardened his hands on the fence posts that ringed the old corral. He called himself El Diablo de Sinaloa. His stepfather called him a dick and a clown, for which Armando beat the old drunk till he couldn't stand, stole what money the family had managed to save, and left for Tijuana in complete ignorance of just about everything.

He lived at first with a second cousin, in a room with half a dozen other *nacos*. The word denotes undisguisable Indian blood and carries with it the usual connotative aspersions—ignorant, irredeemable, mustachioed, and generally appalling . . . And if Armando had never exactly thought of himself as any one of these things before, then he would learn to do so here, in the Zona Norte, amid the colored lights and banda music, amid the hookers and slumming white boys, in this apartment with his coppery brethren.

The men in Armando's apartment spent their days in the service of the Japanese, assembling televisions in one of the many factories that ringed the city. Some of them tried to talk Armando into joining them. Armando, not yet convinced that he was one of them, went on with his plans. He went in search of a gym where he might be discovered, for a lovely prostitute with whom he might fall in love. He did not have to go far. There was a boxing club around the corner and prostitutes aplenty, a block away, in the heart of the old red-light district. The club was located on the second floor of a crumbling wooden building, above a bar known as El As Negro, and it was here that he made the first in a series of unfortunate discoveries. He discovered that the other fighters were tougher than he had imagined. They did something the fence posts around the old corral and his drunken stepfather had not, they hit back. And by the hard light of day, his nose packed with gauze, he made the further discovery that the hookers all were fat, many appearing to be dwarfs or hunchbacks. Still, he persevered. His nose refused to stop bleeding. In a strip mall replete with palm trees and a McDonald's restaurant, a doctor removed the cartilage. At least he said he was a doctor. Armando learned from a nurse that the man's specialty was injecting rich white women with live cells taken from the organs of sheep. The cells were meant as a kind of tonic, a fountain of youth. Armando was reminded of the execrable sex-strangler Goyo Cárdenas, reputed to have brought one of his victims back from the dead through the use of adrenaline obtained from the adrenal glands of another unfortunate. Armando would have liked to ask if this were possible. He would have liked to ask about the cells. The doctor, however, was short on time. He dismissed Armando's curiosity with a brief grunt, a wave of the hand, then wielding an instrument that might have been used to shuck oysters, removed the boy's cartilage without ceremony, after which conversation was all but impossible, took the last of Armando's money, and sent him packing with half a dozen pain pills in a small white envelope.

Winter came shortly upon the heels of this humiliation and with it the rains. The city turned to mud. The canyons with their vast encampments of the homeless ran with raw sewage and the toxic waste of factories. Entire neighborhoods slid away overnight. The air stank. Training was difficult if not impossible. His money had gone the way of the cartilage in his nose. He no longer had any. He wandered down reeking, rain-slick streets, one more *naco* in jeans and a cowboy shirt. He walked the alleys of El Centro and Zona Norte, drifted among the new high-rises, the banks and shopping malls of the Zona del Río. He walked the Boulevard of Heroes, among the fierce statues of the great chiefs, glorified in stone while their descendants did what Armando did, prowled the streets in cheap clothing with empty stomachs, the invisible multitudes. On every corner there was a sign: *Se Solicita Personal.* And in the end, he did what every other *naco* had done before him. He shined up his boots and rode the blue bus to the Mesa de Otay. He went to work in a factory that produced leather-covered steering wheels and gearshift knobs. Accessories de Mexico, owned and operated by Cline Technologies.

The company occupied a cavernous building in an industrial park on the outskirts of the city. The interior of the building was divided into workstations. Armando was put to work in the assembly area of the plant, where he stood at a table with thirteen other workers. The workers were like him. They came from Oaxaca, from Michoacán, from Sinaloa. They came from hard lives. They came from places that no longer existed. In Tijuana they applied themselves to the assemblage of televisions, of videocassettes, of leather-covered steering wheels, of Miss Piggy dolls, of a thousand other mysterious and superfluous objects. Some dreamed of returning to the villages that no longer existed. Some dreamed of moving north. No one planned to stay in Tijuana. Much of what everyone talked about was leaving. But few ever did. They stayed. And they worked.

Armando stayed too, covering his steering wheels, thirty a day. It was a simple mindless task. It was both easy and difficult. The plastic wheel was removed from the cardboard box in which it arrived and attached to a metal base. Next it was covered with yellow glue. The yellow glue sat on tables in open containers and was applied with a brush. There was also green glue and white glue, together with a powerful solvent, and these too sat on the tables in open containers. The glue was applied to the wheel in short rapid strokes. When the wheel had been covered in a thin film of glue, Armando would place the brush on the table. He would take a piece of pre-cut leather from a container at his feet, inspect it for flaws, then begin to pull the leather onto the wheel. This was the most difficult part of his task. The glue began to set up quickly and it was necessary to keep the leather centered in such a way that when it came time to stitch it the seams would wind up on the inside of the wheel. If the seams wound up in the wrong place the wheel was ruined. When the leather was in place, there was one last piece of business. It remained to clean any excess glue from the leather. This was done with a rag or sponge dipped in solvent.

So all day long Armando worked with the glues and solvents. No one wore gloves. Armando's work would not have been possible with them. He would not have been able to feel the leather. Nor were there masks or goggles. Everyone's eyes burned. Their noses bled. They coughed. They passed out. Managers walked the floor, figuring quotas, flirting with the workers, most of whom were young women not yet out of their teens, encouraged by the management to dress to the nines—stiletto heels and fishnet stockings beneath blue work smocks. It made for a crazy, sex-charged atmosphere, stoned on fumes beneath leering eyes, ghetto blasters spewing sound from every table, the entire factory rocking to techno-house with a Tex-Mex beat . . .

In time, Armando was one of the best assemblymen in the plant. He could do forty wheels a day, for which he was paid two dollars and sixty-nine cents. By the end of a shift he could barely lift his arms. His hands achieved a permanently red and swollen look, the skin cracked and bleeding from constant exposure to the solvents and glues. But there was money enough to scrape by on and he believed that perhaps, in time, he would rise to the rank of manager. This was an impossible dream. Mexican universities had made a cottage industry of turning out mid-level managers. Armando, with his fourth-grade education, his *naco* looks and manners, would never be more than an assembly-line goon.

There were days when Armando would leave the factory so high on fumes he was scarcely able to walk. Sometimes it was even funny. Then one Sunday, in a month he could no longer recall, he found out something about himself. He had gone to the home of a fellow worker to watch a football game. Other workers from the factory were there. Someone had pilfered a can of the yellow glue. It sat uncapped on the floor at their feet and before the afternoon was over, they had all gotten high on beer and glue, watching the Oakland Raiders and the New York Giants, on a stolen big-screen television perched upon an engine block in a shack made of tin and cardboard on a hillside in the Distrito de Florida, overlooking the city of Tijuana, its gargantuan national flag flapping in great undulating waves above crumbling rooftops, and it was good. That was the thing he learned, that it was good to have beer and glue. It was good to be high.

He was not alone in this discovery. In the weeks that followed he often heard his fellow workers inhaling deeply at their workstations. Days passed as in a dream. Summer settled upon the city as if to smother it. The breezes that had blown throughout the spring across the Tijuana River Valley failed and the air hung trapped among the brown hills for days at a time, unmoving. And every week or two one of the city's great and improbable dumps would catch fire and the stench of burning waste would choke what was left of the stagnant air. In winter the factory had been freezing. Now it sizzled, a din of noise, fumes, and smoke. In the stitching area, where the women worked to sew the leather to the wheels, the accidents multiplied.

Armando had often thought of the women as so many featherless birds seeking flight, their arms rising and falling as they performed the elaborate maneuvers necessary for securing the leather, long, hooked needles slicing the air. Body parts were pierced. Eyes were lost. Mexican law required that each factory employ a nurse. The drug of choice was aspirin. The factories took the young. When workers began to age, or became injured, they were sent to the junk-yard—that part of the building where older or maimed workers were assigned the most menial of tasks before their firing, which was inevitable and irrevocable. Yet all through that summer of smoke and fumes the banda music played on—songs in praise of peasants become drug lords and of the crops that had made them wealthy: *"Me paso la vida sembrando mota . . ."* And indeed Armando would have been more than happy to spend the rest of his life tending marijuana. Unhappily his mota was in short supply. What came in its place were more steering wheels, more leather, more glue.

The work groups within the factory were referred to as cells. There was a woman in Armando's cell by the name of Reina. On a summer night during the peak of the season she was declared the winner of the wet T-shirt contest the managers had contrived to stage in the parking lot behind the factory and when the contest was over she left with Armando. She might have gone after a man-ager, but in fact she and Armando had been flirting for some time in the sweltering summer heat and that night she had chosen him, in front of everyone. Armando had taken her to a restaurant in the Zona Norte where the band was loud and the fish prepared Sinaloan style. He'd blown a month's wages in a night but they had danced on the street beneath colored lights and afterward she had taken him to her home on the southern flank of Cerro Colorado.

The home did not amount to much, situated upon a steep hill-side, half a mile from the nearest water, built of wooden pallets and cardboard boxes, but the plot of land it occupied was registered in Reina's name, which meant that not even the city itself could evict her. In time, Armando moved in. They added on to the house—

more pallets and boxes, a cast-off garage door. They cooked outside over an open fire. They used oil lamps and candles to light the house and they got their water from a truck that chugged along the highway then stored it in a fifty-gallon drum salvaged from a nearby dump.

It was not the life Armando had imagined, riding the buses that had brought him north. But it was the life he had. A woman. A house. An unbearable job. They said a teaspoon of sugar made the medicine go down. Armando had beer and glue. By the end of summer it had become apparent that Reina was with child.

They were married on a sweltering Sunday afternoon at the Church of the Purest Conception, in the shadow of the great cultural center in the Zona del Río. On Monday Reina was fired. They had known this was coming. Women at the Cline plant were expected to show used tampons to floor managers on a monthly basis and Reina had been unable to do so for some time. But she had been a good worker and they had waited until she began to show before cutting her loose. Children were frowned upon by the managers at Cline Technologies, at least until they reached the age of fourteen or fifteen and could themselves be put to work.

So while Reina worked at making a home of their shack on the hillside, Armando carried on in the factory, redoubling his efforts. He was up to fifty steering wheels a day when his wife gave birth. It was the day that changed everything. A moment of terror and wonder. The infant was a boy, with dark, liquid eyes, jet black hair, and a huge tumor that ran the length of his tiny back. In his face, Armando thought, his son looked normal, regarding the world with inquisitive eyes. But of course one couldn't just look at his face. The condition was diagnosed as myelocele and the family remanded to the hospital in Reynosa, in the state of Sonora.

✦   ✦   ✦

The hospital occupied the high ground along a barren and windswept plain where for days the couple waited on metal folding chairs, in gleaming corridors bathed in fluorescent light. There were five surgeries in all. Somewhere between the fourth and fifth surgeries a revelation occurred. A doctor appeared, stating that the child did not have any more blood in his veins. That was how he put it; there was no more blood in the baby's body. He asked Armando to come down to the lab for some testing, to see if he would be able to provide blood for the coming operation. But Armando failed the test. That was the revelation. They told him that his blood was poisoned and that they could not use it. They declined to tell him how or why this had come to be, but that was their way. They were not long on explanations.

Armando wandered the blinding corridors. He met other families. He discovered than an entire wing of the hospital had been given over to children with anencephaly, that is, children born without brains, the children of factory workers. The doctors went ahead with the fifth operation. The boy died and was buried in the Pantheon of the Cypresses overlooking a truck yard. Armando and Reina stood on a small square of Astroturf as a Sister of the Immaculate Conception said a rosary, then they boarded the bus that would carry them back to Tijuana, past the factories that lined the border.

In Tijuana, in the Colonia Solidaridad, on the hillside overlooking the city, Armando and Reina were visited by the manager of human resources, an employee of Cline Technologies. The man's name was Ramón de la Christa Cortez. He was a small, misshapen man with a humped back all his own and a thin, wispy beard that fluttered like strands of moss in a brassy afternoon wind. Armando greeted him upon the wooden pallet he used as a porch.

"You know that I have heard about your child," Ramón de la

Christa Cortez said. "I hear that he passed away. And I am very sorry. But I don't want you to feel that it was because of the workplace. It is not because of the thinner, the Varsol, or the solvents . . ."

"How about the glue?" Armando asked him.

The manager smiled sadly, as if he were talking to a child. "No," he said. "Your child was born like that because, well . . . it is a part of nature."

"I know what I know," Armando said. "Before the factory I was in fine health. Reina also. I was in training to be a fighter."

The manager seemed to give this some thought. "Did you know that I once trained for the priesthood?"

"How would I know that?" Armando asked.

The manager ignored Armando's question. "I studied religion," he said. "All kinds of religion. And the books of religion. In the Jewish religion there is a book called the Talmud. And in the Talmud there is a blessing one is to say when one sees someone deformed from birth. The blessing is this: 'Blessed art Thou, O Lord our God, King of the Universe, who changes the creatures.' Perhaps what happened was due to some injury. Perhaps it was hereditary. Perhaps somewhere in your family line there have been others with such problems. Perhaps it is in the genes. You will never know. It is better, when looking at the photograph of your son," for he had seen that in fact Armando was holding a picture of the baby boy, "to recall this blessing." And he repeated the blessing one more time, looking at the photograph in Armando's hand, then turned to go.

Armando watched as the manager made his way back down the hillside to the dirt road that ran along the floor of the canyon, aware only of the pain in his head. He had never heard of the Talmud. He knew only that he was in need of beer and glue, and that he wanted to kill Ramón de la Christa Cortez, to work out on his head the way he had once worked out on the fence posts around the old corral where the Río Mayo made its way into the Gulf of

California, and he doubted the manager would hit back as hard as the fighters in Tijuana or be as hard to hurt. The men in Tijuana were like him. They came from hard lives. And Armando had looked once more at the photograph of his son. The boy was on his side, facing the camera, swathed in a large white bandage that allowed his arms and shoulders to be free, and he was smiling. A remarkable thing, that smile. It prompted Armando to dig a stone from the ground at his feet and throw it after the departing manager. The man was already too far away, but the stone got his attention. It caromed off a metal trash can and rolled on down the hill. The manager never looked back. He did, however, quicken his pace.

Back in Tijuana, Armando could no longer find work. Because he had complained about the conditions in the factory, because he had thrown a stone at the manager of human resources, he was blacklisted. In spite of their multinational character, in spite of the diversity of their products, the factories hired managers from the same pool, and the managers were, for the most part, all in the same club. They kept lists. They named names. Reina kept her mouth shut and was hired almost at once. She went to work in a factory owned by the Japanese, where conditions were not so bad as at Accessories de Mexico.

Armando stayed home. He slept during the day. At night he went in search of beer and glue, the colored lights blurred by pain. He asked Reina to bring glue from the factory but she told him there was none to be had in the new plant. She encouraged him to find work, any kind of work. He walked the streets instead, as if in search of something he had lost. He wandered the alleys of El Centro, past hookers—many of whom he now recognized as factory workers moonlighting to make ends meet in the new Tijuana.

Sometimes he walked the mesas, waiting for Reina, watching as the shifts changed in the factories, watching the armies of women. He did so with a mounting anger, for he had begun to think of the women as so many whores, in their fancy undergarments beneath their little blue smocks, selling themselves to the bosses while their men waited at home or loitered in the streets—the world as he believed it should be stood on its head to pay the piper. For her part, Reina did little to assuage these pangs of resentment. When she was not working extra shifts she seemed to have little time for Armando's attentions. She was one of them now, one of the employed, and Armando was back on the other side, once more in league with the unwashed multitudes.

From the street kids he learned the knack of pouring a little paint thinner into a soda can then carrying it with him at all times—little whiffs now and again to ease the pain. He was tormented by images of his son. He became increasingly suspicious of Reina, of the extra shifts she insisted upon working. He began to accuse her of various transgressions. He began to blame her for what his life had become. He might, he concluded, have been a great fighter after all, El Diablo de Sinaloa. Regret dogged his boot heels, midnight ramblings at the edge of the mesa, lone *penitente,* the lights of the city arrayed at his feet like valuables fallen from his pockets—the glories of a life not lived. The nights became indistinguishable, one bleeding into another, black on black, Armando on pathways always descending . . . till that moment of dim illumination by which he dared to hope once more, this now spectral medium, his dreams held in trust, for a second son conjured of fumes. He rushed home to inform Reina, invoking scripture. Why, even the Son of Man had come once to suffer, once to suffer and once to rule. Armando would train the boy himself. Years from now their progeny would make them rich. His wife recoiled in horror. She bore her memories like a crown of thorns. Armando was insistent.

So was she. Armando had no choice. He claimed his due by force, on this night and others like it, till the night she clubbed him with an iron poker, fleeing on foot from their shack on the hillside. Armando took up the poker himself, from where it had fallen to the dirt floor, and gave chase. She lost him somewhere near the mouth of the canyon, where the lights of a new convenience mart fired by a belching and farting generator, for there was no electricity yet run to this quarter of the city, burned above a barren lot and a crew of miniature cholos who crouched there like rodents over marbles on the ground and who, when asked if they had seen a woman, barefoot and running, had erupted in a cacophony of laughter and insult, digging stones from the hardscrabble ground, turning him from the chase.

Armando was the better part of a week in finding her. It took a man he'd known from the factory to direct his steps, a fellow casualty in this new incarnation of war between the sexes. The first thing Armando needed to understand, the man assured him, was that Reina had not conspired against him unaided, for so had it been with his own wife, and he told Armando of a group of women in an old part of Tijuana, in a house known as Casa de la Mujer.

The man had an address as well and by sunset of the following day Armando had found it, on a narrow side street, in a neighborhood of houses that actually looked like houses, with stucco walls, iron gates, and bars on the windows.

He'd stood in the street for a quarter of an hour, stymied by the walls, proclaiming his presence with insults and lamentations till a number of women had come out to confront him. It was then that he had seen Reina, in the arms of some Madonna, wrapped in a shawl as though she were no more than a child. The sight had inflamed him further and he had charged the gate. The women of

Casa de la Mujer had driven him back, hammering him with broomsticks as might some coven of witches while Reina, unmoved, remained huddled in the arms of her Madonna, in the shadowed arch of a door.

The noise of battle brought neighbors into the street and Armando had fled, fearing the arrival of police, but he had not given up. Night after night he stalked the neighborhood, occasionally shouting at the barred windows, hoping for a second opportunity to confront Reina outside the walls. But he did not see her again. In the end it was the Madonna herself who met him at the gate, where standing thus, he saw her for what she was, scarcely more than a child in her own right, yet straight and fearless behind her iron bars.

"You have to stop coming around here," she told him. "You're making a spectacle of yourself and your wife is gone." Her black hair, fallen to her shoulders, framed the delicate angles of her face, the dark eyes from which she regarded him with a measured contempt to which he was no stranger. Yet still, he thought, her beauty only added to its sting.

"Gone where?"

"Gone. It was what she wanted. She's had enough."

"What about what I want? What about my son?"

"You should go now," she said. "If you come again I will call the police."

"I want my son," Armando told her.

She stood in the doorway, a white peasant dress following the curves of her body, touching the floor, the bars still between them. "Your son is dead," she said finally. She spoke softly then turned and went back into the house, the door closing behind her.

Armando had remained on the broken pavement, staring into the yellow light that spread from barred windows, imagining such rooms as lay beyond, inner sanctums of womanhood, distant as the moon . . . And then a voice . . .

"I can tell you her name," the voice said. It issued from shadows at the mouth of the alley that ran along one side of the house. Approaching it, Armando caught sight of a blue light flaring beneath the bowl of a pipe, avicular features lit from below, bones like something blown of glass. Moving closer he saw that it was the man who had directed him, his compadre in loss. Armando's first thought was that the man had followed him, but the man shook his head. "I come here too," he said, and offered the pipe.

A single hit snapped Armando's head around like a punch.

"They took my child as well," the man said.

"What?"

The man waved toward the street where figures could just now be seen, approaching in the dark. Some carried torches or signs. Some were dressed in white, streaked with red. Still others carried children's dolls impaled upon sticks. They came like ghosts from a lost time. Maybe it was the dope. The torches flamed like planets cast down. A mounted policeman rode nearby—the clip-clop of shod hooves echoing between the buildings.

Armando was aware of the man at his side, whispering in the dark: "See the Guardians of Christ."

The marchers formed a line, chanting slogans in support of the unborn.

"There's a girl in there tonight," the man said. "They've found out about it." He nodded at the marchers. "They've come to keep out the doctor."

"The doctor?"

"The abortion doctor, fool. Why do you think the women go there?"

Armando stared into the face of his companion. The man's eyes gave off a dull sheen. "You didn't know," the man said and the idea seemed to amuse him. "You didn't know why the women came, why your own wife came . . ." The man laughed, his breath like something already dead. At which point Armando punched him in the solar plexus, hooking from the hips. He never had liked a harbinger of bad news. He took the man's works and smoked the rest of his stash right there on the street, a mounted cop not fifty feet away. The drug raised his skullcap to the stars. He felt the wind off the earth's rotation through the bones in his face. The man clawed at one leg. Armando dragged him further into darkness then cut his throat with a cheap Tijuana switchblade. The blood spurted and pooled. A light steam rose above it. The cop never saw a thing.

He went that night to a place he'd found upon the western flank of Cerro Colorado, to a high place overlooking the city and the great national flag, luminous above blackened rooftops, and to the west a vast darkness he knew to be the sea though no feature of that august body could be in any way discerned for it was a moonless night and the sky a featureless waste. He had come to mourn the passing of his son, unnamed and unborn, to meditate upon the depths of Reina's treachery and of those who had aided her; and he thought back over all that had transpired since coming to this godforsaken place, of two children already in the grave, and it seemed to him as though the wheels of that dark profundity beneath which he crouched had been set against him, as surely the moving pieces of that same profundity are akin to the machinery of a watch and so set against all men from the moment of their birth. And he felt that he'd come finally to the end of a long road, but that some new road lay yet before him. He did not imagine that what lay ahead would be in any way as varied or as long as what lay behind, for already he carried within him the signs of its ending and there would be none after it by which to continue. Of that he was certain and yet the road was not arbitrary. Its ending was in death and there was death as its marker. These things were as clear to him as the youthful dreams that had drawn him forthwith. And while the former seemed now as fraudulent as a whore's smile, the latter seemed both inevitable and irrevocable for it was part and parcel of the workings of justice and was in itself an aspect of that profundity he had so named and was endemic to its mysterious dispensations, and there issued from back of his parched lips the words to a prayer, the only one he knew: "Blessed art Thou, O Lord our God, King of the Universe, who changes the creatures." And before that night was over he had used the knife, the same with which he had taken the life of the factory worker, to scratch her name into the flesh of his arm, this Madonna, so as not to forget it amid some delirium to come.

9

THEY SENT the e-mail before dawn. Fahey's main phone was broken and his cell phone lost.

"How does one break one's phone?" Magdalena asked.

Fahey told her that he'd been sitting near the porch when last he'd used it, that he had placed it on the ground then run over it with his pickup. It was, she was beginning to see, a Fahey kind of story.

They were drinking coffee from cracked mugs, the eastern sky shot through with a sickly yellow light, or so it appeared to Magdalena. Perhaps, she thought, something had broken over there on the Mexican side of the fence, some great piece of subterranean plumbing, like a severed artery pumping tainted blood to stain the sky. She elected to share the observation with Fahey, this and others like it, elaborating upon her view of the maquiladora industry as a parasitic organism attached to her country, sucking away its life's blood.

Fahey looked toward the sunrise. His face was puffy in the bad light. There were white shavings in his beard and hair, stubble on his cheekbones where his beard was in need of trimming. He stared into the mesa for some time without speaking then rose to get more coffee. The maker from which he produced refills, like pretty much everything else on the property, save for the hula girl lamp, was held together with duct tape.

Magdalena watched as he poured. He was wearing a T-shirt. His arms looked tan and strong yet she detected a slight tremor of the hand, the latter eliciting some reflection upon her earlier enthusiasm. She was beginning to think that his aid might be more difficult to enlist than she had heretofore imagined. She was thinking too about what he'd looked like, in the dead of night, waking in something close to a blind panic, though she supposed some measure of the blame for that condition was her own. She'd begun by tapping at the window with her fingertips, then slapping it with the flat of her hand till a small piece of glass had fallen from a corner to break upon the floor. Fahey had come bolt upright at the sound, hitting his head on the sawhorse with enough force to dislodge his work in progress then casting about with a wild-eyed look she would just as soon not have seen before finding her at the window. She'd looked away as he struggled from the bag then heard his voice through the damaged pane, a single word. "What?" he'd asked. She had found his face within inches of her own, his hands cupped about his eyes. "I need a phone," she told him.

Which was when she learned that his was broken, though he did not say how just then, but motioned her around to a door and let her in, asking if a computer would serve, pulling boxes from beneath his workbench, not waiting for a reply.

Magdalena had taken the opportunity to examine the photographs on the walls. Many had been cut from magazines but others had not and many of these, like the one in the trailer, were photographs of Fahey himself, for she recognized the muscled shoulders, the flowing hair, the positioning of the arms. In a corner of the room, just above the light switch, there was another photograph that caught her attention. It was a picture of the young Fahey—that is, the Fahey of the waves. A young woman stood by his side and between them a grinning dog. Fahey and the girl were standing at the back of a pickup truck. The dog was seated in the bed. The picture appeared to have been taken at the side of a road, at some elevation, for below and in the distance one could make out a strip of white sandy beach and beyond it a turquoise sea very nearly indistinguishable from the sky above it. The color scheme suggested Baja, though the photograph had obviously been on the wall for some time, exposed to the elements, and its colors had taken on a delicate, milky hue that made their original intensity difficult to judge. Still, there were the faces of Fahey and the young woman, the grinning dog. One might have written "happy campers" somewhere beneath it. The other thing about the photo that caught Magdalena's attention was the girl. She was lithe and dark and quite obviously a Mexican.

She was still considering the photograph when Fahey announced that his computer was ready for use. She turned from the picture to find that he had cleared a place on his workbench where an ancient laptop now sat among more tools and shavings, its keypad black with an accumulation of dirt and grit.

Fahey sat on the floor, pulling on sandals while Magdalena typed out her message to Carlotta. He never asked what it said. Some of it she told him anyway, that it was extremely urgent she communicate with a friend in Tijuana, that quite possibly it was a matter of life and death, which is why she had taken it upon herself to wake him in the dead of night and for that, together with the breaking of his window, she had apologized profusely. He'd received both her story and compunction in silence, with nothing more to say till she was done, and they were left facing one another at the center of the cluttered room. It was an awkward little moment, ended by Fahey when he asked her about the coffee, namely if she would like some.

"You're not going back to sleep then?" she asked, the words no sooner out of her mouth than she was struck by the absurdity of the question.

Fahey said that he was not.

She said that she guessed she wouldn't either and they had repaired to the tiny kitchen, where everything was broken, then come outside to watch the sun rise above the mesa, for it had proven to be later than she had imagined, sitting for the most part in silence, though from time to time Fahey would direct her attention to the call of a particular bird, a clapper rail, a least tern, a western flycatcher . . .

"That's what you were doing on the beach," she said. "You were yelling about some bird."

"Snowy plovers," he said. He told her about their dwindling numbers, the delicate nature of the nests.

Magdalena listened. Her memory of the snowy plover was not an altogether pleasant one. "I don't think I've ever been shit on by a bird before," she said.

"It's how they defend themselves," Fahey told her. "Imagine the experience if there'd been a hundred instead of half a dozen."

"Thanks. I think I'll pass."

"That's what the coyote said to the fox."

Magdalena smiled. "You're quite the expert."

Fahey shrugged. "It's the valley," he said. "I know this valley and what's in it. You get me outside somewhere"—he waved toward the distant mesas as if the entire outside world was contained therein—"I don't know shit."

"What I know about is all over there," she said, and she told him a little about what she did. She told him about Vista Nueva and the boy who had died of lead poisoning.

Fahey listened but did not speak, as if these subjects belonged solely to that world beyond the valley, the world of his professed ignorance, and were not washed by the same polluted sea or warmed by the same yellow star.

"Maybe we should have some breakfast," he said.

He made scrambled eggs and toast. There were tomatoes and tomatillos mixed in with the eggs. He told her that the vegetables had come from the valley.

"From your garden?"

"Just from the valley. They grow here, if you know where to look."

Magdalena blanched. "I don't see how you could eat anything that grows here," she said.

"They're fine," he told her. "You just wash them off."

"They grow wild?"

"They come with the sewage."

She just looked at him.

"The seeds pass through the people that ate them. They wind up in the river. The river brings them here. Tomatoes, tomatillos, squash, melons . . . This was great farming land for many years. There was a time," he said, "when you could live off this valley. You could live here and this would be all you needed." He told her about Hoddy Younger, his shack of driftwood and whalebone, his traps for lobster, his crossbow for game, the patch of ground he'd tilled to plant his garden. "You should've seen it then," Fahey told her and so rhapsodic did he wax in the telling that by time he was finished she wished that she had and she was willing to say so, to which Fahey only shrugged. "Too late," he told her. "You missed it."

"I don't know . . ." She was thinking that maybe she'd been rather harsh in her judgment of what the valley might produce. "It doesn't seem so altogether bad. You live here."

But Fahey wouldn't hear it. He shook his head as the boughs of an oleander scraped at the side of his trailer. "This is nothing," Fahey said, "It's not even good leftovers."

He did his dishes then went to work in the shed, where he said he was making a surfboard. Magdalena dozed on the porch to the sound of an electric tool.

By noon there had been no answering e-mails and she was beginning to worry. She went to the shaping room once more, where she found him still working on the board, covered in the white dust, head to toe, wailing away with a power sander.

"I need a phone," she said.

Fahey said that his had been broken.

"Yes," she said. "I know. You ran over it with your truck. And your cell phone's been lost. But I have to make a call. Perhaps one of your neighbors . . ." Her voice trailed away. Deep in the cottonwoods and oleander it occurred to her that she had no idea whether there even were neighbors. It next occurred to her that if such neighbors did indeed exist, they were probably a lot like Fahey; their phones would have been destroyed or misplaced. It was that kind of place. It was, she thought suddenly, a lot like Mexico.

Fahey turned off the sander and hung it upon a wall. He used an air hose to blow away the dust, from both the board and himself, then spent a few seconds looking over his creation, lifting it, sighting down its edge as if inspecting it for flaws. "There's a phone in town," he said finally. "What do you think this is, some kind of backwater? I'll look in on the herd, then we can go."

She waited while he checked his windrows, feeling them with the flat of his hand, taking their temperature, adding water.

"You've got to keep the worm beds moist," he told her, "but not soaking wet."

He opened the passenger side door of the old rusted-out Toyota, clearing away the debris that seemed to have collected in the front seat since last she'd ridden there—a variety of newsprint, paper bags, empty beer bottles, the dried blossoms of pink oleander. When he was finished she got inside then watched as he walked around the front and slid in behind the wheel. He was still on about the worms.

"The pH is very important," he told her; "you've got to keep it between six and seven. The better the conditions, the more the little beggars will eat. They can eat up to half their weight in a day— anything that was once alive and is now dead." Fahey counted off several items on the tips of his fingers. "Paper, coffee grounds, table scraps . . ." As a parenthetical thought he noted the exclusion of meat or dairy products, then went on with his list, ending with mention of lawn clippings and manure from larger animals. "It's funny what they like," he said. "I talked to a woman out in Perris who feeds her worms crushed black walnut shells, says it makes them more lustful."

Magdalena watched the yellow trailer and the rows of old surfboards shrinking in the mirror on her door. "Lustful is not a term I would have thought to associate with worms," she said.

"Worms are hermaphrodites. In theory they could mate with themselves, but that does not seem to happen. They mate with other worms, romantic little bastards. Once impregnated, the female part gives off capsules, which develop into worms. What I've been into lately is trying to get a gray worm to mate with a red worm. The point would be to get a bigger red worm. Some entomologist out at UCSD told me this was impossible. So now I'm trying to prove him wrong. I'm experimenting with different combinations of animal manures, produce, feeds, supplements . . . Nothing so far, but there is this amino acid I'm pretty excited about. My capsule productivity has risen by twenty-five percent."

Fahey paused and Magdalena raised her eyebrows, making a shape with her mouth, nodding her head, hoping to appear interested, watching as the last of Fahey's farm slipped from view. One bend in the road and the entire place was lost behind layers of vegetation, nothing to mark its location save the trees with their limbs of dust and spider's webs, and if you did not already know what lay beneath them you would not think there was anything there at all. It was a place to hide, she thought, to hide from the world, and she thought of the worms, cozy in their hermaphroditism, at least in theory, each a little self-contained collection of opposites, not unlike the man who tended them. And that, it occurred to her rather suddenly, was what interested her. She was interested in Fahey and whatever it was that had gotten him here, from the waves to the worm farm, living small in his own little corner of the world.

She was still pondering such questions when she realized that he was sneaking glances at her as he drove, possibly in anticipation of some response, and she cast about for a moment or two, trying to remember exactly what it was that he had been telling her—something about the world's largest red worm. So she asked him why. It was the best she could come up with.

"To corner the bait market," Fahey told her, a satisfied smirk on his dusty face.

Magdalena nodded. "Of course," she said.

They rode in silence.

"So tell me about all those surfboards," she asked, "the ones you've built your fence out of."

Fahey shrugged. "My old quiver. I wasn't sure what else to do with it."

"Quiver?"

"Different boards for different waves and conditions."

"You must've been really into it," she said.

Fahey drove on, the truck rolling above ruts, marsh grass, and weeds, vegetation she could not name rising up ten feet high on either side of them, white dust floating in their wake.

"Yeah," he said. "I was."

"I saw your pictures. They're very nice. They seem to be of professional quality."

Fahey nodded.

"Were they taken here, at the river mouth?"

"Some were taken in town, by the pier. Some are from Mexico. A few from Hawaii. I guess you don't want to know any more about worms."

She looked to see if he was smiling, but it was hard to tell. He was watching the road.

"I guess not right now," she said. "Do you mind if I ask how you got the photographs?"

"I surfed in a few contests one year. I traveled a little. I got some attention. It was a long time ago."

He seemed unwilling to elaborate without further coaxing. She was tempted to ask about the photograph of the woman and the dog but thought better of it. She did not doubt there was a story there to tell, but she was still a little gun shy in the wake of her ordeal and she worried that the story might not be good for her. She could imagine the subjects of Fahey's photograph ending like Fahey's phones, one damaged, the other lost.

They drove on, a certain amount of the fine white dust raised by Fahey's tires finding its way into the cab. Magdalena cracked a window. A light breeze caressed her cheek. The dust swirled about. The sky burned hot and blue above the chalk white road, which must, she thought, have spent at least part of the past winter doing service as a riverbed, for it was littered with stones and articles of junk and old tire casings and these of a uniform color, caked in dried mud like articles borne on water and arrived here from some-place else.

"I've always wondered what that would be like," she said, finally.

"What what would be like? Growing worms?"

"Surfing," she said.

A roadrunner darted from the brush then ran on in front of them, the sun at its back, its body slanted longwise into its own shadow, nearly parallel to the ground before vanishing as quickly as it had appeared, back into the dusty vegetation.

"A greater roadrunner," Fahey said. "A kind of cuckoo, actually. You don't see them here as often as you used to." He slowed a bit, starring into the brush where the bird had gone, then added as a kind of afterthought, "There's nothing else quite like it."

"Nothing else like what? Worms, surfing, or roadrunners?"

Fahey smiled. "You pick," he said.

She studied his profile in the dusty cab. "So I guess your bumper sticker is right . . ." for she had seen the old decal on the stern of his trailer. "There really is nothing a day of surfing won't fix?" She thought this a clever remark that might engender further comment, but watched instead as the smile faded from his face.

"Yeah, there is," Fahey told her. "It took me a while but I found it."

10

A T SOME TURN in the road they were afforded a fresh look at the mesas that marked the southern edge of the valley, a perspective from which one could see the cars winding their way along Mex One, tiny dots of color shimmering above the steel arc of the fence with its gridwork and bracings.

"It looks like a carnival ride," Magdalena said.

Fahey glanced to see what she was looking at.

"The cars, the fence. You ever think that?"

"Maybe. I guess."

"I almost died up there."

"You almost died in the ocean."

"And then there were the dogs. That's three. You believe in nine lives?"

"I believe whatever happens happens."

"I forgot one," she said. "I almost died in Las Playas, where the fence runs into the ocean. It broke when I hit it . . . Do you know how many people have drowned there?"

Fahey maintained his usual silence in the face of such questions.

Magdalena studied the fence a moment longer, vanishing into the west, and upon whose ending she'd so nearly seen herself impaled. She noted too the trucks of the border patrol, perched in various nooks and crannies atop the mesas. She called the trucks to Fahey's attention. "What about them?" she asked. "Do we still need to worry?"

"Most of them know my truck," Fahey told her. "They're not going to come down for it. If we happen to run into someone, I'll just tell them you're a friend. Your English is so good I doubt there will be any question . . ."

"If they ask for identification?"

"It's back at my trailer?"

"If they insist on going to look?"

"Then we're fucked. But I don't think they will." He looked up at the green-and-white trucks. "They'll sit there all day, till their shift changes. The action's all at night, less of it now that there's the fence."

"And yet many people die because of it."

Fahey said nothing.

"But I crossed without trying," Magdalena said. She couldn't quite leave it alone. "The fence just crumbled away . . ."

"It does that out there on the beach sometimes. The ocean is rough and the saltwater eats away at things."

"But in Mexico, there are the names of the people who have drowned there, pinned against the fence by the currents."

Fahey nodded. "If you had been trying to cross, it wouldn't have happened for you like that. You would have been caught," he said. "Or the fence would not have broken."

Magdalena just looked at him. "Is that so?"

"It's the way life is."

"The way life is?"

"I believe it has something to do with the irony of human action."

"I didn't know you were a philosopher."

"I'm a worm farmer."

They kept to dirt roads, cut among a variety of grasses and tall reeds, the ubiquitous willow. Fahey called out various points of interest as they passed—a stand of wild radishes, eight feet high, a sandbar willow he thought to be of an impressive size and shape. They came to a place where the taller vegetation dropped away. In its place there was greasewood and sage then waving fields of orange poppies and a bright yellow flower Fahey named as sumac.

"This is quite lovely," Magdalena said.

"You think so?"

"Yes, I do." Across the undulating sea of flowers one might glimpse the tops of the dunes, sparkling white in the sun, and beyond these the craggy shapes of the Coronado Islands—blue shadows upon the horizon.

"Later I'll show you something," Fahey said. "Later on."

She turned to look at him. His eyes were still on the road, his hands atop the wheel. The wind of their passing was in his hair, lifting it from his face, and she was reminded of the photographs she had seen in the trailer—the young Fahey, a blond Adonis on a board. It wasn't a bad profile, she thought, you cut away some of the beard, you got rid of the dust from that board he was making, you scraped away the years and whatever it was that made him say that if she had been trying to cross she would have been caught.

"So what are you going to show me?" she asked.

"Just something."

✦ ✦ ✦

Eventually they came to paved road. They drove though tract homes that would have been nice for Tijuana but seemed quite shabby here, in California, in the Promised Land. She said as much to Fahey.

"Not down here," Fahey told her. "This is the end of the line, the only beach town in California no one wants, where the sewage meets the sea."

They drove down a main street anchored at one end by the No Problem Bar, and at the other by a bizarre collection of Plexiglas sticks rising above a number of stubby-looking benches that were shaped more or less like surfboards.

Fahey provided narration. The No Problem was a favorite haunt of the Navy SEALs who trained a few miles north, out of Coronado Island. "They used to train in the valley," Fahey said. "Did a lot of stuff right at the river mouth, for years. But the pollution got worse and they began to drop like flies. The toughest of the tough. They were losing it to amoebic dysentery and flesh-eating bacteria. So they gave it up. They still come to the bar, though. This time of day the place is okay. You go in there after midnight with an attitude, you'll be lucky to come out alive. It's like a Western movie . . ." Fahey turned to look at her. "You know about Westerns?"

Magdalena just laughed at him. It was perhaps the first time she had done so in his presence and he was struck by the beauty of it. "Yes," she said. "I know about Westerns. The Gunfight at the No Problem Bar."

"More likes fists and knives, but that's the idea."

He parked near the colored Plexiglas.

"They call this place Surfhenge."

"As in Stonehenge?"

"Unhappily, yes. It is intended as a tribute to the men who surfed the straits."

"Where I nearly drowned."

"You would not have been the first, believe me. I used to lifeguard here, here and in Rosarito . . ."

"You lifeguarded in Mexico?"

"For a while."

Fahey pointed out a pay phone near some public rest rooms at the entrance of the pier. To reach them it was necessary to walk among the Plexiglas sticks. "What are these things?" Magdalena asked. She was standing beneath a brilliant, electric green arch.

"I believe they are meant to represent waves."

"You seem dubious."

"Well, Christ, look at the place. It looks like a fast-food restaurant, without the food."

He had a point. She noticed a number of small bronze plaques scattered across the sidewalk at her feet. The plaques had names written on them in raised letters.

"And these?" she asked.

"The names of the surfers." He ticked off several of the names on his fingers, a dozen or more, without looking at the plaques. Many had colorful nicknames and she asked him about these as well. Fahey paused to smile. "Surfers are like sailors," he told her. "They love their stories. They love mythic waves and mythic characters, mysterious events that defy explanation. A good one enters the canon. It gets passed on."

"What about this guy, Kayak Jack?" She was reading from a plaque.

"Of Native American ancestry, reputed to have ridden Third Notch in a kayak."

"I see. And Third Notch?"

"There are basically three breaks out there. An inside break, a middle break, and an outside break. They call them First Notch, Second Notch, and Third Notch. The notches are canyons in the mesas. But you get out there a few hundred yards . . ." He gestured toward the ocean south of the pier. "They look like notches. And you can use them to tell you where to wait for the waves by lining them up with the old lighthouse in Las Playas. On a small day, when only the inside is working, you put that lighthouse right in the first notch, and that's where you wait; on a bigger day you move to second notch, and so on . . ."

"That's rather ingenious."

"Hoddy Younger," Fahey said. "The man I told you about. He was the real pioneer, the guy who figured it all out, as much as it could be figured . . . There's a fourth break out there too. Way out. Lots of the old-timers called it the Mystic Peak. Hoddy called it Outside the Bullring, because that far out, none of the lineups work anymore, and that, Hoddy would say, was when the straits were really the straits, meaning that if you chose to go for it, you were always going to be in harm's way. You blow it that far out, it's still no joke. But in his day . . . before wet suits and leashes . . . It was Hoddy who gave the place its name."

Fahey looked at her and laughed. "He rigged up this contraption once, fifty feet of line, an engine block on one end, a weather balloon on the other, rowed it out to where he thought the lineup might be for the Mystic Peak, and heaved it overboard. The next big swell washed it all away. There's still no real way to know if you're in the right spot or not. If you're too far outside, which is almost impossible, you can't catch the wave. If you're too far inside, you'll get nailed." He shrugged. "Not that anyone still cares."

"They built this," she said. "What happened?"

Fahey looked out across the beach. You could see the ocean from where they stood, a narrow band of blue whipped by the wind. "The waves are still there. The water got bad. It's surfed on occasion, but no one's ridden Outside the Bullring in more than a decade."

"It hasn't broken?"

"Not clean. Not epic. There's a lot of elements that have to come together, the right storm, the right tide, the right weather pattern. You might get it like that two, three years in a row, then not see it again for another decade."

"But you've seen it? You've been there?"

Fahey nodded.

"Is your name here then, on a plaque?"

"No."

"But you've surfed the straits?"

"I grew up surfing the straits."

"And you did it well."

Fahey gave this some thought. "In the world of surfing there is the concept of the waterman. I don't know if these kids coming up now think much about it anymore, but there was a time . . ." He paused. "Let me put it like this. Surfing is just one thing. I mean it may be the jewel in the crown, but it's still just one thing. Being a waterman was about more than one thing. It meant you not only surfed, you swam, dove, sailed, fished . . . It was about a life lived in harmony with the sea, with all of the elements, really . . ." He went to one plaque in particular, as if he'd been there many times before. The plaque bore a single name. "Hoddy Younger," he said. "Now there was a waterman."

"In his house of sticks and bones."

"Driftwood and whalebones, with a roof of palm fronds. It was pretty cool, really. And he rode the Mystic Peak, as big as I've ever seen it."

"You were there?"

"I was with him. I was sixteen and it was the first time I'd been that far out. I caught one wave. Smaller than Hoddy's, but still . . . It was Outside the Bullring."

"Then your name should be here too," she said. "You should have your own plaque."

But Fahey just shook his head. "I surfed well," he said, and his voice had a kind of faraway quality about it, as if he was speaking as much to the ghosts of the men whose names lay at his feet as he was to her. "But I didn't live well."

He led her among the gaily colored stems and arches that seemed to her to have acquired a rather more somber cast in the course of their passing, then nodded in the direction of the pier. "Phone," he said. He took a roll of quarters from his pocket and placed it in the palm of her hand.

She left messages at each of Carlotta's three numbers then called the women of Casa de la Mujer, where she spoke to a woman named Rosetta, a former factory worker turned activist, learning to her great relief that Carlotta had gone to Mexico City for a conference, that she had left several days ago and would not be back for several more.

"But what happened to you?" Rosetta asked. "We heard about your car. We were all worried sick, Carlotta most of all . . ."

"Too much to tell," Magdalena said, then told her some of it anyway—a truncated version of recent events.

"Holy Christ," Rosetta said.

"What I really need are my files. My laptop and my files . . ."

"Why not come here?"

"I feel safe where I am. I need time to mend, and to get my bearings. I would like to know who was behind this before I come back."

"You may never know."

"I can try. I will also need another amparo. Mine was lost. Carlotta can help me with that when she comes back. In the meantime, if I had my files, I could work right here, uninterrupted."

She heard the other woman sigh. "You may be right," she said. "Not to come back so soon. Another factory girl has been killed."

"When?"

"The night before last. The same as the others."

Magdalena felt the news in the pit of her stomach.

There was a moment of silence on the line, the buzz of a faint static. "But then your files are so many," Rosetta said. "How can you ever get all of them?"

Magdalena felt a momentary despair, the likes of which she had felt that night upon the bluffs at the candlelight vigil for the boy. What good were her files in the face of this new atrocity?

"Are you sure you're all right?" Rosetta asked her. "Maybe it was wrong of me to tell you about the girl. Maybe now was not the time . . ."

"No, no, I'm okay. Really. I was just thinking about the files." And indeed she was, thinking about all that was there, trying to decide if she should wait for Carlotta, yet hating to lose the time, then catching sight of Fahey through one of the Plexiglas windshields that flanked the pay phone, for in the heat of the moment she had all but forgotten about him. Yet there he was, standing some ways out on the pier, looking south, faded print shirt and corduroy pants whipped by the wind. Magdalena watched him for some time. "Maybe I could send someone," she said.

11

ARMANDO AVOIDED the scene of the crime for several days, an act of will he took as evidence of a fundamentally prudent nature. When he finally did return by the light of day, the house seemed different though he could not have told you how or why. Perhaps, he concluded, it was he who had changed. As for the body of his fellow worker, there was only some slight rust-colored smear along the wall of a building at the mouth of the alley to mark his passing and even this appeared as next to nothing in the harsh midday light. It was not even recognizable as blood, and might just as well have been some bit of shoe polish or the paint of a passing car. Such fluids as Armando had last seen pooling in the alley had been hosed down, or washed by rains, the body long gone, a footnote in some street cop's ledger, one more nameless *naco* lost to the night. Armando was a moment in contemplation of this faint talisman, then put the story from his mind and from the world as well, for there was none but himself to tell it.

He came again that night and once more on the following morning but neither of these visits bore the desired results. His wife was gone, as was the Madonna who had taken her.

Throughout this period he had continued to occupy the house on Reina's *terrino*. But suddenly one morning, a man appeared, claiming to be the new owner. The man came with a paper in his hand and he did not come alone. There were others there with him, half a dozen altogether. The men wore work boots and carried pick handles, as if in expectation of trouble. Armando had little choice but to leave. He went with nothing but his knife and the clothes on his back, shuffling down a steep hillside among dust and tumbling stone, the canyon bottom yawning before him—this dark pit of refuse and toxic waste and no place on earth to receive his shambling ruins but the reeking stone corridors of Colonia Subterráneo.

Which is what the Tunnel People called it—that great network of storm channels that lay across and at times beneath the sprawl of the Zona del Río, the new Tijuana. His first night down he was forced to fight for his life—his training above the As Negro making itself truly useful for the first time. His opponent was eager but unskilled, and after the fight, Armando became something of a leader in the tunnels, a man of respect. In time he was doing what the Tunnel People did to stay alive, a little theft, a little extortion. Sometimes they robbed the freights where an American railroad ran close to the fence near the border crossing, leaping to the top of passing flatcars, off-loading whatever they could get their hands on. But there was no real pleasure in it. In a world where babies were born without brains, it was just natural that a man should want to do a little harm. At night he watched the factory girls of El Centro and the Zona Norte as they boarded the buses for work, hunkering upon some cornice along the path of the river circumscribed in concrete, eyes burning like coals in their sockets, his face warmed by the butane lighter held to the bowl of the glass pipe in his hand, for he'd found that with a little money in his pockets, he could indulge in finer highs than beer and glue. In time, however, the American trains began to carry armed guards and were not so easy to take down. Armando left the tunnels and moved into a deserted factory on the edge of the mesa overlooking the Colonia Vista Nueva.

He'd heard about the factory from a man who sometimes came to the channels to traffic in stolen goods, a cowboy with a red convertible who lived next door to the old smelting plant at the rear of an auto body shop and so knew of its availability. And indeed the site was to Armando's liking, with its piles of rotted battery casings, its rusted pipes and cinder-block walls. He cleared a place in a corner of the building where the roof was mostly intact and the walls were thickest and he hung there a hammock and he built a fire ring out of stone and covered it with an iron grate by which to warm his food and boil his water.

Also to his liking were the warning signs posted about the factory's perimeter. The signs made certain of his privacy and those not scared away by such postings were soon enough scared away by rumors of the strange, gaunt man who had taken up residence there, in the midst of such poisons that he was declaimed by some as their very agent and by others as the devil himself. Still others took him for a criminal come up from the channels, a murderer in hiding or perhaps some recreant apothecary.

These tales and others like them were conveyed to him with great enthusiasm by the cowboy in the red convertible. Armando did nothing to dispel them. On the contrary, he was beginning to see how they might be put to his advantage. It was during this time that he took the liberty of having the disembodied eyeball tattooed into the ever-expanding bald spot at the rear of his skull, and he went about armed and dangerous and half deranged from whiffing fumes so that factory girls and workmen alike were more often than not put to flight by his very approach and even the cowboy was at times a little bit frightened by him. In the cowboy's case, however, his fear was tempered with a certain grudging admiration as he, too, was a student of crime with aspirations of his own in that department, and as word of Armando's frightening countenance and dubious accomplishments continued to spread, even into those parts of the city where such things as wanton bloodshed and mindless violence were valued like rare coins, so did the cowboy imagine his own claim, however modest, on the other's ascent.

And indeed it was true that men would sometimes come to Armando with money to pay for favors—a store manager threatened or tortured, a small-time dope seller carved and robbed, a girl to be snatched from one of the factories then sold to the slavers at the border . . . The men who came to see him about these jobs were not the men who paid but the men who worked for the men who paid and they came in fine cars and expensive clothing and often wore surgical masks when approaching his ruins. The money rolled in. The stories multiplied. There came a night, walking home in the wake of some foul deed, that Armando heard a street musician at the door of a factory, the man giving voice to a crude corrido in praise of the exploits of El Diablo de la Mesa, and he stayed himself in the shadows and listened, for it seemed to him that he himself had become the subject of song, which in fact was the case, and he went so far to imagine a shrine built in his honor, such as he had seen in his youth, monuments to the drug lords of Sinaloa. In Armando's case he imaged a pair of boxing gloves dangling from the neck of the virgin, the lost cartilage of his nose arranged at her feet, a small pile of reeking waste and next to this a container of the yellow glue. He might have taken some pride in finding himself the subject of song but in truth he was past all of that now and there was really only a kind of snaking dumb wonder, a standing and gaping, at the awful procession of things as they are.

It should also be noted that Armando took no great satisfaction in the deeds themselves. Nor did he think much about them when they were done. He viewed them as the manager of human resources had once viewed his son, as he'd learned to view the murder of the factory worker who had told him about the abortion clinic, as a part of nature. Though it is also true there were now many things he could no longer remember about his son, or about himself for that matter. The future was a corrido sung high on fumes, a reflection in a bottle, the past a fever dream, punctuated by a single brilliant image—that of his Reina in the arms of her Madonna. For if it is true that each man is a child wandering lost in a forest of symbols as some have said, then for Armando, the little tableau so named had not simply continued to burn in his mind's eye, it had become the lamp to light his way, the marker on the road, and though there were none around him to so state it, one might well have dispensed with the host of rumors as to why he'd come to the mesa and cited only Hades in pursuit of his Persephone as the more direct representation of Armando's intentions. The old recycling plant was at the very heart of the factory district. It was the perfect vantage point from which to resume his search for Reina—the search his sojourn in the tunnels had put on hold—and so had he done, prowling once more among the industrial parks, wandering among the armies of working women, revisiting the neighborhood of Casa de la Mujer. And yet his wife was gone and the Madonna with her, swallowed whole in this city by the sea.

❖ ❖ ❖

Had he never seen either of them again, he might have reached a time when each would have been called into question, and each found wanting, their origins ascribed to some nightmare born of fumes, the scratches on his arm as mysterious as a birthmark. But such was not to be. As out of the blue, the Madonna appeared once more, in faded jeans and a Casa de la Mujer T-shirt, not fifty yards from where he waited, amid his block walls and rotted casings, peering out across the rim of the mesa and the paths of the factory girls.

By some miracle, she had come to his very door. But there was a catch—a miracle with a bit of hooked steel set to snare the eager jaw. There were people with her, a man with a camera, a woman with a briefcase. On the following day she came again, the others still with her. He watched as they moved about the bluff, in back of the factory, taking pictures, making notes. He followed at a distance as they walked the path between the body shop and the factory. He followed as far as the street, where they got into a car, Magdalena behind the wheel, then watched as they drove away.

The cowboy said the woman with the briefcase was an attorney and that Magdalena was her helper, that he had heard them talking to the owner of the body shop and that they were trying to do something about the old plant in which Armando lived. It was unbelievable. His first thought was that she had been given into his hand. He now saw that it was she who pursued him.

Later that night, alone in his hammock, he'd pondered this mystery and others like it till sleeplessness had driven him to the dirt pathway where the smell of tobacco and trace of smoke spooling upon a night sky had led him to Chico in the back of the red convertible, as that was where the cowboy lived, in his car, at the rear of the body shop.

"Who's they?" Armando said. He put his weight against the fence that ran along the path, screening the body shop from the rest of the world, the steel mesh corroded with time, giving beneath him.

He saw the cowboy come bolt upright in the backseat of the car, his cigarette tumbling to the floor. "For Christ's sake," Chico said.

Had the cowboy not already confided his age it would have been impossible to guess it. He might have been twenty. He might have been forty. He had a large Aztec sun tattooed on his stomach, gang-land-style. When working at the body shop he went about in grease-stained rags, missing teeth. Come the weekend he would add a bit of cheap Tijuana bridgework, dress himself in cowboy finery, and go about in his ancient red convertible in search of factory girls to satiate his desires.

"Who's they?" Armando said once more.

"What do you mean, who's they?" Chico asked. He was somewhat disoriented. Armando Santoya made for a disturbing spectacle at almost any hour but even more so by moonlight, in the dead of night.

"You said they wanted to get rid of the factory. I want to know who they are."

Chico looked him full in the face, his own vacant as the moon. Armando was about to turn around and go back the way he had come when some dawning light of recognition fluttered across Chico's face, the bat-winged shadow of dim intelligence above a nearly toothless grimace. "Oh, that," he said. "I didn't know what the fuck you were talking about."

Armando waited, at rest upon the fence.

Chico pulled himself to the rear deck of his car, where he settled upon his haunches, a feral animal awaiting treats. "It's these women," he said. He waved toward the lights of the city sparkling beyond the dark rim of the mesa.

A junkyard dog slunk from shadow and set about barking at Armando. Chico was quick to drive it away with some object snatched from the back of his car, thrown hastily into the night. "They say the factory is bad for the children."

"What children?"

"You know, down there . . ." Chico nodded in the direction of the *colonia* at the base of the hill.

Armando looked off into the night. He saw no children but his own, dead young and dead unborn, vitreous flesh emitting starlight . . . "Casa de la Mujer," he said.

"Say what?"

"The women. It is what they are called."

Chico shrugged. "Maybe. I don't know." In truth he didn't. Not knowing made him uncomfortable. Armando's eyes glinted in the night. He wanted to change the subject. "Is it true," Chico asked, "that the Obregón brothers keep tigers?" He knew the answer to this one but he wanted to hear Armando tell it.

Armando made a vague gesture with one hand, as if to dismiss the subject, though in Chico's case he knew this to be an impossibility. The cowboy harbored an obsession with the Mexican drug lords, both large and small, but especially with those famous enough to appear in the contraband music he played incessantly upon the tape deck dangling beneath the dashboard of his convertible amid a web of exposed wires and tiny glass tubes. That Armando had actually done jobs for a number of these men filled him with both dread and envy. He knew there was a part of the city in which such men lived, in their million-dollar mansions, behind walls of stone, among menageries of wild animals kept for no other reason than that they could be kept, objects of status, like a new car, a fine watch, or a beautiful woman. Nor could Armando escape all blame for his friend's infatuation, having on at least one occasion made the stoned-out-of-his-gourd mistake of admitting to firsthand knowledge of these amazements, though in truth he'd done little more than hear of them in his own right, for he was hardly an invited guest to such halls of power but was rather like some dangerous animal retained on occasion for the dirtiest of jobs. But for now he was willing to move his head knowingly in the dim light, an assent to fantasy . . . "They feed their enemies to them," he said. "You're not careful they'll put a T-bone steak up your ass and lower you into a pit with chains."

Chico shifted his weight, bouncing upon his coiled legs. "No way," he said, the words issued as a chorus, a response to Armando's call, as between a preacher and his congregation.

"These things are the truth."

A solitary tooth glinted in the moonlight. "Maybe you could use me sometime," the cowboy said.

Armando sighed. The man's ambitions bored him and his first instinct was to tell Chico to go fuck himself because rarely did he need help in carrying out an assignment and when he did there was already one that he used, and that child of darkness unbeknownst to any save himself and bound to remain so. But he checked this impulse as something else was at just that moment beginning to occur to him, a new plan of action. He looked into the darkness beyond the rim of the mesa where the lights of Tijuana cast a pale frosting upon the night sky, like breath made visible, as if some great warm-blooded thing lay hidden there, then cast his eye upon the Chevrolet convertible listing before him, among refuse and weeds, faint reek of body odor and gasoline above grease-spattered soil, its owner like a hood ornament misplaced, dangling cigarette clutched in toothless jaws, potential acolyte, partner for a day.

"I'll tell you what," Armando said. For he was thinking now of his Madonna, that if she had come twice, she would come a third time, and for that he intended to be ready. "I'll make you a deal."

12

FAHEY WAS QUIET when they left the pier, as if the visit to the unfortunate monument had turned him inward. Magdalena let him be. She had her own demons to contend with. The news of the murdered factory girl accompanied her like a cloud, shadowing her thoughts. What new evil was this? she wondered. And how long would it go on? How many more girls would die before someone put an end to it? She was mindful of the deaths that haunted Juárez, the other great city of the border, where in recent years, literally hundreds of factory girls had been murdered, where authorities looked on with apparent helplessness as the body count mounted, as the web of mystery and deceit, of lies, false leads, forced confessions, and general corruption that surrounded the bodies of the innocents grew more impenetrable by the hour. Was Tijuana now destined for something of the same? The thought rested in her mind like a splinter, poisoning her resolve. To do just one thing, she thought, to rid the city of just one evil . . . was that too much to ask? She stared into a coloring sky, a dusty orange light above willow and marsh. Perhaps so, she thought, catching herself at an angle, reflected in the mirror on the door of Fahey's truck. "Who do you think you are?" she asked, the question posed in silence, answered in silence, for there were none forthcoming from the quarters into which she stared—the valley beyond her window, as great a repository of bones and dreams as one was likely to find, and above which a flock of shorebirds broke suddenly from beaches beyond her sight. The birds rose in asymmetrical perfection before an immutable sky, their very existence a thing of beauty, yet if one fell to earth, the others would do no more than peck it to death on the beaches below and didn't she know it.

She closed her eyes in the face of this observation, the tips of her fingers pressed into the center of her forehead as though she'd located her mystical third eye and might by such pressure bring it to bear on all such mysteries and speculations, and then proceeded to sit that way for some time, as though by adhering to the pose she was, in some way and at the very least, holding it all together, as if in the end, this was the most that one might ask of oneself, regardless of who one thought one was.

It was the jarring of the truck that eventually diverted her, giving her to understand Fahey had turned off pavement and onto dirt once more. She opened her eyes to find them at the southern edge of the valley, very near the fence and churning along through what appeared to be more of a dry riverbed than any kind of road and clearly not one of the routes by which they had gone to town.

Still, she said nothing. Her trust in Fahey had risen considerably since their first meeting, and Fahey drove on. They had gained in elevation. There was a view, across the scrub of Border Field State Park, toward the sand dunes and beaches, and Fahey was taking them higher still, the hot smell of burning rubber she took for his clutch drifting back to fill the cab. She was beginning to wonder if his truck was up to the task he had set for it when he turned from the climb onto a patch of level ground and killed his engine.

The area was a kind of pie-shaped notch carved by the elements into the northern face of one of the mesas, no more than twenty yards deep, marked by a smattering of grass and three small pine trees of undistinguished character.

Fahey had still not spoken. He unfastened his seat belt and got out. Magdalena did the same. "Is this what you wanted to show me?" she asked.

"I thought you might like to see these," he said. He was looking at the trees. "Bishop pines. Some people would probably think they were Torrey pines, but Torrey pines have larger cones."

The cones on the trees before them were no bigger than the end of her thumb.

"The Bishops are indigenous. They think that about thirteen thousand years ago, there was a forest of them running from at least as far north as Santa Barbara all the way down the coast, on into Mexico. There's still a little forest of them on La Purisima Ridge in Santa Barbara and some more down in Eréndira, in Baja. And there's these, right here."

They stood for a moment before the trees.

"Trees are kind of like animals. You leave them alone, they interbreed; over time they'll form their own little subspecies. These trees are probably unique. Nothing else in the world quite like them. The trees are low because they get most of their moisture from the fog. Check the needles."

He put his hand to the end of a bough, holding the tips of the needles across the palm. "See their shapes. Each is able to create a little vortex around itself, which allows it to hold the air just a little longer, to draw as much moisture as it possibly can from what's available."

Magdalena saw that her first impression of the trees would stand in need of revision. "You know the first thing I thought?"

"They're not much to look at."

"Maybe you should give tours of the valley. You could open a shop."

Fahey gave her a look, then turned to the trees once more. "Yeah, well, there it is, the last of the great forest for two hundred miles in either direction. You disappointed?"

"Are you kidding? I wouldn't have missed it . . . Everything that has happened . . . this makes it all worthwhile."

For a moment they just looked at each other. Fahey shook his head. "You try to share, this is what you get."

They walked to the edge of the little clearing, a good deal of the valley spread out below. They were almost even with the old bull-ring. The Tijuana lighthouse rose before it like a bone, hard-edged in the long rays of light.

"That's where it happened," she said. She was looking toward the fence where it entered the sea, just barely visible in the thickening coastal light, a mile from where they stood. "If I told my story on the Mexican side of that fence, the peasants would build a shrine—Our Lady of Las Playas . . ."

"For you?"

"For whatever it was that pulled me to shallow water." She checked to see if he was listening. "You don't believe that part, do you?"

"On the contrary."

Magdalena waited. One could see the streets of Las Playas from this elevation, windswept and vacant, basking in light the color of old brass.

"But I don't think it was a lady."

Another moment passed. "I think he's still out there some-where," Fahey said. "I think I saw him once. I think he lives among the homeless in Tijuana. But I think he passes back and forth, at night through the canyons, or maybe out at the beach."

As she realized what he was saying, she experienced an actual shiver, like a child listening to a ghost story. Because she thought it might be true? Or because this was what he believed? "Hoddy Younger," she said. "You think he's still alive?"

"He'd be around eighty . . ."

"You're not serious?" But of course he was and she saw that her words might have offended him. She touched his fingers with her own, almost taking his hand but not quite. She could see that Tijuana was not the only place where folktales might hold sway in the light of day. "Then maybe we should make a shrine on the American side," she said, "of whalebones and driftwood."

"The whalebones would be hard to come by." A faint smile turned the lines of his face, the long rays streaking his hair with light.

She saw that he meant to go and this time she took him by the wrist. "Maybe you're right," she said. "I mean there was somebody." She took a long breath. "But now I need to ask you something."

His countenance darkened considerably. What she saw there reminded her of what she had seen the night she had awakened him in the shaping room, with the need to contact Carlotta. It was the look of someone who'd just been told the house was on fire, or something like it. Still, she had come this far . . . She saw no reason not to carry on. "A favor," she said. And she told him about the files, in Casa de la Mujer, in Tijuana, in Mexico.

13

H E WOULD NOT say yes or no on the mesa. He simply walked away. Magdalena followed. They drove in silence to the farm, where Fahey commenced to dampen his windrows and check their pH factor. Keep it between six and seven. They dined on canned tamales, tortillas browned in a skillet.

"I don't know, about this Tijuana thing," he said, as if more than two hours had not transpired since she'd ask him about crossing the border.

They were seated on the deck, the last of the dinner in paper plates held on their laps. Crickets sang in the darkness. There were bats in one of the cottonwoods and from time to time she would see them. They appeared as black, erratic shapes upon a Halloween sky.

"I've got the worms to think about. And there's this guy waiting on that board I'm making."

"I could help you with the worms," Magdalena said, "you tell me what to do."

Fahey looked unhappily into the dark yard.

"I think you could do it in an afternoon, two or three hours, really." She understood this to be an exaggeration, adding that she could not go herself, because of the amparo, which was not an exaggeration. "It would mean so much," she said, finally. "If we can build a case against just one of these foreign factory owners . . . It would mean so much . . . to so many people."

He would not look directly at her, but drank his beer, staring thoughtfully into the night.

"I might be able to figure out who tried to kill me," she said.

"That would be in your files?"

"Maybe, in some way, yes."

Fahey nodded.

"You don't much like it there, do you? Mexico, I mean."

"Not much."

"Do you want to talk about why?"

Fahey looked at her for the first time. The booze was aging him, she thought. Booze and this life he led.

"That might take a while," he told her.

She supposed it was like asking why he no longer surfed, or who the woman was on the photograph in his workroom.

"Maybe I should just put it like this, helping people has never been something I was very good at."

"Ah, yes, the irony of human action."

"You could say. And you would have to be alone while I was gone, here in the valley."

"Is that so bad?"

"You don't know the valley," he said. "Not really. And not at night."

"This is night."

"This is a little oasis, with a chain-link fence, dogs, and a bad reputation."

"Then I should be all right."

Fahey shrugged, looked away. "Maybe," he said.

"It would only be for a few hours." She knew she was pressing it.

"Longer, I get stuck in traffic."

"You pay attention, I can teach you a shortcut."

"That's what they told the Donner party."

Magdalena leaned forward in the wooden lounge chair, her hand moving to touch his forearm. "Lives are at stake," she said. And yet hearing herself say it she wondered if this was really the case, or only what she wanted to be true. For the news of the murdered factory girl had called her into question, herself and her work, all that she was about in the world. It was a gut feeling, she knew, running over reason. Yet the girl had died on a night like this. Who could say that in the morning, there would not be another—some discarded bit of human refuse at rest among the weeds, on the morning to come and on every other morning from now until time indefinite, while Magdalena studied her paper trails and factual reports?

And yet surely, she thought, someone had tried to kill her. And maybe the files would suggest an answer. Maybe it was only her own life that hung in the balance, and she wondered briefly if that was enough.

Fahey sat with her hand upon his arm, for some time, watching the yard in which there was little to watch. But in the end he turned, he let his eyes find hers. He knew it was a mistake. Yellow lamp light from inside the trailer was running along the edge of her jaw, the fine straight line of her nose. "I guess I could have the cowboys look in on you," he said finally, hearing his own words, not quite believing that he was actually saying them. But then he could hardly tell her the truth, or at least could not bring himself to do so, that even going to Tijuana for the meds had provoked such panic attacks as he had suffered in the maze and this on a trip that had scarcely taken him beyond the gate.

He finished his beer and rose to get another. The beer helped. He snuck a pill while still in the kitchen. The odds improved. He could probably do it, go and come in an afternoon. No one would know. Except her, of course. She would know if he went and know if he didn't. She would judge him accordingly and he would judge himself in her eyes. Who would have thought it? Thank God for Valium and beer. In sufficient quantities he might just pull it off, a fool for love in the city of the lost. It was classic Fahey—everything he had always been, and everything he had promised himself not to be, ever again, for all that it had gotten him in the past.

"I guess I'll have to think about it," he said finally. He was standing in the narrow doorway that separated the kitchen from the room she was in. "Maybe I can talk to the cowboys in the morning. They're early risers."

He went outside after that. She watched him go. The smallest of the two dogs ran out from beneath the trailer and bounced along at his heels, a white spot in the night. She watched as he stood at the side of his windrows. It seemed to her that he was there for quite some time. Eventually though he went into the shed and after a while she heard the familiar buzz of his sander and a boom box playing Chet Baker.

She lay in the dark, a blanket pulled up to just beneath her chin. She lay there without sleeping. The music and the sander went on for a very long time. At last she dozed, then woke near dawn and looked outside.

It was quiet. The yellow bulb still burned in the shed and for a moment she believed that he must be asleep. And then she saw him, at the farthest reaches of the workroom light. He was out there in the dark with the board he had shaped, naked save for what was either a baggy swimsuit or boxer shorts. The board lay on the ground—a pale sliver against the dark earth—and Fahey stood next to it, apparently engaged in some kind of little dance. At least that was what it looked like. She watched as he cross-stepped, forward and back, with quick, almost dainty steps, then stopped, turning his shoulders, swaying at the hips. She watched as his arms rose above his head, exposing a bit of a paunch around his middle, yet she could see the rounded muscles of his back as well, their hills and valleys shaded by the faint light, as his arms drifted down till they were nearly parallel to the ground, rather, she thought, like a gull in flight, and she understood then what it was he was up to—this little dance at the side of the board. The bit with his hands had given him away. Fahey was surfing, or at least pretending to, alone in the dark, a good two miles from the nearest wave.

14

THE DEAL WAS fixed on the Mesa de Otay, on a sweltering September afternoon, not fifty yards from where she had first appeared. Armando and Chico, together now, hunkered over beers in a corner of the body shop, squatting above the grease-spattered dirt like plungers at a game of craps, the slinking curs who guarded the place lying nearby, tongues lolling, snapping at flies, bellies pressed against dirt blacker than coal, the corrugated tin roof beneath which they had all come for shelter useless before a sun already low enough in the west to have come between it and the ground, igniting the polluted airs that lay between as though some angel of the Apocalypse had poured out his bowl upon the sea.

At the heart of their agreement was a simple plan. When she came again, Chico, who had some skill as a mechanic, would do something to her car, anything that would cause it to break down, but not in front of the factory, anywhere but there and hopefully somewhere on the outskirts of town. Armando and Chico would follow in the red convertible. After the car had broken, when Magdalena got out to investigate, Armando would swoop down to grab her.

What he had in mind after that was more complicated, yet he had prepared a place to receive her, an old mining shaft east of the city, where her screams would go unheard, where even the witches of Casa de la Mujer could never find her. To what end she might come there, or rather by what circuitous paths she might reach it, for he reckoned the ending was known well enough, would have been harder to predict. Still, he'd spent long hours alone in this pit, lost in the meticulous arrangement of those articles he'd deemed appropriate, many pilfered from dumps or stolen outright from places he'd gone in performance of the jobs that Chico so envied, trinkets to which their owners could no longer lay claim. He brought candles in abundance and pieces of cloth, brightly colored. To these were added all manner of ropes and chains and assorted bric-a-brac, including a stuffed owl in a rusted birdcage, the former dressed as a child's doll with a lace doily upon its head. And there were other things too, things he had carried on his person for as long as he could remember—a photograph of Reina taken on the day of their wedding, a scrap of paper from the hospital in Reynosa upon which a doctor had written something he could not read but that he guessed was about his son and this crumpled as an old bill, as was the photograph itself. He arranged these by candlelight, affixed to beams amid walls of dirt so that over time this hole had come to resemble the burial site of an ancient king, or perhaps the gathering place for flagellants, secrets, whose ceremonies in their minutiae were hidden even from the builder of their chapel. What he knew for certain was that some ceremony would take place there, a ritual of blood, in whose performance particular events could be assigned their rightful place in the economy of a universe that was none but his own. He knew this and one thing more. It was a ceremony in which her attendance would be required.

The riskiest part of Armando's plan was the apparent necessity to execute it in broad daylight. But then he had seen the logo of Casa de la Mujer on handbills attached to telephone poles all over the mesa, handbills alerting him to the candlelight vigil. It was better than anything for which he might have hoped and he rushed to inform Chico, at work on a six-pack, in the stifling heat of late afternoon. "Tonight's the night," Armando had said. And they had finalized the last details of the plan. "And after this, there will be others," Chico said, their business concluded.

Armando shrugged, rising from his haunches. "We will see," Armando told him. "We will see how you do."

Chico grinned, watching as the other man walked away. He was certain he would do just fine, though he had little interest in this Madonna, as Armando liked to call her. That she was pals with some attorney even made him a little nervous. But he had seen the rolls of bills in Armando's hands, spread between those grease-blackened fingers with their bitten and splintered nails, and when thoughts of the attorney made him uneasy he would try instead to imagine the halls of the drug lords, exotic animals pacing in jungle-like settings behind walls thick as those of the Alamo. And he would make sure that after tonight, after this thing with the woman, there would be other more lucrative partnerships and that he would begin to make his way among at least some of those men now immortalized in song.

For his part, Armando could see the gears working through the holes in Chico's head. The truth was that he had no intention of partnering up with Chico for more than a night and fully intended to rid himself of the man as soon as the job was done. For in essence the cowboy was like too many he'd known already, just one more child of the streets, quick and mean, less trustworthy than a jackal. His skill as a mechanic and his car, these were the things that made him valuable, and if, in the end, he was more difficult to be rid of than Armando had heretofore imagined, he might just feel compelled to make a particular introduction, and in fact began to take such perverse delight in that imagined confrontation that by the time he had returned, later that afternoon, to the old factory, where he had intended to nap, he went instead to work, clearing a place among the piles of debris to make way for the red convertible.

What Chico failed to appreciate was that Armando survived by knowing how to be silent. The men who hired him knew where to find him and it was they who came to him when they needed something done, never the reverse. They set the price. Armando never questioned it. He never pestered or begged. Chico had not yet helped out on a single job and already he was a pain in the ass, already asking for more. And then of course there was the other part of the equation, the thing the young cowboy could hardly be expected to know, that Armando was already in possession of a partner, when such a partner was needed, a partner who would never ask for more, who would not wish to meet the men from whom the money flowed, about whom the men would never know—Armando's secret weapon, strong as a bull, faithful as a hound . . . Armando had already taken steps to see that he would be waiting at the mine shaft to meet them, ascending from that black hole as though provoked from the very depths, face scarred to the point that it appeared only half formed, as if its owner was a piece of work still in progress, yet damned even so, like some junkie's child, born to addiction and thereby censured prematurely, sharpened screwdrivers and rusted church keys dangling from silver chains . . . Armando caught in his mind's eye, as though it were a thing already transpired, the exact look on Chico's face as he saw it coming, this denizen of such menageries as the cowboy had not yet thought to name, the instrument of Armando's will, for such had he become and so was he likely to remain, till such time as comes to all men, when each is reclaimed by darkness . . .

Still, it was just Armando and Chico the night she got away, following in the old convertible, the instrument of Armando's will, together with such introductions as were sure to follow, scheduled for a later date. But later never came.

Chico said she was drowned. There was no other way, he said. His voice sounded as though he were talking from the bottom of a drum, the Madonna having broken his nose. But then Chico had said the car would break much sooner as well. All Armando had needed was to get her away from the factories. But the car had gone on and on, to the highway above Las Playas, where they had nearly lost her to a head-on collision, Armando pounding the dashboard with his fist, Chico bug-eyed with fear, visions of future paydays destined to make him a wealthy man crushed upon the highway.

But she had survived the crash. Chico had reached her before Armando, an oversight for which Armando would be a long time in forgiving himself. And then came the second truck, and Chico losing her. Christ, he should have taken her arm himself. Eager to show his worth, the cowboy had shown his weakness instead. Imagine having to grab your nose just because it was broken. Imagine how far that would take you among the fighters above El As Negro!

The driver of the truck had proven to be obnoxious and Armando had been forced to shoot him, had shoved a belly gun into that soft spot below the buckle and blew chunks of the man's spine across two lanes of Mex One, after which they had given chase, right down to the line, then watched, helpless, as she ran into the sea, her head vanishing below the water not fifty feet from the great fence.

And yet Armando could not quite believe that she was dead. Her luck ran too good. With the coming of morning he moved into the rafters of the old bullring then hunkered there as if fixed in stone, shit on by pigeons, joints on fire, eyestrain running through his head as if electrodes were what held his eyes to the base of his skull, peering though stolen binoculars by the hour, sweeping the valley below.

Chico said he was crazy. He wanted the rest of his money.

Armando told him to go fuck himself.

Armando stayed in the rafters. He supposed that he had been lucky in his choice of viewing glasses. What he knew of binoculars could be written on a stamp yet these had come from the rear of a Mercedes limousine, black on black, as were the glasses themselves, with printing upon their parts that was in neither English nor Spanish. They were only slightly smaller than a toaster oven and through them he saw wondrous things. He saw the border patrol chase down *pollos*. He saw birds raiding nests, a weasel fighting with a snake, coyotes on the prowl. He saw a naked man, of no more substance than a scarecrow, engaged in a kind of dance at the top of one of the mesas.

Chico made repeated visits. He wanted his money.

"I don't know that she's dead," Armando told him. "And anyway, even if she is dead, she didn't die right."

"If she's dead, she's dead."

To which Armando said nothing.

Chico stood below him, sullen, shouting up into the rafters. It was the third or fourth time that he'd been there. He saw that Armando was eating a hamburger. He thought about the distance to the nearest eatery. He tried to imagine Armando's coming down and found that he could not. He tried to imagine Armando's having a friend. This was equally difficult. There was no point in asking. He had discovered that Armando could say nothing for hours at a time.

Still, Chico redoubled his visits. The results were predictable. And then he screwed up. He was there when Nacho brought the food and this was how they met, not exactly the meeting Armando had fantasized, but Chico went mute as a stone nonetheless. And who could blame him, taken unawares by such an apparition—that great bald dome, save for a few stray tufts of hair, bobbing among such shafts of light as fell from between the bleacher seating of the old bullring. In fact his appearance was no doubt augmented in this setting, wherein the slatted light found not only his great, thatched head but the metal stars upon his shoulders and these affixed to the epaulets of a leather jacket which might have contained the hide from an entire cow and beneath this a myriad of chains and church keys and sharpened screwdrivers swinging in discordant harmony as might the accoutrements of an old-fashioned cooking wagon.

Armando made introductions from fifty feet above their heads. "Nacho takes care of things for me," Armando said. "You'll get your money when the woman is dead. You want it sooner, talk to Nacho."

Chico declined. It was time for him to go. Armando thought that perhaps he had seen the last of him but Chico was back the next day, albeit more subdued. Armando owed him money. Armando had connections. The cowboy would wait it out. An uneasy alliance held sway in the shadows of that aging arena, as among desperadoes beneath the eaves. "For the love of Christ," Chico asked one day. "Where did you get him?" His voice was cast upward, as if calling out to the Almighty himself, and Nacho nowhere in sight.

"Where do you think?" Armando asked, for in truth there could be but one such place.

"Colonia Subterráneo . . ."

And so it was. Whatever name his mother had given him was long forgotten by the time they met. Or perhaps there never had been a name. What he went by was Nacho, which meant little one, still a boy and already in excess of three hundred pounds. Armando had come upon him in a vacant lot by the rail line, where the youth had managed to ignite his face while filling his mouth with lighter fluid then spitting it at matches. The trick had gone awry and Armando found him rolling in the dirt, howling in pain and terror while a dozen other children of lesser size looked on with apparent nonchalance, as if this too was a part of the act and not to be interfered with.

Armando had used his own jacket to smother the flames and Nacho had taken to following him about like a lost dog. The flames had left him scarred. Whiffing fumes had left him simple, but he was built like a water heater, strong as an ox, loyal unto death. "You could learn some things from him," Armando told Chico.

"What's that?"

"To keep your mouth shut and do as you're told." He supposed that he was a leader in spite of himself. He had acquired a gang.

On the fourth night there were shooting stars, the naked man dancing, a red dawn. On the fifth day he saw her, near sunset, on the rim of a small mesa. A man stood at her side. The big binoculars even showed him the scratches on one side of her face. The man wore a Hawaiian print shirt, corduroy pants with white dust on the legs, huarache sandals like those you would buy from the street vendors in El Centro. His hair was to his shoulders. The glasses were so good Armando could see what was on the front of his baseball cap—a bright yellow worm with a cowboy hat and dark glasses. The worm was sitting in a lounge chair and smoking a pipe. He had no idea how far away they really were but when he lowered the magic glasses he found that he could still see them—no bigger to the naked eye than the candied lovers atop a wedding cake. He studied them for some time. He had no use for the glasses now. There were other ways of getting a closer look. One need only go to America to make it happen.

15

DEEP IN THE heart of Tijuana, Fahey thought of a county jail. He was feeling rattled and could not, at just that moment, have said which one, yet in all other matters he could remember it quite clearly. He remembered it at the edge of a great plain. He remembered its five hundred inmates in their seven tiers. He recalled what it was like, trying to sleep in such a place, trying to exercise, trying to eat, trying to do anything. The noise never stopped—radios blasting, men crying, men having sex, men having nightmares, men talking shit at the top of their lungs, night and day . . . One of Fahey's strategies for survival in such places had been to control his immediate sphere, that is check out who was next to him, who to watch, who he might speak to, offer a sandwich to—jailhouse issue, of course, peanut butter on white, no frills. The trick was to orchestrate one's surroundings to one's advantage, to find an ally—a man to take your back, and you his. Could you find two? Could you trade sets of push-ups? Could you do a hundred? Could you stay in shape? Talk about one's own sphere . . . Talk about control . . . One passes quickly though denial in such a place. One comes quickly to the realization that one is a speck of shit in a vast system. The system proceeds in accordance with its own architecture and law. A sane man could be nothing but an interloper, a particle adrift in the blood works of an unimaginable host, waiting only to be found out, waiting to be crushed.

It was how he felt upon crossing the border, each time, without exception. Mexico was like bus therapy. Things went bad in Mexico. They got out of hand. They descended into weirdness. Take that dog pack, for instance, the one that had been trailing him for the better part of an hour, and he looked once more into his rearview mirror . . . seeking in some small way to take the measure of his immediate surroundings, to control his sphere, because, well . . . maybe it was them. Maybe it was the dog pack that would in some way cause him to tip his hand, to force an error. Maybe it was they who had his number.

Only here of course could such carven beasts even begin to exist, wall-eyed mongrels every one, of indiscernible color, shapes born of genetic experiments gone badly awry. One dog had the body of a wiener dog, the head of a German shepherd. Another had what appeared to be a chicken bone sticking out its ass. They ran with the endurance of coyotes. Two miles or more they had trailed him, up whatever nameless canyon into which he had driven, in the execution of Magdalena's errand, lost of course, her map ground into the floorboards at his feet, the tracks of his rubber-soled sandals all but obliterating whatever lines, street names, and numbers she had composed there for his edification, the shortcut that had led him here.

He found it hard to say now just where it had all gone wrong, quite possibly in the great traffic circle known as the Five and Ten, where every road in Tijuana intersected with every other road in Tijuana, looking desperately for one called Agua Caliente, and/or the restaurant Carnitas Urapana, whichever he could see first, as one was the gateway to the other. And in fact he believed that he might actually have glimpsed such an establishment, at about that point where the sixteen-wheel garbage truck nearly crushed him, forcing him into a turn before he was ready, across two lanes of traffic, horns blaring, voices hurling insults in a foreign tongue. There was nothing for it but to keep going, down one-way streets, past junkyards and liquor stores, hoodlums on corners, dogs at a gallop, past crumbling stucco houses, their colors like the electuaries born of bad acid trips, trying to get back to the Five and Ten, but spiraling ever deeper into a gradually deteriorating urban landscape, across dwindling amounts of asphalt until the road had turned to hard-packed dirt. And finally even the dirt was gone, giving way to red rock and sand as though what he'd entered upon was a dried-out riverbed, a repository of blown tire casings and cast-off appliances, the skeletal remains of those vehicles unfortunate enough to have found these barrens before him, and which in so doing had found their ends as a part of the bargain.

The sun caromed about this harsh landscape with an intensity that was nearly audible, like clashing cymbals—in defense of which, the tape deck dangling from beneath his dashboard oozed Chet Baker. Fahey chewed Valium—ten-milligram blues, two at a time, washed them down with the beer held between sweating thighs, and these taken from the six-pack at his side. He used a forearm to wipe still more sweat from his eyes and saw the narrow box canyon into which he had driven ending in spectacle a short distance ahead.

There were houses here if you could call them that—tin-roofed shacks of cardboard and chicken-wire mesh, sliding down from the mesas above but inhabited nonetheless. A copious amount of water ran from the mesas as well. It gathered on the floor of the wash in a fast running little brook Fahey now sought to straddle with his tires. As he did so, a foul reek rose from the floorboards at his feet.

But all this was about to end, as dead ahead there stood a man in a spacesuit, bone white in the noonday sun at the side of a bone white truck with some kind of symbol on the door. The man held what appeared to be a small glass vial aloft in one gloved hand, peering at it as though it were a toy through which to see the light.

As Fahey watched, a fat woman with sores on her legs wobbled forward to spit on the man in the suit. The man did his best to ignore her. The woman circled like a buzzard, her jaws at work. Dogs and children played about the edges of the brook. Fahey could see the pack that had trailed him gaining ground in a hurry.

He had no choice to but stop. The dwarf dog with the head of a shepherd bit his tire. A throng of cholos in baggy pants, stocking caps, and chains seemed to appear out of nowhere, standing at what might have passed for a street corner, a barren patch of soil at the foot of the cliff, at the edge of the foul little stream.

Fahey sat behind the wheel of his truck. The cholos were checking him out, grinning like wolves. A number of women appeared before one of the houses. Two came forward to restrain the spitting fat woman. The rest stood in the yard of the house, a kind of leprous hut from whose outer walls great patches of stucco had fallen away to expose not only the framing, but the interior as well. The effect was that of a large-scale and derelict dollhouse—the plaything of maleficent giants.

Fahey's clutch had begun to smoke. The engine was running hot. The gas was running low. The gauge was notoriously inaccurate, and at just that moment when he tapped it with the back of his finger in hopes of producing a more favorable reading, the engine died out altogether. The dogs went wild with glee. The shorter animals yanked at his tires, the taller ones scratched at his doors. The cholos began to laugh. The man in the white truck had apparently gotten what he came for. He wanted out. And who could blame him? But Fahey's truck was blocking the path. The man shouted in Spanish. Fahey grew nauseous.

"*¿Habla inglés?*" Fahey asked through a crack at the top of his window.

The man stared at him through the plastic faceplate in the white hood that covered his head—a look of such naked contempt that Fahey was reminded of a long-ago girl left to her fate in a canyon much like this one. One more dope deal gone bad. *Federales* with guns had made them run but kept the girl for sport. The man's face reminded Fahey of the faces of the soldiers, nothing but malice. One might just as well have appealed to the currents of Las Playas for mercy. Fahey had never seen the girl again. He'd broken cold sweats then, too, and run for the border.

The thought occurred to him that he might run just now, though at this precise moment he could not have told you which way the border was. The man in the spacesuit had begun to pound on the hood of his truck. The dogs swirled about the spaceman's legs, bouncing as though held upon strings let down from the heavens, oblivious to everything save Fahey himself, in his truck, out of options, out of gas, out of luck. He played a hunch. He scooted across the seat. Beer cans tumbled to the floor. One sprang a leak, spraying the rubber mat. The reek of beer filled the cab. The dogs redoubled their attack. Fahey rolled down the passenger side window just enough to shout through it. He shouted at the women in front of the house.

"*¿Dónde está Casa de la Mujer?*" Fahey shouted.

The women looked at him.

Fahey repeated the question.

A woman approached the car, wading through the dogs. She came to Fahey's window.

Fahey repeated his question for the third time.

The woman looked at him, with some mixture of curiosity and pity. "Yes," she said. "I know."

The women were remarkably resourceful. One even had a can of gas in the trunk of her car. One shooed away the cholos on the corner. One drove away the dogs. Another actually got in beside Fahey and turned the truck around. The man in the spacesuit bolted. The woman with the sores on her legs threw rocks at the departing truck. But the immaculate vehicle was soon gone in the dust, a white speck at the red mouth of the canyon. The Valium and beer were coming on strong. The woman behind the wheel gave Fahey a long look. "I'd better drive you," she said.

It was how Fahey arrived at Casa de la Mujer. He'd overdone it with the pills and booze. Two more women helped him inside—a modest home in an old residential district, at the corner of an alley. He rested on a couch, looking up at the array of small tapestries that covered the wall nearest where he lay. A woman was produced who spoke English. "My name is Connie," she said. She knelt at his side. "We've been expecting you. You're the man Magdalena said would come."

Fahey said that he was.

Connie smiled at him. "She said you might have trouble finding us."

"More than trouble," Fahey said. He told her about the canyon. "You're the first good luck I've ever had in this town," he added.

She looked at him, puzzled, then shrugged. "If the man from the environmental agency had not been there, there would not have been such a scene. You would have simply turned around and driven back out. You would have found us in time."

"I don't think so," he said. His head felt like a brick. "Coffee?" he asked.

The woman smiled. "In time. I think maybe you'd better just lie here for a bit."

"Magdalena . . . She's alone in the valley."

"Is that so bad?"

"I asked one of the cowboys to look in on her."

"A cowboy? Then I'm sure she will be in good hands."

Fahey tried to imagine her in good hands. The tapestries danced about his head. "Maybe if I can just nap here for a few minutes," he said.

The woman patted his shoulder. "You nap all you want to," she told him.

Fahey slept like a dead man, beneath the tapestries that in fact were the work of Chiapas peasants, done for the great march on Mexico City. He slept on the couch, amid boxes and posters, the drawings of children. Eventually he dreamed about the girl in the canyon. The girl morphed into Magdalena, beneath the totems of Surfhenge, the bronze plaques at her feet. She seemed to be asking why his name was not written among the stars. "There are some things," Fahey said, "you never come back from." Then he woke with a start, drenched in sweat, to the wrong kind of light, to the image of Magdalena, alone in the valley.

16

UNDER NORMAL circumstances, Armando would only have taken Nacho to cross the border, but Chico, persistent as a case of the clap, proved useful one more time. He had a cousin on the other side, hiding out in a place called Garage Door Tijuana, right down in the river valley. You could see it from the rafters of the bullring—the garage doors, anyway. What lay behind the doors was a mystery—a dark labyrinth from which one might glimpse the occasional white plume of pampas grass, together with a few stunted palms.

And Chico also knew where to cross—an old concrete storm pipe recently excavated. The pipe was said to leave Mexico near Las Playas, running parallel to Yogurt Canyon, but opening farther into the valley, far enough beyond the line to have thus far escaped the attention of the border patrol. The pipe was old and dated to well before the fence, to a time when such secret routes of passage were not so sought after. Even still, the pipe was said to have enjoyed a certain iniquitous history and was from early on a favored haunt of smugglers, right up to the coming of the new fence, when American engineers had found it and filled it in. But in recent months the pipe had been reopened—the work of drug runners using forced labor. The men who had done the work were rumored to be buried at its mouth in the Tijuana River Valley, on the American side. It was also said there was even a little track in the tunnel, like what you might find in a mine, and that on this track there was a cart with steel wheels able to move more weight than any man could carry and that the track and cart were, like the tunnel itself, artifacts from another time, but now pressed into service once more.

Sometimes the crankster gangsters who controlled the tunnel entrance on the Mexican side would let a few *pollos* cross if they had the money to pay tribute. Sometimes they would take the money then wait till the *pollos* were inside, cut their throats, and bury them with the men who had done the digging. Sometimes they would throw them in the river on the American side of the fence, on its way to the sea. It depended on how they were feeling. But Armando could pay their tribute. In the company of Chico he had negotiated a price. On the night of the crossing, he would take both Chico and Nacho with him.

He could not see where the Madonna and her man had gone. Those parts of the valley most exposed to his lookout beneath the bullring were the beaches and marshlands south of the river. When the man and woman had left the mesa they had done so in a rusty-looking pickup that had carried them inland, disappearing beneath the trees in a gathering dusk, and that was the last he had seen of them, but it was clear that she was alive, living somewhere in the Tijuana River Valley. And the Tijuana River Valley was not that big. There were only so many places one could hide. And only, or so one might hope, so many caps like the one worn by the big American with the flowers on his shirt, perhaps even only one.

They made plans to cross on the evening of the following day. Near sunset they wandered the streets of El Norte and the old red-light district, within sight of the fence. As shadows grew so did the number of peasants hoping to escape the gravitational pull of the great land mass from which they had come, hoping to survive the crack addicts and thugs of Colonia Subterráneo, to outrun the border patrol, hoping to survive whatever assortment of bandidos, gang-bangers, and vigilantes the night might array against them, for the number of their enemies was legion. And so you would see them, scarecrows with frightened eyes loitering in the shadows of the fence, along the cement walls of the flood control channel, at the bottom of every gully, clear to Las Playas, where they huddled amid the reek of excrement in the shadow of the bullring at the edge of the old people's park, fingering rosaries and counting out their luck.

Armando might have pitied them, but somehow their vulnerability invited only his contempt, that and a certain satisfaction that in spite of everything that had befallen him, or perhaps because of it, he and his compadres could sit by, nonchalant, drinking beers among the strippers till the time had come for them head out to Las Playas and their chosen route of passage, where they would cross at their leisure.

A dozen street thugs were gathered at the tunnel entrance, not far from an overpass, the cars on Mex One rumbling by in the night. Money exchanged hands. Armando carried a .45 automatic in his jacket, a switchblade in his sock. His binoculars he left at the battery plant, for he reckoned them as excess baggage, that when next he met with his Madonna it would be face-to-face. Chico was armed much like Armando. Nacho went with the strength of three, brass knuckles and a straight razor in the pocket of his coat, together with such accoutrements as have already been noted dangling from their various chains. The street thugs gazed upon him with wonder and there was no trouble at the door. A kid with a mouthful of silver teeth took their money and saw them in, smiling only at what they had brought to light their way.

Once inside, the tunnel went on for longer than Armando would have guessed, every inch filled with reek and sweat, the ghosts of those who had died here breathing down their necks, the single pin light they carried too weak to do more than light the air around it. As a consequence of which they went like blind men, stumbling over rails and each other and other things—rolling unnamed and unseen beneath their feet, the occasional scratching of some rodent or whir of insect mixing with the sound of their own labored breathing until the scent of wet marsh and the sea beyond it told them they were nearing an end.

Armando drew his pistol, stumbled over some final impediment fixed in earth the consistency of stone, the great hulk of Nacho slamming into him from behind, knocking him through a tangle of hanging vines that hid the tunnel entrance on the U.S. side. He tasted America before he actually set foot in it, crawling on all fours through some kind of bog, spitting sand and grit, a great swarm of mosquitoes buzzing in his ears, descending, ravenous, upon his balding head.

Chico's cousin was there to meet them as promised. He led them quickly into the trees and from there they made their way eastward among canopied trails, among willows and arundo cane double overhead, bowed to hide the stars. They crossed the river in a narrow place among reeds, on a pair of planks kept hidden in the grass and mud, and when they had made use of this makeshift bridge they pulled it in upon the side to which they had crossed and buried the pieces much as they had found them.

In a short time Garage Door Tijuana loomed before them, a wall without end. The cousin produced a door, as if by magic. A narrow chasm yawned before them, a passage run between walls of wood and tin or built up out of old tires stacked twelve feet high and past the backsides of trailers packed like sardines, opening at last into a wonderland of house cars and televisions where men sat smoking in plastic lawn chairs, drinking from bottles and strumming guitars. There were children at play. Women cooked food on great sheets of steel over open fires.

Armando wiped the last of the mud and grit from his face and looked around him. People were smiling. There was laughter and song. One might almost say that a festive air obtained. Garage Door Tijuana, Armando concluded, was like a day in the park. And why not? The people of Garage Door Tijuana were living large in the USA, in Southern California, for Christ's sake, in happy ignorance of what had only now entered among them.

17

A BLANKET OF FOG lay upon the valley floor, too dense to see more than ten feet in any direction save up, where the fog was shallow enough for the admittance of starlight, where planets shone like gems though a vast and diaphanous vale. As far as Deek Waltzer knew, and he had traveled to a good number of places, the phenomenon was peculiar to the Tijuana River Valley and reminded him of his days driving for the Blue Line, if for no other reason than that it was a good night for running illegals.

There was a six-pack on the seat next to him and the great halo of his headlights traveling with him as though he'd been called to heaven as opposed to inching along the Dairy Mart Road on his way out to the Fahey worm farm, thinking about the Blue Line and those early days in the valley. Funny how often he recalled them now, as if they were some golden age, as opposed to the last days, which was pretty much how they had seemed to him at the time—recently divorced, house gone, job gone. Fifty years old and every expectation confounded. No money. No hopes. No plans. But he'd gotten a rush out of those runs to the border, thinking then there was really nothing left to lose and he supposed now the happier for it. Later would come the valley itself, Jack and the horses, the modest job and the trailer among the Oaxacans who had taught him something about life in the moment, which was, as near as he could tell, pretty much how one ought to live it—a far cry from the philosophy that had driven him in his previous life, selling real estate in the heart of Orange County, juggling mortgages on three properties, balancing his portfolio and looking toward retirement . . . storing up treasures where moth and rust corrupt, just like the good book said.

He laughed out loud and cracked another beer. He thought about the rodeo slated for the coming weekend. He enjoyed the hell out of those rodeos. He enjoyed the Mexican rodeos with their emphasis on roping and riding, the judging based purely on artistry and skill, different from the American rodeos with their bull riding and bucking broncos, their ticking clocks that were the final arbiters in all events.

He also enjoyed the horse races, and there was a man bringing in some Andalusians fresh from Spain that he was eager to see. But what he enjoyed most was simply the spirit of the Oaxacan people. They would turn out early in their Sunday best, betting money on the horse races till all the horses had been run, by which time they would be drunk enough to take off their shoes and run against each other, pounding down the Mexican quarter-mile track in their bare feet, middle-aged men who'd not run more than a block since childhood. They would bet on those races too. And when they were too drunk and tired to run they would draw a circle in the sand and box one another bare-handed till every cent they'd busted their asses to earn for the past month was gone like snow in the spring. And there would be beer and barbecue and tacos cooked from scratch and Deek would don his dress boots, his white Stetson, and strut around like he owned the place, possibly even getting laid in the bargain, though that happened less frequently these days than he would have liked or at least less frequently than he seemed to remember it happening when he was a younger man—fifty, say, driving for the Blue Line, running the Oaxacans from the border to San Diego and parts north.

He turned off the Dairy Mart Road and onto one of the unnamed dirt trails that would take him to the Fahey worm farm. He was not sure what all of this was about, or why it was him doing it instead of Jack, who was Fahey's friend, inasmuch as Fahey could be said to have friends.

The former surfer and convicted felon had come around one evening past to say he would be going across the border for an afternoon and wondered if one of them would mind looking in on a guest who was staying at his place. Deek had taken it as a given that the job would fall to his partner, but then Jack's horse had come up lame riding trail in the valley and Jack had taken it to a vet, asking Deek to look in on Fahey's visitor.

"For Christ's sake," Deek had said.

"Oh, go on and do it," Jack told him. "I'll buy you a six-pack."

"One today and one tomorrow."

"Deal."

So here he was, a day's work behind him, the fog coming in early, halfway through the first of Jack's six-packs as the lights of Fahey's farm came into view. He drove up before a locked gate and tooted his horn.

To his surprise, a woman came out of the trailer. Also to his surprise, he saw that she was a Mexican. He noticed this as she passed within the lights of his truck, the dogs at her heels. She came up to the gate. There were keys in her hand. She wore a flannel shirt, several sizes too large, and sweatpants that were of roughly the same proportions.

"You must be one of the cowboys," she said.

Deek saw that in spite of the clothes, which rendered her appearance somewhat clownish, she was both young and attractive and this surprised him even further but he allowed that such was the case; that he was, indeed, one of the cowboys.

"I thought that he would have been back by now," she told him. "I don't suppose you'd have a cell phone."

Deek just looked at her. "You know something," he said. "I had one of those damn things. But I lost it."

They sat in Fahey's trailer. She sipped tea. Deek drank another beer, looked at the photographs on the walls. He was not altogether sure how long this "looking in" on someone was supposed to take. "So I guess these are him," he said. He waved at the pictures.

"Some of them." She pointed to her favorite, Fahey at the base of the big blue wall, his hair in the wind.

"My partner, Jack . . . he says he used to watch him surf, back in the day, says they called him the Gull. But I guess you knew that."

Magdalena shook her head. "I've only known him for a few days," she told him.

"You don't say?"

But the woman only smiled. She was well spoken and clearly educated and he could not for the life of him imagine what it was that she was doing here. He noted the little cuts beginning to heal across one side of her face, the remnants of a bruise around one eye, remembered Fahey asking about the medication and the bad water. There was a story in all of this, he concluded, in the wounds on her face, in the clothes that were obviously Fahey's, in her saying that she had not known him for long . . . and just maybe, he thought, maybe one day he'd hear more about it from Jack Nance because he doubted he would hear much more of it tonight from this woman seated across from him in Fahey's trailer.

"What do you suppose happened?" Magdalena asked. "To him, I mean." She waved toward the pictures.

Deek would have preferred to know what had happened to her and why she was here but it was not his nature to pry if the information was not volunteered. "You mean what happened to make him late?"

"No, I mean what happened in a more general way, to him," she said.

"You would be better to ask Jack about that. I believe he has a theory on the subject."

"That's your partner?"

Deek nodded.

"Sam said there were two of you."

"That's right, Jack and me. And Jack and Sam were friends."

"But not you and Sam?"

Deek squirmed on one side of the small L-shaped couch that filled the small room. He sat on one side of the couch, Magdalena on the other.

"I knew some things about his father," Deek said at length.

"What about him?"

Deek thought about that for some time. The truth as he knew it made for an ugly story and in the end he guessed that he was not the one to tell it, nor, he felt, was this the time or the place. He shifted his weight yet one more time on the tiny couch. He looked at his watch and finished his beer. "I should say that I heard some things," he said.

Magdalena sat waiting. "Yes?" she asked.

"I heard he was a bad one," Deek said.

✦ ✦ ✦

An hour later saw him back on the road, window down to catch the wet scents of greasewood and sage, to blow away the feel of Fahey's trailer. She'd pressed him some on the subject of Fahey's father, but the look on her face as she asked made him wish that he had not brought it up in the first place. In the end, all he had said was that the man had a bad reputation among the Indians, that he was known as a liar and cheat, and his farm a place to avoid. And even this news, general as it was, seemed to darken her mood. So he'd done his best to lighten things with tales of the Mexican rodeo. He told her about the music and some of his favorite parts. He told her about the mounted horse roping, how the caballero would sit astride his own horse, sixty feet of rope coiled about one open hand, the rope looped once about the horn of the saddle, the leather smoking as the line paid out, as the wild horse on the other end of the rope galloped toward the far end of the guitar, where it would pull up before the fence, then make a circle of the big part of the guitar before the event was called and all the while the caballero seated on his own horse, holding position in the center of the ring, enveloped in the rising smoke and the horse he sat upon dancing to the music of the musicians that would be there dawn till dusk, with their guitars and guitarrones, their fiddles and accordions. And when he had told her about the rodeo and finished the last of his beer, he'd asked her if she wanted him to stay longer and she had said no, that she would be okay, to which he'd asked if she was sure and she had said that she was.

He'd invited her to the rodeo, her and Fahey too, standing in the foggy dark, in front of the trailer, the little dog jumping at his leg, the old dog lying off somewhere in the black shadows of the trees.

"They last all weekend," he'd told her. "Starting Friday afternoon. But Sunday is probably the best. If you want to come."

"Maybe we can," she said.

Deek thought she meant it. "You sure you'll be okay now?"

"I'll be fine. There's the fence, and the dogs."

To which Deek had smiled. "That old dog's about as much use as I would be," he'd told her, which struck him now as a perhaps overly self-deprecating thing to have said, flummoxed no doubt at such unadorned beauty.

"I'm sure he'll be home soon. I'll tell him you came."

And Deek had nodded, not wanting to tell her he had no interest in Fahey's gratitude. "Okay," he said. "And don't forget the rodeo."

She said that she would not. She thanked him again for coming. He left without ever knowing what had brought her there or why she seemed to harbor some affection for Sam Fahey. It was funny, he thought, driving away, and thought about it again just now, how some people seemed drawn to that man . . . his partner for one, and now this girl. But then ruins were like that sometimes. And there were women, and men too, who were just not happy unless they had some wreck of a human being to fawn over and look after, and if that was the case with this Madonna in rags, then Deek supposed she had come to the right place.

In time the smell of the corrals found its way into his window and soon after he could hear the horses in their stalls though neither were visible in the fog. He found the entrance to the driveway by senses other than sight and turned down it, the wheels of his truck grinding over rutted gravel till the siding of his trailer rose up before him, as broad and white as the forehead of a whale. He killed the engine, which ran on for a few seconds anyway, suggesting a manifold leak he supposed he would have to attend to at some point in the near future, then got out with his spare six-pack tucked beneath an arm.

The door of the trailer was open to the night. This did not surprise him. He'd been stripping some wooden cabinets in the kitchen and he'd wanted to air the place out. He had no worries about doing such a thing in Garage Door Tijuana. The Indians he lived among were honest people who had never given him a day's trouble and indeed he felt safer here than in just about any other place he might have named.

It was not until he was inside that he sensed something else was going on. There was an odor he could not name, a felt presence. These things were followed by a sound—a kind of rummaging in the kitchen. And yet even then he was not overly alarmed. His faith in his neighbors was absolute. In place of subterfuge he was inclined to suspect some foraging animal, or at worst a local youngster, too green to know better. It was really not until he'd come through the living room and seen the back of a grown man going through his cupboards that he realized something very much out of the ordinary was happening to him and the bad feelings began. Perhaps it was the disembodied eyeball tattooed in the bald spot at the back of the man's head.

Deek put the six-pack on the floor at his feet and lifted one of the bottles by the neck. He could feel the pulse in his hand, against the glass. "Excuse me," he said.

The man turned to look at him.

Deek thought, Christ Almighty.

A floorboard squeaked at his back. And something struck him from behind—a good deal harder than anything had struck him in a long time. The entire Milky Way galaxy danced before his eyes. He believed he must have fallen because the next thing he knew he was on his back and there was a man looking down on him—

from a dark place Deek had not known about—and he suddenly found himself thinking about his good friend and partner, Jack Nance, and that thing he used to say about Sam Fahey, reprobate, the part about endless night . . .

18

MAGDALENA WAITED throughout the night, without recourse to phones. Near dawn she dozed on the couch, wrapped in one of Fahey's flannel shirts. She woke hours later to the sound of his truck, looked through cracked glass to see him at his gate. A feeling of relief washed over her. Thoughts carried her back to her arrival at the farm and how she had looked upon him just there, at the gate, and her in the seat of his truck, too weak to move, yet filled with dread, taking him for some denizen of the streets, possibly deranged. Funny how time had changed things, for she watched him now with some measure of affection, this Fahey, with his shaggy hair and broad shoulders, his impossible past.

She was waiting for him in the yard. She could see the boxes containing her files in the bed of his truck. Fahey slipped from behind the wheel, his hair combed back wet as if he was not long from a shower. Their eyes met. He held up a hand before she could say a word. "It's a long story," he said.

✦ ✦ ✦

He told it in the kitchen, as she was cooking eggs. She listened, grateful for the women of Casa de la Mujer, but grateful for Fahey as well. Clearly, things had not gone as smoothly as they might, though she guessed he was omitting a few details. Still, he was back and the files were with him.

When he had said about as much as he wanted to, he took a beer from the refrigerator then sat with it at the tiny kitchen table, watching as Magdalena began to chop tomatoes and green onion.

"Those are from the valley," he told her.

"You just wash them first," she said.

They ate on the deck. There was a nest of sparrows in the branches of one of the tamaracks. Eggs had hatched in the course of Fahey's trip to Tijuana and the morning was filled with the chirping of tiny birds, the hot damp smell of vegetation, like something ripe seeping up out of the ground at their feet. Fahey's irrigation system was in play above the windrows and the air in that quarter of the farm sparkled with tiny rainbows.

Fahey looked out over the narrow lines of castings and moist earth. "I could break into the black this year," he told her.

He went on to say that with the advent of his larger-than-life red worms there were already several bait-and-tackle shops scattered around the bay waiting for shipments. And he'd recently connected with a big organic farm on the outskirts of Julian looking to buy his topsoil and their own worms for recycling. He pointed to a number of the white boxes he used for shipping.

"Those are for the folks from Julian. And there's the wave of the future, worms for composting and recycling."

"I didn't know you thought about things like that," she said. She was half joking with him.

"Things like what?"

"Recycling. The future."

"Oh, I think about the future now and then."

"And what do you think about, when you think about the future?"

Fahey finished the last of his eggs. "Sometimes I think about the waves. I wonder what would happen if it broke big again, Outside the Bullring."

Magdalena remembered the sight of Fahey half naked, mind surfing in the darkness, at the side of his board. She wondered if that was the kind of wave he had ridden then, Outside the Bullring.

"I was under the impression that you didn't surf anymore."

"I go out there sometimes at night, on a full moon, paddle the length of the valley, from I.B. to the border, keep my swimming muscles in shape."

"Surely there's more to it that that."

"Once you surf, you surf . . . Smaller waves are more about timing and flexibility . . . In big surf, if you're in good enough shape to get to the waves, and you know the spot, know how it breaks . . . You'll get a wave." He looked at her and smiled. "At least that's what I tell myself."

"So you would really try?"

"You only get so many chances at a place like the Mystic Peak."

"I don't know," she said. "You're not going to tell me you wouldn't be taking a chance, that it wouldn't be dangerous."

Fahey shrugged. "I think everyone would like to leave some mark on the world, something that said you were here, something only you could do."

Magdalena gave this some thought.

"It's funny," she said. "That particular way of making your mark on the world. It's a very different way of seeing one's role on the planet, different at least from what I've grown up with."

Fahey just looked at her.

"I can imagine the Sisters of the Benediction saying that riding big waves is just about you."

"Maybe that's the point."

"And what about everything else? What about the rest of the world?"

"You mean the ills of humanity?"

"You wouldn't deny them."

"I guess I always figured that I'm something I can actually do something about." Though as he said it, it struck him that he'd not really done very much about it so far, unless one considered adding to the world's already vast supply of turpitude an accomplishment.

They sat for a moment in silence. Fahey drank his beer. "Windrows are in good shape," he said. "You did a good job."

"You did too, Sam."

Her words seemed to give Fahey pause. "I don't think anybody's called me Sam since my father died. Except he liked to stick an *h* in there and call me Sham. I believe it was his idea of a joke."

Magdalena thought about what the cowboy had told her. "I've never heard you mention your family," she said.

"There was not much of it to mention. Me and the old man."

"What about your mother?"

"She left when I was young. My father never spoke her name. I no longer know it myself."

"You're kidding me," she said, then judged by the look on his face that he was not kidding her at all and was sorry she'd said so. "And what did your father do?"

Fahey looked at the floor. "That's a difficult question to answer," he said. Time passed. He saw that she was still waiting. "It's difficult for me to talk about," he added. He might have told her that his father had failed at everything except killing Mexicans but he decided against it. He kept that one to himself. When they had finished break-fast Fahey went to his shaping room and worked on his board.

◆ ◆ ◆

The next couple of days passed in a pleasant haze, different than anything Fahey had experienced in some time. He continued to work on the board for Jack Nance, shaping it the way Hoddy had taught him to, for the big, open ocean waves that came from Outside the Bullring. Magdalena looked through her files, searching for names. They seemed to take some pleasure in one another's company. They shared meals, walks in the valley. Fahey took her to the top of Spooner's Mesa to show more about how the waves broke at the straits. "The Mystic Peak has never been photographed," he told her. "In the old days, not that many guys shot from the water and it would have been hell getting out there with a camera. You'd just about have to shoot it from a helicopter, and the kind of guys that do that are all over in the Islands, shooting the outer reefs, or working for Hollywood. No one thinks about this place anymore. The water scares them away. People know about the Mystic Peak, but since no one's ever photographed it . . . There's probably not more than a dozen people in the world at this moment who really know what it's all about."

They were standing close together, their arms almost touching. She could not help noticing he'd trimmed his beard, that he had brushed the shavings from his hair. He studied the swell lines beneath them from behind Ray-Bans patched with duct tape. She noticed, however, that the tape was new. When they turned to go his fingers brushed the back of her hand.

That night he sat with her in the living room, which she had turned into an office, as he had done on the previous two evenings, drinking his beer, watching as she worked before going to bed in the old work shed. It was almost, Magdalena thought, like they were a couple. A couple of what would have been harder to say.

"What are these?" Fahey asked. He had taken at random a thick sheaf of paper from one of the boxes near where he sat.

Magdalena looked at the box to see how it was labeled. "Factual reports," she told him, "on deserted industrial sites along the border."

"Like the place you told me about, the old battery plant."

"The recycling plant, exactly. That place is owned by a man named Hunter, an American. There's a point of American law known as Minimum Contact. If I could discover that he was still doing business in Mexico, he could be prosecuted, here in the States. He could be forced to clean up the mess. That's more or less what all this is about, making a case against him, or someone like him."

"You getting anywhere?"

Magdalena shook her head. "I don't know. Someone tried to burn our offices. Someone tried to kill me. Why? I keep thinking the answer is somewhere in these files . . ." She looked over the papers scattered around the floor. "If it's not, then why am I here?"

Fahey had no answer for that. "So where do you start?" he asked, finally.

"My car was tampered with outside the battery factory. The men on the road were Mexicans. I've been looking over everything we have on that case, going back to the original inspection reports, getting as many names as I can, supervisors, workers, whatever . . ."

"But you don't know the names of the men on the road."

"No, but I believe I could identify them. They had tattoos. That much has come back to me. One had an Aztec sun across his abdomen, the other an eyeball on the back of his head. I'm sure of it. And if I can get some names for Carlotta, she can go to the police. We have at least one friend there." She was thinking now of Raúl, the man who had taken her to lunch, willing, for the moment at least, to reconsider him as an ally. "He knows the streets," she said. "He might be willing to see if any of the names go with the tattoos . . ."

"He might?"

Magdalena shrugged. "Mexico wants to be a friend of business. They don't care what the human costs are. I mean, what do you think you saw up that canyon the other day?"

"You mean the astronaut?"

"Exactly. The little river running through that *colonia* comes straight from the factories above. It's filled with pollutants. The people in that canyon are all sick from it. And they complain. So some environmental protection agency sends out that guy you saw. Clearly he knows the whole place is toxic. He's dressed for the planet Mars. He jumps out and grabs a vial of water to be analyzed. You want to guess what his agency will determine?"

"The water is safe?"

"To find otherwise might work some hardship on the factory. They might have to stop dumping whatever it is they're dumping. They might have to clean up their wastes. They might think that's too expensive. They might close their factory and move to another country."

"A country even more friendly to business."

"There you are. So anyone seeking to hold these people accountable is immediately seen as being opposed to progress . . ." She paused for a moment, then added, "Let's just say the situation can make for reluctant officials."

"And lots of enemies."

"And that too. But now think about the guy that owns the battery place, where the car was tampered with. The cost of cleaning that up would be enormous. It might ruin him financially. He might go to great lengths to hang on to what he has, maybe even hire a couple of his old workers to take out the people responsible for shutting down the plant, for losing them their jobs—which is probably how they would look at it. Forget that the jobs were killing them."

"I guess hiring hit men would pass for still doing business in Mexico . . ."

"If they could find one of these guys . . . And if that guy talked . . . That's attempted murder. Screw Minimum Contact."

"You'd like to nail this guy, Hunter."

"You bet."

"Of course it might not be him . . ."

She looked over the boxes filling the small room. She smiled. "No," she said, "he's just a place to start. There are lots of others."

"Tell me about it. It took me an hour to load all this stuff, another hour to tie it down. I didn't think the truck was going to be big enough."

"That's a good thing," she said. "I've got you doing your part."

Fahey smiled, but she was only half joking. He could read it in her eyes. He reminded himself that she had been raised by nuns.

"I'm serious," she told him. "I mean, here you are. In this valley, where a man used to be able to live off the land . . . Where you used to be able to ride your waves . . ." Magdalena broke off. "I guess I'm proselytizing," she said. She thought about her lunch with Raúl. "I can be a bore . . ."

"That's not possible," Fahey told her.

"It's just that, usually, when I try to talk to you about what I do, you never have much to say, like you're not that interested, and yet . . ." Her voice trailed away once more.

"Yet here I am."

Magdalena just looked him. "Here you are."

"Here I am," he said. "At least there's something we can agree on."

"You're making fun. But what happens if the valley gets any more polluted? Then where will you be?"

"And what if you give everything to this cause and never get anywhere? What if that's your life? What if this thing you struggle with is just the sweep of some big evolutionary process . . . I don't mean to say that makes it good, or desirable, just hard to do anything about."

"And that's a reason not to try?" It struck her that for the first time since coming to the valley they were actually talking about something.

Fahey cracked a fresh beer. "One can try, I suppose. But one needs to be realistic. I mean you could fill your life with these battles. Next time someone messes with your car, you could die."

She looked him hard in the eye. "To give up would be to die," she said. "Giving up is letting them win, letting them take your soul."

"The world is run by people for whom power is everything, that's how they rise to the top. When evolution is on their side, it makes them hard to stop. But you can always ignore them."

"Like you?"

"There was this surfer, Mickey Dora. He's gone now but they've still got his name on the wall at Malibu, long live Da Cat. He had this riff about riding a wave, about the lip of the wave, the part that's throwing out over your shoulder." Fahey made a motion with his hand, as if he were flying across the face of a wave and the motion was meant to indicate that part of the wave so named. "That stuff in the lip, that's everything that's out to get you—cops, teachers, priests, bureaucrats, everything that would say your life has to be this or that, everything that would limit and define human experience, it's all just going by, and you just keep on riding, keep tapping that source, 'cause that's where it's at, always was and always will be, life in the moment . . ."

She was trying to see if he was messing with her. In the end, she concluded that he was not. "But if everyone thought that way, there would come a time when there was no place else to go, when these power junkies you're talking about would have it all . . . There are people in the world who feel that their life only has meaning when they are engaged in a struggle for it."

Fahey finished a beer, tossed the can into the trash, and got another. "Well," he said, "it's your world, Magdalena. I'm just passing through."

To which she balled up a piece of paper and bounced it off his forehead. "That's the bullshit gong," she said. "It just went off."

Fahey smiled, but there was something sad about it.

"I thought we were having a conversation," she said. "It was fun."

"Fun?"

"Okay, nice . . . you pick a word."

He answered by popping the top on a fresh beer, then sat looking at the hole he had made as if some deep truth were contained therein.

"What happened, Sam? There are other waves in the world besides the Mystic Peak. You talk about surfing. You love it, but you don't do it, not really, not anymore . . ." The directness of the inquiry surprised even her. Fahey looked for a moment as though he'd been struck, then turned away. "That's a tough one," he said.

Magdalena sighed. The sight of him peering without apparent hope into the depths of his beer seemed to have momentarily eviscerated her gratitude. The lapse shamed her. Who, after all, did she think she was? She was trying to fashion some response by which to reclaim their conversation, but already he was on his feet. She watched as he took the rest of the six-pack from the refrigerator—three cans dangling by the plastic nooses that bound them together as though they were some ornament to be used in ritual—then stood with them in the tiny kitchen at the side of his tiny door. "I hope you find what you're looking for," he said. "I really do. I hope you win." After which he went outside.

She saw him through the window, through the dirt and grime, the strips of silver duct tape, walking toward his work shed with its ever burning yellow light, the cans trailing from his hand as it swung from his arm. She saw him open a door and go inside. In time she heard the jazz, and finally the sander, its piercing, high-pitched whine drowning out all else.

19

No one knew there was a dead man in the trailer. But then the locals were engaged in high living. The week was ending and a rodeo was coming to town. The women cooked outside on their grates over open flames. Armando and his companions camped beneath the stars in front of Chico's cousin's shack. Armando had never seen the world from this side of the border. He was reminded of the old corral where the Río Mayo made its way into the Gulf of California. In the ghetto sprawl of Tijuana, it was a place he had not been reminded of for a long time.

None of the Oaxacans seemed to know anything about a man with a worm on his cap. But that was okay, for the moment. It was a small valley. He could not be far. And in the meantime there was the approach of rodeo. There was beer and food. There were women in dresses who showed their legs when they danced. And there was more. Chico's cousin had been a fisherman on the peninsula, where he had begun to traffic in sea turtles. The turtles were an endangered species and catching them was illegal. But Chico's cousin had found that there was a market for them among the roving gangs of drug runners moving up and down the coast. At first the drug runners paid in cash, later, after Chico's cousin had gotten a taste of what it was they were moving, they paid in crack.

The man went from fisherman to crack addict in less than a month. Half the village went with him. Their yield went down accordingly. Drug runners took everything they had in trade. They stole their fish, raped their women, set fire to their boats for sport when the local turtle population had dwindled. Chico's cousin packed up his habit and crossed the border. He landed in Garage Door Tijuana, out of which he worked in the fields as far north as the Coachella Valley but got his stash right here at home, in the parking lot of the Palm Avenue 7-Eleven, from a kid with a head shaped like a peanut and a hoop through his nose.

Armando, Nacho, and Chico sampled his wares, stayed up days running, right into rodeo, where they staggered about like drunken novitiates amid costumed gallants, where they ran in foot races, boxed, ate, danced, and fucked, or at least jerked off, and for a time, forgot even among themselves the dead man in the trailer.

Come the dawn of their fourth day in the valley and Armando was running on fumes, harsh yellow light that tolled the morning slashing though scattered clouds and a sky that smelled of the sea. Armando was wobbling across what was left of the quarter-mile track, barefoot in the churned dirt, high as a kite, when he noted the Indian checking out a window in the cowboy's trailer.

"Hey, compadre," Armando said.

The guy looked at him.

"What gives?"

"Something smells," the guy told him. "I think it's in here."

"You don't say."

"Check it out."

The man turned to the window.

Armando walked up behind him. "Check this out, *cabrón*."

He stabbed the man in the kidney, then stepped to his side and stabbed him in the liver. The man looked him in the eye, his own beginning to glaze, their question left unformed.

But Armando leaned just a little forward and whispered in the man's ear, *"Hijo de la chingada."* It was perhaps the most melancholy of Mexican curses for it was more than the sum of its parts and was also the registry of a people, or so Armando had always imagined it, for the people so indicted were none but his own.

"Son of the fucked," was what Armando whispered to the dying man. But he might just as well have spoken to himself.

20

MAGDALENA WAS up early on the following morning. She had not slept especially well, replaying her conversation with Fahey throughout the night. She did not doubt her own part in it, for she had chosen her path. Given the circumstances of her childhood it was difficult to see how it could have been otherwise. The battle, after all, had been brought to her door. Still, she had overstepped her bounds. There was some wound in the man and one needed to be mindful of it, for it was a thing time had not worked to heal. His battle was not so much with the world at large as with his own past and such demons as it had spawned. And yet it was also her judgment that all this isolation was not good. He was too alone here, too cut off from the rest of the world with nothing but the past and his worm farm to occupy his mind, and these things had not brought him to a good place. The man's business could break into the black nor not, Sam Fahey was hanging on by just a thread.

✦ ✦ ✦

Such were her thoughts as she went about what seemed to have become their domestic routine. She would rise before him, or at least before he had made any appearance at the trailer, make coffee, then go outside to see where he was. He was generally up, either attending to his worms or working on the board.

On the morning in question she found him doing neither, but seated in the shed, hunched over his laptop in an attitude of such intense concentration she simply stopped in the doorway and stood there for some time in silence for fear of disturbing him.

A chemical odor she would later learn to recognize as the scent of fresh resin hit her full in the face. It was strong but not particularly unpleasant. Still, her work among the factories had led her to associate any such odors with suffering and decay.

This morning's fumes seemed to issue from the surfboard Fahey had been working on and it appeared that he must have worked throughout the night for the board seemed finished and still wet, its freshly coated fiberglass surface shimmering in the light that streamed from the open doorway at her back.

Fahey, intent upon his computer screen, had still not seen her.

"Sam," she said, finally. She held a cup of coffee in each hand, one for herself and one for him.

He still did not turn.

"Sam," she said once more.

"Come look at this," Fahey said.

She put her own cup on the workbench and took the other to where he sat, perched on an overturned five-gallon drum, the computer resting on another such drum before him. She touched his shoulder with her hand, looking over it. "What?" she asked.

"This," he said. "It's a storm."

She saw before her a colored screen, shades of blue and green superimposed over what appeared to be a map.

"Jack Nance's been telling me about this," he said. "I started tracking it last night."

After their conversation, she thought. "You've been working on your board too," she said.

"I couldn't sleep," Fahey told her.

"Nor could I."

If her remark registered he did not show it. "This is a big storm," he said. "It will generate some very big waves, waves that will reach the straits."

He made some adjustments with his mouse. The map shifted. "It started moving off the coast of Japan, six, seven days ago. It seems to have peaked over Hawaii, then turned toward Alaska." He brought up another screen, a graph with numbers. "Buoy readings," he told her. "They are already posting small-craft warnings up and down the coast."

She was more interested in him than in the screen. His face, she thought, was slightly flushed, fixed with an intensity she had not seen there before, not even on that first morning, on the beach, when he had killed the dogs, and she saw that it was not their conversation that had kept him awake, it was this, the map on the screen and the prospect of waves, though perhaps there had been something in their conversation that had made him want to look, as opposed to dosing himself with pills and going to sleep, or in his case, what passed for it.

"Will it be as big as before?" she asked. "When you and Hoddy rode Outside the Bullring?" She felt compelled to participate in the moment.

"We rode Outside the Bullring more than once. But that first time, that was the one."

"When Hoddy got his wave?"

"When Hoddy got his wave."

"Will it be like that?"

"I don't know."

"And will there be rain?"

Fahey shook his head. "There's high pressure inland. I believe the rain will all be to the north."

She stood for a moment in silence.

Fahey turned from his computer.

"You said it was twenty years ago."

"I guess."

"It was an El Niño winter?"

"I don't believe we called it that then, at least I didn't. Why do you ask?"

She made a little shrugging motion with her shoulders. "Twenty years ago . . . A rainy winter . . . It's quite possible at least some of those waves you rode came with the storm that killed my mother." She hardly knew what had inspired her to say it.

Fahey had no idea how to respond. "I'm sorry," he said.

Magdalena shook her head. "I guess that's not really anything you needed to know. I don't know why I said it."

"It's okay," Fahey told her.

"I just had this feeling . . ." which in fact she had. It had come upon her suddenly and continued to linger. One might say it was a premonition. "I brought you your coffee," she said. It was only then that she noticed her hand had been shaking badly enough to spill some of it, and that she had burned her fingers.

"Really," Fahey told her. "It's okay."

But she was not so sure.

21

H E SUPPOSED IT had been a mistake, leaving the cowboy in the trailer. They should have taken him when they took his truck and this sold to a meth chef in Chula Vista for three hundred dollars. They could have disposed of the cowboy along the way. Failing that, they should have buried him in the valley. But then Chico's cousin had warned them to be careful of the valley, as it came under constant surveillance by the border patrol. Still, Armando thought, in the wake of his encounter with the Indian, his mind still moving at something like the speed of light, the valley would have been better, under the trees, where the ground was damp and good for digging, and before the morning was much older it was where they put him.

With Nacho to wield a shovel he was underground in no time at all and the Indian with him. They had carried them there in sleeping bags taken from the trailer and no one paying much attention to anything in the aftermath of the rodeo's opening, everyone sleeping it off, everyone not tweaked to their eyeballs on Chico's cousin's little brown crystals. God have mercy. In truth there seemed only one person in all of Garage Door Tijuana still able to think on his feet and that was none but Armando, and while he reckoned them lucky in their disposal of the cowboy and the Indian, he saw now that there was also the trailer to contend with, tin charnel house of bodily fluids and bloody fingerprints and God knew what else . . . a smell that would never be entirely gone. In the end, he soaked a rag in gasoline and stuffed it into a bottle filled with the same. With Chico and Nacho standing lookout, he broke one of the trailer's windows with an elbow, put a match to the rag, and tossed the bottle inside. Within minutes the thing was engulfed in a roiling pillar of flame. The ensuing fire took out half the neighboring corral and killed a horse. The flames brought fire engines and a car from the San Diego sheriff's department. Armando deemed it a good time to go into town, where Chico's cousin had already agreed to take them to meet his man. He was, he concluded, still thinking clearly. He was riding a streak.

Town was Imperial Beach. It reminded Armando of Tijuana, the new part, in the Zona del Río. It was filled with the same Mexicans. The predominant language was Spanish. Homeboys loitered on corners. There was no old town, however, no El Centro with its clubs and whorehouses. There were only gas stations and strip malls and fast-food joints, islands amid a seemingly endless sea of tract homes where greenery was as scarce as it was across the border.

To Nacho's eye, the tract homes appeared as mansions and this is what he called them.

Chico's cousin, whose name Armando could never quite remember, thought this was very funny. "You think these are mansions, *cabrón?*" He looked at Nacho in his rearview mirror. "These are some cheap shit, man. The cheapest shit you can find."

Nacho didn't much like being laughed at. He stared back into the mirror with an evil look that Chico's cousin would have done well to have paid more attention to.

"These are the cheapest pieces of shit in all of California," Chico's cousin said, expanding upon his earlier pronouncement. "Only an idiot would think they were mansions."

"You shouldn't laugh at Nacho so much," Armando said. "He doesn't like it." He figured the cousin was high on his own shit, as high as Armando. He was trying to give him some good advice. He was feeling magnanimous.

Chico's cousin looked once more at the hulking youth in his rearview mirror. He shrugged. "He shouldn't say stupid shit," he said.

"Neither should you," Armando told him.

The cousin shot him a look but kept his mouth shut. Nacho looked like something out of a horror movie but Armando was the one he was afraid of. He pulled into the parking lot of a 7-Eleven store, then around back by the Dumpsters. In a short period of time the guy they were waiting for showed up. The guy wore a black leather motorcycle jacket. His head was indeed shaped more or less like a peanut and there was a silver hoop the size of a silver dollar dangling from his nose, just like the cousin had said.

They bought some goods. Armando bought his own share. He was living large on money he'd found in the cowboy's trailer. The sale of the truck was chicken feed in comparison. Nacho went into the store by himself. He came out with a bag of pork rinds, a bottle of white port with lemon juice, and a short dog of Silver Satin.

The stuff was all tucked away in various parts of the oversized army jacket he wore.

The guy in the motorcycle jacket was gone now. It was just the four of them, in back of the 7-Eleven, among the big blue Dumpsters.

"What the fuck," the cousin said as Nacho began to pull things from the sleeves of his coat. "You stole all of this shit?"

Nacho's face twisted into a kind of grin.

The cousin just looked at him, his own face flushed with disbelief. "How stupid can you be?" he asked. "Did you forget you've got no papers? You get caught doing something stupid like this we'll all be back on the other side before nightfall. In jail. You don't got papers, they take you straight to the border police."

"Fuck the border police," Nacho said.

The cousin stared at him once more. "Fuck the border police? How about *chinga tu madre?*" Meaning how about fuck your mother?

Nacho reached for one his chains, quick as a snake. There was a flash of silver. Chico's cousin stumbled backward, clawing at his throat where he had been stabbed with a sharpened screwdriver, then went down at their feet, his hands wrapped around his own neck as if engaging himself in some manner of struggle and this act accompanied by weird gurgling sounds. When he puked it came out the new hole in his throat. He rolled facedown, blowing bubbles in blood and puke, until the bubbles stopped.

Nacho and Armando put him in one of the Dumpsters, shuffling things around until he rested on the bottom. Chico looked on. He wore the expression of a man who'd just been kicked in the stomach by a horse.

"He was not long for this world anyway," Armando said. He was hoping to put things in perspective. "Not with the shit he was doing." He looked at Chico's cousin's car, which was some kind of old American sedan, a rusted hulk on sparkling chrome rims. "What is it?" Armando asked.

"What do you mean, what is it?" Chico was still a little shaky. Nacho passed him the short dog.

"I mean what kind of car is it?"

"It's a Pontiac."

"I always wanted one of these," Armando said.

Chico took a long drink of the Silver Satin, staring at the car as if he were seeing it for the first time.

"And now we have a use for it," Armando said. In yet one more moment of lucidity it had occurred to him that things were maybe getting just a little out of hand over here in the land of the free. It was time to do what they had come to do and go home. It was time to get serious about finding the worm man.

22

FAHEY HAD said that he was not hungry and Magdalena ate alone, on the deck of the trailer. Near noon, she noted that he had not yet run the sprinklers above the worm beds and when she went to the shed to ask him about it, she found him as she had left him that morning, seated before his laptop, tracking his swell. If he had done other than move the mouse on his computer she could not tell it. The new surfboard still sat nearby, gleaming upon its drip-laden sawhorses, above the scattered mounds of dust and shavings that had fallen away before its sleek, needlelike shape.

When she told him about the worm beds, he looked up as though emerging from a trance, then shuffled outside in sandaled feet to attend to the herd.

Magdalena walked with him.

"Carlotta was due back last night from Mexico City," she said. "I'd like to go into town, give her a call. I know it's a bother . . ."

Fahey looked at her a bit sheepishly. "You have an e-mail," he said. "It came in early this morning. I was online. I looked to see if it was an order. When I saw it was for you I printed it out then went back to the storm and I forgot about it. The outside buoys are beginning to show, by the way. You asked if these waves would be as big as the ones I told you about. I believe they will be."

"The e-mail," Magdalena said.

Fahey nodded and led her back to the shed. "I should've told you," he said. "I'm sorry."

It took him a few minutes to find the pages, which were already buried in clutter. He dug them out and handed them over, watching as she walked with them back to the trailer, reading as she went.

He was back on the buoy readings, a full five minutes later, when he heard something break in the trailer. The sound was followed by a sharp cry. He toppled the can he had been sitting on then covered the distance between the shed and the trailer at a dead run. He arrived at the trailer door to find her inside, in tears, seated on the floor, in the midst of the clutter she had created with her papers and files. Fahey's Hawaiian hula girl lamp lay in ruins at her side.

"I'm really sorry," she said. She had seen Fahey at the door. She paused long enough to wipe her nose with the sleeve of one of Fahey's shirts. "I broke your fucking lamp."

It took some small amount of coaxing to get her started. Fahey did so as he collected the pieces of the plaster hula girl and dumped them in the trash.

"The Guardians of Christ the King," Magdalena told him.

"I'm not sure I follow you," Fahey said.

"That's who started the fire in the office."

Fahey just looked at her.

"This fringe group of Catholic extremists." She shook her head, took a breath, started from the beginning. "There was this girl, all of fifteen. She was raped by her mother's boyfriend, some middle-aged crackhead. It was very brutal, very ugly. The doctors had reason to believe the girl would not be able to carry the child. But it is very difficult to obtain an abortion in Mexico. Carlotta took this case; it was tried in Mexicali, and in the end we were successful. The girl was granted the right to abort the child. But the case got a lot of press. A number of demonstrations were staged outside Casa de la Mujer, where the girl had stayed for a while. This was months ago. Then just last week, while Carlotta was in Mexico City, while I was here, someone tried to firebomb the house you visited in Tijuana. They caught the men in the act and no harm was done. But there were two of them, and they've admitted to the fire in Carlotta's offices. Also, in Mexicali, one of the attorneys we worked with had the brake lines in her car cut . . ."

"They've admitted to that, too?"

Magdalena shook her head. "Not yet. But they're from Mexicali, that's where this group is based. There were two men on the road that night. There were two men who tried to firebomb Casa de la Mujer . . ."

They sat with this for a moment in silence.

"Carlotta seems to think these are the guys. She says if I come back to Tijuana, maybe I can identify them . . ."

"Surely the Guardians of Christ the King consists of more than these two guys."

"Sure. But the group's been identified. Their actions are out in the open. Even if the guys who came after me on the road are a different pair, it's unlikely they'll try anything else, not with two of their members in jail."

"I don't think you should go back," Fahey said, "not yet. How about e-mailing Carlotta? She can find out if either of these guys have tattoos."

Magdalena responded by kicking one of her boxes. Factual reports and old case studies slid across Fahey's carpet like spilt entrails.

"You don't like the idea?"

"Sure. Right. We'll send the e-mail." She shook her head. They sat for a moment in silence. "You don't get it, do you?" She looked up at him, her face flushed. "Don't you see? I thought I was getting somewhere with all this." She picked up a handful of papers, twisted them in her hand then let them fall. "I don't care about the Guardians of Christ. History will dispose of the Guardians of Christ. I want to make a case against the owners of one of these dumps, make them clean it up, so maybe the other owners will be spooked into cleaning theirs up as well, so maybe, just maybe, some lives will be spared." She shook Carlotta's e-mail in his face. "I thought I was on to something. I thought finally . . . I thought some big shot was out to get me. I thought I could use everything that's happened to me to help nail him. It's all just stupid," she said finally. "A stupid waste."

"You still don't know that for sure. And all this work you've done"—he waved his hand to include her great heaps of paper—"it's good work. I mean, it could pay off at any time . . ."

"One gets tired of waiting," she told him. She tossed Carlotta's message to the floor, then leaned down, her forehead upon the heel of a hand.

"That's what happened to my lamp?"

"I slammed the door. It fell over. I'm sorry . . . Truly . . . It was practically the only thing you owned that wasn't broken . . ." She stopped talking when it became apparent that Fahey was smiling at her.

"I could make you a list."

"Of what?"

"Things that still work around here."

She wondered briefly if his list would include himself.

"Forget the lamp," Fahey told her. "When you're surfing—you know how you get outside, on a big day?"

Magdalena just looked at him.

"You have to want it. Oh, you try to read the water, to choose a path. You try to use your head. But mainly you just really have to want it. So you put your head down and you paddle. Your mouth goes dry. Your lungs burn. Your arms turn to rubber. But you keep on paddling. And in the end . . . you do that long enough, and hard enough . . ."

Fahey got to his knees on the floor beside her and went about collecting her papers, arranging them in a stack that he placed by her side. "You'll get there," he said. "You'll get one of these guys. You're smart and you're persistent. And you want it."

Magdalena sighed. She turned to the window, giving him her profile—the thrust of her chin, the delicate sweep of her jaw, the fine straight line of her nose. He could see the pulse at the side of her neck. Her hair fell across her brow, hiding many of the little cuts left by the accident. His impulse was to touch her, to let the tips of his fingers draw the hair away from her face. He wanted it in a way he had not wanted anything in a long time, with a longing to constrict the heart. He would never have done it. Suddenly, however, she turned and leaned against him, her head pushing in upon his chest. He could feel the warmth of her tears through the fabric of his T-shirt, caked with dust. And then, very slowly, because he had not done anything like it in a very long time, like the Tin Man gone to rust yet recalling a gesture from a time before, his arm moved to circle her shoulders. My God, he thought, she was no bigger than a child. He let his head bow down, the tip of his nose touching the part in her hair, smelling her skin, afraid to move.

"You must think I'm a fool," she said.

Fahey stroked her hair.

They stayed that way for some time, their breaths coming and going together, her tears upon his skin, the scent of her hair in his face. She draped an arm across his chest and put a small, warm hand upon his arm. Now you've done it, Fahey thought. Days and nights of unbearable loneliness that would surely follow in the wake of her passing appeared before him, stretching out as far as the eye could see. His knees ached, sending little spears of pain up into his legs. But still he held her. Anyone would have. He wondered for a long time if there was something he ought to say, rummaging about in his head like a blind man searching for something in an empty room. He was afraid of appearing pathetic.

"Will you try to ride these big waves?" she asked.

Neither of them had spoken in a very long time. Fahey would have had the time last longer. "I don't know," he said.

He felt her sigh.

"I guess we should send the e-mail," she said. "You are right, of course, that's the way to do it. Carlotta can find out about the tattoos."

The words stabbed at Fahey's heart. He felt in them the beginnings of her long absence. Dumb shit, he thought, it's only what you get. "We'll do it," he told her. "And then we should celebrate."

She turned her face to his.

"I'll take you down to the pier," he said. "We'll drink a beer, or two, or three. We'll eat fish tacos and watch the swell. It should start coming in sometime tonight. We'll watch it by the light of the moon."

She put her head upon his chest once more. "It would be kind of like you were taking me out," she said.

Fahey sat with this one. Seconds passed. "I guess it would," he said finally. He was watching the light outside his window. "It would be kind of like that."

23

A SIGN AT THE end of a dirt road read MEET THE PICKERINGS. The sign had two little birds—long-billed clapper rails, if you knew what you were looking at, carved at the top of it, one in either corner. The birds had names, Dot and Don.

Don Pickering was well into his seventies, still able to mend fence and track the feral animals that from time to time found their way onto his land. Dot was nearly the same age, a little crippled with arthritis but still able to tend the garden. They'd lived in the Tijuana River Valley for some fifty-odd years. They'd raised four sons and two daughters, an unknown number of chickens, horses, and cows, though in recent years the land had gone mainly for crops, Brazilian lettuce and organic strawberries.

Having lived in the valley for such a long time, there was not much that had gotten past them. They remembered Lucian Fahey and his notorious farm. They'd known his son as well, for their own boys had grown up surfing near the mouth of the river and from them they had learned of the exploits of Sam the Gull Fahey and his strange mentor, one Hoddy the Dog Younger, out there on the beach in his shack of driftwood and whalebone, and considered each a bad influence from day one. Sam Fahey had visited their farm on several occasions, in the company of one or more of their sons, and they remembered him as a skinny, towheaded boy with a defiant look and little to say. Their opinion even then was similar to that held by Deek Waltzer, whom they also knew; they found it hard to believe that any good would ever come from the likes of Lucian Fahey and so believing had not encouraged his son's presence among their own.

Later, when the ridiculous submarine sank off Rosarito Beach, when the math teacher put a bullet through his head and the stories about the Island Express were filling the local papers, the name of Samuel Fahey prominent among them, and when the same Samuel Fahey was sentenced to prison and gone from the valley, they felt their suspicions confirmed and were glad they had nipped that boy's friendship with their own sons in the very beginning, before further harm could be done. And later, when old man Fahey died and left the worm farm, by then little more than a garbage dump, to his only son, fresh from his second stint in the penitentiary, they were not inclined to roll out any red carpets. As far as they were concerned, the sooner he failed with his worm business and went away the better off the valley would be, for surely, they thought, no good had yet come from the presence of a Fahey in their midst, any Fahey at all, nor could they imagine this was likely to change anytime soon.

The Pickering property was less than a mile from the Fahey worm farm, near the middle of the valley, within sight of the river, and over the years the Pickerings had been made witness to many strange things. They'd seen entire families running through their fields by moonlight pursued by men in flying machines and on horseback. They'd seen drug runners of every ilk, shape, size, and disposition. They'd lost untold nights' sleep to gunshots and cries for help, to the barking of dogs gone mad, with grief or rage, none could say. And come mornings they'd often found the leftovers of what they'd heard in the night. They'd found the bodies of men tortured and slain. They'd found women robbed and raped, wandering shoeless on bloodied feet through fields of mud. They'd found stashes of drugs, marijuana mostly, left where they had fallen upon the ground, or ditched among the brush. Once they'd found a backpack filled with marijuana, a severed hand still clutching to one of the straps.

It might also be said that life in the valley had taught them to recognize trouble when they saw it, so that when Don Pickering looked out of his front door late one afternoon in the even later autumn, the sun already beginning to smear colors across a western sky as though some child of God had been loosed among the reds, pinks, and yellows, and saw there two strangers arrayed before him, like figures come for trick or treat on the wrong day of the year, before the sun had even a chance to set, he knew that something was amiss.

He rose from the chair he'd been seated in, crossed the living room floor to retrieve the shotgun kept standing and loaded in an umbrella rack just inside the front door, and went out onto his porch to meet them, life in the Tijuana River Valley having conditioned him to a certain degree of self-reliance. Nor would this be the first time he'd been called upon to send strangers packing.

Yet even Don Pickering, never known to his neighbors as anything but a hard case, was a bit nonplussed by such characters as now confronted him. They were two in number, and one, a ragged scarecrow of a man, fixing him with a silver smile that had no warmth or humor in it, with eyes sunk deep in their sockets and threads of thinning hair hanging down on either side, long enough to touch the uppermost bones of his chest; and the other standing nearby, enrobed in a garish cowboy shirt that he wore unbuttoned, and nothing under it save the Aztec sun tattooed across the ribbed muscles of his naked abdomen. In point of fact it had been some time since he'd encountered such rough trade and the old man was vaguely aware of the dull throb of his heart and supposed that he'd been remiss in not having called out to Dot to phone the border patrol, of which his own son was now a member, or at least to watch his back, and this even before it occurred to him that no dog had barked, nor had any workman raised a voice from out near the gate that by this time of day ought to have been shut and locked. Still, he had come this far and he knew better than to show weakness in the face of such rabble, so he came onto the very edge of his porch and down the three wooden planked steps to stand in the dirt, the rifle pointed slightly down, held loosely in the crook of his arm, and said in perfect Spanish to the men arrayed before him, "What can I do for you, boys?"

And though he would never have guessed what they were after, he could not say he was surprised when the scarecrow he took for the leader launched into some manner of tortured inquiry with respect to a big man with a worm on his cap. And he might have answered straightaway just to be rid of them, for there could only be one to fit such a description, and he could not think of a single reason to say otherwise. But it was in just that moment when he was about to speak that he caught sight of something in one of the trees near the entrance to the drive. So stunning was the sight he could not immediately be certain his eyes were not playing to his paranoia, that there really was a dog, one of his own, hung there by its leash among the shadowed limbs.

Once verified, the sight seemed to affect him as might a blow, sapping the strength from his hands, so that the gun seemed not to rise smoothly as he brought it to bear but to swing at the ends of his arms as though it were an instrument for finding water and thereby subject to powers not altogether his own. In fact, the entire world seemed altered somehow in the arrangement of its parts, and yet if he knew just one thing with any kind of certainty at all, it was a thing he had known in the abstract since the day he'd heard about that accursed worm farm and the ex-con coming home to claim it, that the presence of a Fahey in the valley, any Fahey at all, would never spell anything it had not spelled out already many times over. The thought rifled through his mind even before he saw the third man, the size of a goddamn water buffalo, coming around from the side of his own house, not six feet from where he stood, rooted, the shotgun in his hands not yet parallel to the ground and the man already mid-swing with that rusted old machete he'd left out by the tool-shed, meaning to either get rid of it for scrap or take it to be sharpened on his next trip into town, which he saw now was apt to be a long time coming.

24

THE EVENING SO decided, it occurred to Magdalena that she didn't have much of anything to wear for dining out. She'd been going about in either the flannel shirt and sweat clothes that Fahey had provided or the jeans she'd come in, but these were torn and stained. The sweater she'd worn was beyond use altogether.

"We're going out to the pier," Fahey told her. "You can probably get away with the jeans and sweatshirt."

"But it is a celebration," she told him, and she was doing her best to see it as such. "It would be fun to do better than 'get away with.'"

Fahey appeared to give this some thought. "I think there are some clothes in the house," he said finally. "I believe they were my mother's, but I'm not sure. And I don't know what kind of shape they're in, but I know where they are. There's an old cedar chest in one of the bedrooms. We could look."

"Are you sure you want to do that?"

Fahey shrugged. "If that doesn't work we could find a strip mall somewhere. But this would be quicker."

"And what about the bees?"

Fahey said he thought these were confined to the front porch and living room. He also believed they were worse during the day, which was just about gone, and that he was willing to risk it.

He'd not set foot in the house for more than a year. In truth he had not lived in it since he was a boy. When his father had died, leaving him the land, he'd purchased a trailer from the owner of the stables where Deek now lived and gotten Jack Nance to help him drag the thing across the valley and set it up at the edge of his holdings. He had concluded there were simply too many associations with the old farmhouse, which was no more than three bedrooms and a bath, for him ever to feel at home there, and he guessed that one day he might have the money to gut it of its sordid history and remake it in some new image that was more to his liking but had never done more along these lines than to convert what had once been an enclosed back porch to his shaping shack. The rest of the house was as his father had left it and there were even his father's clothes with dust on the shoulders of old sports coats and a single suit with frayed cuffs and the little holes made by cigarettes smoked thirty years in the past and shirts thin as palimpsest shaped to the hangers upon which they hung. There were old ties dangling from hooks like things killed and hung to dry and old dress shoes that seemed to contain in them the very essence of old age so that in looking at them one thought almost immediately of old men on park benches. There was a shoehorn made of bone or perhaps the horn of some animal with a brass knob at one end with a short leather strap through it—some little bit of finery purchased in some no doubt illusory moment of happiness.

He passed a dresser and mirror that caught his reflection upon smoky glass before he could turn away. He saw cuff links and a long-handled comb beneath a brass lamp whose shade contained a map of the world. He went among these things in utter silence and with great effort, which was really the effort not to see them at all, for each was more than the thing itself and in each lay the starting point in such concatenations as could only end in feelings for which he could find no proper name.

There were three bedrooms in the house; one for each of them and one for the mother who'd not lived there for more than a month but whose room had been left as she had left it herself and which Fahey had not seen since he was a boy. For in the musty air of these sad rooms he felt that he had come to the place of his own beginnings, that in some measure he was made from these things and all the sadness and darkness that had come with them was carried still in such chambers of his own heart where thought and feelings dance their Sabbath.

The cedar chest was as he had remembered it and he thought that anything in it was likely to be fairly well preserved though he saw too there were also a few articles hung in a closet like his father's and a second dresser with articles scattered across the top, but he did not care to look at them. When Magdalena told him she thought there was enough here for her to work with he left her to see what she could find or would want and went back out through the house as quickly as he could, as though dogged by its very ghosts, and into his trailer, where he sorted out such things as he intended to wear, then went to the sink and removed his beard. After which he showered and dressed and went outside.

What she found was a red dress and a pair of ivory combs. In place of shoes she wore the leather sandals Fahey had found for her and so added a slightly bohemian flair to the dress, which was vintage something and altogether astonishing—a summer dress of simple cotton with thin straps at the shoulders. She tied a scarf around the waist to pull it in but it all worked somehow and done up in it she looked like what she was, a beautiful Mexican girl dressed for fiesta and dancing in the streets. The simple fact was, she took Fahey's breath away and he watched her cross the yard in changing light, as though some vast and apocalyptic fire was raging just beyond the gray-green shadows of the valley. The sky was the color of her dress, and standing, he was aware of the pitch of the earth beneath his feet.

Walking to meet him, she found herself trying to take some measure of exactly how she felt about what had so recently transpired, her head upon Fahey's chest, his arm about her shoulders. The truth was, she was not so experienced in affairs of the heart as one might have thought. Raised by nuns, her life thus far had been composed of school and more school, of work and the cause. She had even missed her Quinceañera. It was what Mexican girls got when they turned fifteen—a coming-out party harkening to another age, an event, like the debutante's ball, replete with dinners and dancing and expensive gowns. There had been a few dates since starting college, a brief and unsatisfactory sexual escapade with one of her professors that had left her gun shy for months to follow. The last man for whom she had felt some real attraction, as opposed to what she had felt with Raúl in the restaurant overlooking the valley, was a young lawyer out of San Diego with whom she and Carlotta had pursued a case. Physically, however, the attorney was very much like Raúl, nearly her own age, a handsome Mexican, trim and dark, with an easy smile. Fahey was nearly twice her age. He slept with the lights on. For some absurd reason she found herself thrown back on Scripture . . . He was a man meant for pains and for having an acquaintance with sickness . . . And yet if that was what drew her, there were those aplenty in the country to which she was returning and she supposed it was a good thing that she was going there soon. Though perhaps, she thought, they would remain friends, she and Fahey. It was then that she caught sight of him walking to meet her. She saw him in the last light. He had showered and shaved. He'd put on a pair of white canvas trousers, a flowered shirt, socks and brown leather loafers. And as he walked, the wind lifted the sun-streaked hair from his face, and the years with it, so that for just that moment the Fahey she saw in the sunset yard was the Fahey of the photograph on the wall, the one she had gone about clutching with both hands. He would have been just about her age then, she guessed, in that picture, carving his turn from the base of the wave, triple overhead. He would have been something.

He escorted her to the truck. He opened the door for her and made a show of doing so. She clutched at a handful of the red material, lifting it so as to save it from being caught as she slid onto the seat and he closed the door behind her.

They went by dirt roads among deepening shadows, the light running before them. They passed the old Pickering place and the wooden sign with its long-billed clapper rails fashioned in wood and a lowered Pontiac on chromed rims parked off-road, among the trees.

Fahey noted the car. He noted the rust spots and California plates, the powder-puff dice, baby blue, dangling from a rearview mirror, and the steering wheel, fashioned of a silver chain. It could belong to none but a Mexican and so was attributed to one of the Pickering workmen. The old man was forever fiddling with his property and Fahey guessed that someone was working late, which was not altogether inaccurate. It was the nature of the work in progress that escaped his imagination, much as the hanged dogs escaped his sight, for they were hung well back from the road, amid gathering shadows and, like all the rest of it, too dark to see.

25

T HE SUNLIGHT was all but gone as they drove down Ocean
Boulevard toward the pier in downtown Imperial Beach.
Fahey had thought to watch the sunset from the pier itself but saw
now that he had mistimed it. Still, the moon was rising above the
Mexican mesas and the evening was shot through with a delicate
beauty, the great dome of the sky going from some deep shade of
midnight blue in the east to ashes of rose over the black and craggy
shapes of the Coronado Islands—an airbrush job of epic proportions, hot-rod art writ large as if Big Daddy Roth had been permitted some say in it.

The swell Fahey had predicted had indeed begun to show, the
pier shuddering beneath their feet as they walked its length toward
the small restaurant at its far end, Woody's at the Pier. To the north
lay the tip of Point Loma—a deep black landmass from which a few
yellow lights had begun to shine like planets in the night sky. Three

miles to the south were lights marking the end of the border fence, where it entered the sea, and beyond that those of Las Playas.

Magdalena pointed to the lights of Point Loma. "You've got to wonder," she said, "if any of those are his."

Fahey assumed she was talking about Hunter, the owner of Reciclaje Integral.

"I mean, he lives somewhere in the county. What if he can actually see the lights of Tijuana from his house? Could someone do that? Could they look at the lights in Mexico and know what they had left behind was killing the children of this little town?"

"People find ways," Fahey said. "They find ways of letting themselves off the hook."

"Or they just don't care."

"Or they just don't care."

"You think I'm naive."

Fahey shook his head. "I read somewhere that by the time people are about five years old, they've asked all the important questions. They're the questions that can't be answered."

They arrived at the restaurant and went inside. It was small and cheaply appointed, something just shy of a take-out joint but somehow warm and cozy nonetheless with views of the lights and sea in all directions and the aroma of cooking food.

"This place is not much to look at," Fahey told her, "but the food is good."

A man came out from behind the bar to slap Fahey on the back. "Sam the Gull," he intoned, and seemed genuinely pleased to see him. "I'm glad to see you still get out. I thought you'd forgotten us."

Sam introduced him to Magdalena. His name was Bob. Bob brought complimentary beers. "Any friend of Sam Fahey's," he said. He looked at Magdalena. "A bona fide local legend." He left them with menus and went back to his kitchen.

The place was pretty well filled with people. She could feel some of them looking her over, her and Fahey. The walls of the tiny restaurant were covered with old photographs of the town and the surrounding beaches. Among them she saw many old black-and-white photographs of men on surfboards. "They like you here," she said.

Fahey pointed to a photograph not far from where they sat, a grainy black-and-white in which a dark-haired man who looked as if he might have been chiseled from stone and who rode what appeared to be a long, wooden surfboard glided with apparent ease across the face of a long, rolling wave.

"That's him." Fahey said. "That was Hoddy Younger."

Magdalena looked at the photograph. She looked at Fahey, looking at the photograph. Something made her want to touch his hand.

They ate fish tacos, beans and rice. They drank the beers and ordered two more. Below them the big waves continued to crash against the pilings. Fahey looked often into the night. "I had a girl-friend once," he said. The comment came out of the blue as he had been watching the waves but he turned now to face her. "She was a Mexican. I saw you looking at her photograph in the shaping room."

Magdalena was not sure what to say.

"She used to translate for us sometimes, making deals in Baja." And he told her about the Island Express, about running drugs in the valley, about getting busted and doing time. "When I got out, we started seeing each other again," he said. "She was clean by then, going to some kind of college . . . But I talked her into coming back, a one-shot deal, translate for me on a meet in T.J. The Mexicans had the pot. I had the buyers." Fahey paused to look out the window. "A dozen crooked *federales* came down on us, took everything . . . I thought they were going to kill us too, but they didn't. They let everybody go but the girl. They kept the girl."

There was a long pause, the chatter of other customers, the crash of waves.

"We left her up there in that canyon."

Magdalena looked at him, a long beat of silence spooling out between them. She had come to think of his eyes as the color of the sea and the judgment had pleased her, till this moment, when the comparison seemed to fold back on itself, evoking little more than a cold and melancholy waste.

"The men had guns."

Fahey shrugged. "They were soldiers."

"What could you have done?"

"I could have found someone else to translate that night. Failing that, I could have fought to save her."

"And died."

"It was an option. They say you are made by your choices."

"Did you tell anyone?"

"We tried. Some Mexican cops. Mainly they just wanted to know what we were doing there. They were fucking with us. I began to envision whatever happened to her getting hung on us. I started thinking about life in the prison at La Paz."

"So what happened?"

"We ran. They were trying to get us in a car, but there were three of us and two of them. One of them was on his car phone. It sounded like he was calling for backup. We knocked his partner on his ass and we ran, got back to our car, ditched it out by the beaches, and crossed through this old storm drain I knew about. I had an apartment in I.B. but I never went back to it. I fell in with some guys who were cooking meth on the Otay Mesa . . ." And he told her the rest of it. He told her about his father and the scattered bones. He even told her about how he got busted, something he'd never told to another living soul . . . He wanted her to know it all, every ugly little thing there was to tell, that he'd failed even at cooking meth, that everything he'd told her the other night, all that stuff about Dora and the wave . . . that wasn't what he was about. What he was about was being scared, scared of age and scared of failing, scared of things he couldn't control, scared of going back. "Every guy I did time with is dead or back in," he said. He stopped to laugh, but it wasn't pretty to listen to. Some unspecified amount of time went by, just the thunder of the surf, the interior lights finding their reflection in the glass. "I was planning to kill my father," he said at length. "I mean really planning it, then I got out and saw him. Time had pretty well done the trick. But you know what? He left me that land. And that land has been the difference, the difference between me and those guys that are dead or back in . . . Because I had this one thing to hang on to— this one crappy little piece of shit in the middle of nowhere to build on, to watch the waves from . . ." He paused for the last time, still looking out the window. "The waves," he murmured. He turned to face her. It was hard to be certain in the room's dim light but it looked as if maybe he had begun to cry. "And here they are."

She supposed it was what she had been asking for. And now she sat with it, speechless as a loon, in her red dress, in the restaurant on the pier with the crash of the surf and the aroma of cooking food. She should have been a nun, she thought. Maybe then she would have known what to say.

"And the girl's family?"

Fahey seemed to collect himself. "She lived with an aunt," he told her. "I didn't really know her. I thought about trying to find her, to tell her what had happened . . . but then, in a way . . . I always figured maybe she was better off . . ."

Magdalena nodded. She would have liked to look him in the eye but found that she could not. She was beginning to feel just a little sick.

❖ ❖ ❖

They sat for a while longer in silence, drinking the last of the beers. Fahey paid. Bob told him not to be a stranger. Magdalena found another photograph of Fahey on the wall of the restaurant, this too in black and white and Fahey as thin as she'd ever seen him, hair bleached white by the sun. He was standing side by side with Hoddy Younger. The men had surfboards laid out in the sand before them. Hoddy was older in this picture than in the surfing photo. The black hair was a little more ragged, graying at the temples. The deep-set dark eyes appeared somehow troubled, peering out from beneath a scowling brow. She was tempted to say there was some-thing just vaguely familiar in that dark visage, in the way the older man held himself. She remembered Fahey's story, his belief that Hoddy was still out there somewhere. Yet in the end she said noth-ing. There was another photograph of Fahey, surfing. This picture was in color. The colors were the colors of the photograph on Fahey's wall, the colors of Mexico.

They left the restaurant in silence, walking back now along the pier where lights high as street lamps let down pale shafts to pool upon the white water as it broke against the pilings, swirling about their mussel-encrusted trunks, razor-sharp shells glinting black amid churning foam while farther out, away from the pier, great black mounds could be seen moving to and fro—dim, primordial shapes, as if some menagerie of caged beasts had been freed there to roam.

"It's not a pretty story," Fahey said at length. "But I wanted you to hear it."

Magdalena nodded. She might have said something about understatements but she didn't. She touched his hand with her own, but neither made an effort to keep it there. Tomorrow she would ask him for a ride, as far as the border. Carlotta would meet her at the crossing. The files would go as well. The two men in the Tijuana jail would have tattoos or they wouldn't. She had waited as long as she was going to wait. It was time to go home, time to get back into the fight. She looked into the lights of Point Loma. Some men let themselves off the hook. Some men didn't care. Fahey at least had suffered.

"I think you should try to find that girl's aunt," Magdalena said. "I think maybe she would like to know."

To which Fahey said nothing at all.

They rode in near silence back though town and into the valley that lay beyond it. In an odd way the place had begun to feel like home, though tonight she knew her home was over there, beyond the fence.

In time they came to the unnamed dirt road she had learned to recognize even in the dark and turned down it but as the trailer drew near she came to realize just how much she was dreading being there. It was more than confronting the files still scattered across the living room floor. There was what had transpired there, herself in Fahey's arms. A kind of spell had been wrought and yet the evening had undone it and it was the absence of that which she did not want to face, not just now.

The trees came into view. In the light of history they appeared as gallows and she supposed he had told her more than she would have wanted to know. And yet again she supposed that he had been right, right to tell her and she could not say that she was without respect for his doing so for surely he had guessed what the story would cost. Still, the trees came on, and now the fence . . . A lonely night yawned before her—Fahey in the shed, herself alone in the old trailer. She heard the whoop of Fahey's terrier, the low bark of the old hound, whereupon she remembered the day of the week and something to go along with it. She remembered the Mexican rodeo and the cowboy's invitation. Her hand went to Fahey's arm. They had not spoken since town.

"What would you think about going to a rodeo?" she asked.

She felt him study her in the dark.

"Deek invited us. He said it went on all weekend."

Fahey stopped in front of the gate, headlights falling across the windrows, the cast-off appliances, the fence of faded surfboards. To Magdalena's eye it was as though some great ship had broken up here and gone down, swallowed by the earth, and these were the things that had risen. It was how she had come to see the place, as an assemblage of wreckage in the wake of some terrible catastrophe.

"You don't think it's a little late?" Fahey thought no more of Garage Door Tijuana than he did of Mexico in general and for similar reasons.

"He said it goes on day and night, from Friday till Monday at dawn."

Fahey looked out across the ruins of his farm. "You know Deek's not there, that his trailer was burned."

"When?"

"A day or two after he looked in on you. I ran into Jack Nance in downtown I.B. at the little market . . . No one's quite sure how it happened. He'd been stripping some cabinets in order to refinish them and they think maybe he left some rags inside that combusted in the heat. He hasn't been around to ask."

"He wasn't hurt then."

"Not so far as anybody knows. Guy's a loner, comes and goes pretty much as he pleases, but Jack's worried. He thinks it's a little weird, even for Deek."

"Maybe he'll show up," she said. "It is Saturday night. Maybe he'll come back for the rodeo." She felt a slight tremor in her voice and wondered if Fahey had heard it. She watched the set of his jaw in the pale light of the dash, his hands upon the wheel. She guessed they both knew she was pushing it. She guessed they both knew why.

In the end, Fahey put the truck into reverse and backed them down the road upon which they had come. He did it without a word. She guessed they were going to the rodeo, in Garage Door Tijuana. It seemed appropriate enough. She was just a little drunk and she had begun to think once more about her failed Quinceañera. Perhaps it was the dress that had provoked the association. She'd never worn a prettier one, although the color was wrong. The celebration was one of purity. It was demanding of white. But then the night itself was demanding and she too had been found wanting. She should have been some Holy Mother, chartered to hear his confession. She supposed one could only deliver so much. And it was like her to have things a little turned around. Church was to have come before the dinner if this were her Quinceañera, and after it the dance. Clearly their timing was a little off. Still, she thought, it was only the shank of the evening, and the dance was yet to come. "You never know," she told him, "it might be fun."

PART THREE

26

THEY RODE amid a strained silence and words left unspoken. Fahey cut through the valley, along roads of dirt and gravel where the dust of their passing rose in a lambent cloud among the branches of eucalyptus, tamarisk, and sandbar willow. He had thought to come into the compound off paved road by way of Saturn Boulevard but found that entrance blocked by a variety of cars and trucks—enough to suggest there was indeed some celebration still in progress—so he circled around to the dirt road that bordered the compound to the south.

The combined mass of Spooner's Mesa and the Border Highlands rose up before them, the lights of the great fence spooling out from behind their shadowed brow, running south into darkness at the edge of the sea. On one side of this road was the compound, on the other a crop of Italian lettuce where scarecrows stood slanted on pointed stakes like miscreants hastily impaled and beyond them the skeletal remains of a few avocado trees that marked the entrance to Smuggler's Gulch, the remains of an old grove condemned by the opening of the Rodríguez Dam and the same floods that had taken the mother of this woman now seated at his side, wrapped in a silence he scarce dared to touch, though he supposed he would never see these trees again and not think of her, and of this moment and of what had transpired and of what might have been.

He parked in the dirt and got out to open her door. She let him do it, as though this were still a date and not some sad facsimile thereof. She was luminous in the night and his heart clutched in his throat. Her skin was the color of copper and the dress as she stepped from the truck was the color of flame and was in itself an object of great mystery, like some artifact from a world of dream as it had come from among his mother's belongings—this woman whose very name was lost even to him, her firstborn, and yet the old man had kept these few things, hidden like her name even to his own son, and he must, Fahey thought, have sat with them from time to time, in the midst of his long decline. For why else would he have kept them, alone with such thoughts as were now difficult even to imagine? Though in point of fact Fahey supposed that he knew them well enough after all, that in the end they were no more than the thoughts that came to all men caught in the jaws of such traps as they had made of the world, their own and the greater one in which all others were so contained. And from there it was no great leap to imagine some future aspect of himself, come into yet one more darkened room, alone before his own collection of artifacts and talismans and this dress now among those, having passed from one set of failed dreams into another and him taking it to his own face as that wizened old man must well have done before him—a diorama too grim even for contemplation, so that he set about leading her down a narrow causeway between the backsides of trailers and clapboard fencing, where they passed amid the sweet smell of growing onions and the rank stench of manure and the more distant scents of smoking fires, of seasoned pork and chicken on iron grills over open flames, and he began to talk as they went, regaling her with arcane facts, snippets of history, anything really that came to mind . . .

He spoke of Smuggler's Gulch, where it cut between the mesa and the highlands, naming it as the route by which the fabled Serra once made entrance into the region on his way to founding the mission at San Diego, adding with a poetic flourish that on a night such as this, one might still imagine the ghostly rattle of armored riders, the indigenous Kumeyaay looking on, their fated ending laid bare as the riders drew up their mounts in admiration of the fine pastureland and pleasant river so noted in the diaries of the old priest. Though it now seemed to Fahey that all such reveries rang false, even as he engaged in them, that recent events were too calamitous, the blight upon the land too complete, that any vestige of spirits so removed must surely have long since been swept away by the multitudes coming in their wake, and he went so far as to share this observation as well, for he was determined to hold forth against this silence and might have run on even longer had she not put a hand on his arm, stopping him mid-sentence in the midst of yet one more inane proclamation.

"It's okay," she told him. "Really. You're a good man." Fahey stood stock-still, mute as a wax dummy in a Hawaiian shirt. In a moment they went on. They went now in silence, past chicken-wire fencing and a pen of ostriches feeding upon heaps of moldy tortillas. The birds looked up, naked heads swaying on the long stalks of their necks, gawking feeble-eyed while others slept, heads enfolded beneath their wings, and in the dark these looked like rocks sunk in the muddy, putrefying soil. An ancient Texas longhorn, kept there for as long as Fahey could remember, marked their passing, the lower part of a bony white face shoved between the blades of a sorry wooden fence while the horns floated above the fence's uppermost edge in such a way as to make it appear as if the animal was composed of parts ill-fitted and the whole apparatus raised to an unnatural height for it was not the ground upon which the animal stood but rather the aforementioned manure Fahey could remember his father remarking on as a boy, complaining even then that the old Mexican who owned this place had not removed a single shovelful, nor had any been shoveled since. The truth was that much of Garage Door Tijuana was built upon these layers of dung, trailers parked upon it, animals roosting, fence posts sunk slanting at crazy angles . . . They came now among the crops of onions in great wooden bins covered in plastic sheeting, the night air filled with their sweet reek, and finally between walls built up of old tires stacked one upon the other like bricks, ten feet high, drawing close together in a final narrow passage that opened at last upon the event for which they had come, this secret *charreada*, beneath palm and eucalyptus, the incongruent lighting of a dozen tiki torches flaming in the night.

They came first upon the wide curve of the guitar where a pair of drunks ran in circles with a weary bull so that it was impossible to say in just what manner the chase was configured. The bull was missing its tail and sported bloodstained flanks still glistening in the moonlight, and one drunk ran shirtless, clutching to the neck of a bottle, and the second lumbered barefoot with what Fahey could only imagine as the animal's tail held aloft, whooping as he went, drunken celebrant, like a winner at bingo.

Which is to say that for the most part the rodeo events were over for the day and the party had moved from the guitar to a wide yard before an old hacienda in sight of that part of the compound where the ruins of Deek's trailer sat half charred, tires melted by flame, undercarriage conforming now to the idiosyncrasies of the earth itself and rushing no doubt to become one with it for it was unlikely that anyone would ever think to haul the wreck away but would go on living with it till it was like the manure and old appliances and countless other bits of refuse left here to form the soil upon which the community rested.

A band held forth in front of the house, done up in the cowboy finery typically associated with mariachi. They were a guitar and guitarrón, a trumpet, an accordion, and a lead singer, his voice high and nasal, amplified by way of a sound system hastily arranged.

A hundred weary revelers were scattered across this open space. The rodeo was done and the horse races and the footraces and fistfights that had no doubt followed, so that what remained was more eating, and indeed flames still flickered in the odd corner where women cooked over iron grills, but mainly now the party was made up of dancing and drinking though of course the drinking had been going on for the better part of two days so that Fahey and Magdalena had some catching up to do, if, that is, they wanted to enter into the spirit of this event they had driven to attend.

Fahey bought them beers fished from a barrel of ice and they walked about with the glass bottles cold in their palms and when these were done they drank two more. Fahey stood to one side as Magdalena inquired of a resident if anything had yet been seen of Deek, the owner of the trailer that had been burned, then translated the woman's answer for the benefit of Fahey, which amounted to no more than he already knew, that Deek had not been around.

He was aware of some of the men staring at Magdalena, this Indian beauty in the company of the gringo, hatless in a flowered shirt, and wondered if she would be asked to dance and wondered what she would do if she was. But on the few occasions when it looked as if someone might approach she would take Fahey's arm as though they were together.

Fahey snuck a pill, drank more beer. They wandered aimlessly, killing time. The party swirled around them, waxing and waning, finding its own way, much as water will find its way among impediments, in obedience to the dictates of such principles as will determine that way to the exclusion of all others. But suddenly the band picked up its cadence and a new wave of energy coursed through the crowd, these peasants of Oaxaca, nary a one over five foot five . . . the men built like barrels or thin like spiders and their women built the same, a sea of Western-cut denim, boots, and cowboy hats white against the shadows, and the women in white, their dresses brocaded about the hems and throat, with sashes and shawls and black hair flying . . .

The accordion now moved front and center, cranking out a polka beat as though attendant to some Bavarian beer fest and the dancers moving in time—a step to the right and hop, a step to the left and hop, the women's legs beneath lifting skirts. For a time the dancers danced in pairs but as the music grew both in tempo and in volume the people moved to form a chain, each person with hands on the hips of the person before him, winding across the hard-packed dirt amid cooking fires and sleeping dogs, sweeping up everyone still on their feet, pulling them along into the collective dance and on toward Magdalena and Fahey drinking in the shadows.

Fahey could see it coming, could see that they would be engulfed and caught up in it, and that some action would be called for. He was aware of Magdalena looking up at him, the hair swept back from her forehead, held by ivory combs, and these too coming from the trunk she had found, and he saw the hesitation in her eyes. He responded by taking the beer from her hand and setting it aside, along with his own, then getting her in front of him so that it would be his hands on her hips and not some other's.

"How does this work?" she asked.

Fahey smiled. "Who's the Mexican?" he asked.

She answered with a look.

"Just feel the beat," he told her, as suddenly the dancers were upon them and they were one with the crowd. "Step to the right and rock your hip. Step to the left and rock your hip."

And so they did, moving forward in a slow, rocking motion like riding the back of the elephant, down along the neck of the guitar and around the circle where the day's events had transpired and back again toward the hacienda and the singer in the band and the people laughing and singing as well and Fahey and Magdalena rocking along in the line till the band, having brought them back to where they started, changed their tempo once more, downshifting into a slower, more romantic kind of rhythm . . .

Fahey and Magdalena were left facing each other. There was sweat upon her brow and Fahey could feel the sweat upon his own and the shirt clinging to his back and he saw that she was smiling in the wake of the dance and it seemed to make what happened next okay. He took her hand in his and put his other on her hip, and they began to dance once more, Fahey leading, Magdalena apologetic.

"This is a little embarrassing," she said. "I guess I never took the time . . ."

But Fahey shushed her and it was a simple dance. Two steps to the left, a slight turn, then two to the right, sliding across the hard-packed dirt at their feet. He scarcely dared to breathe, much less to pull her close. Her hand was hot in his palm and for a time her eyes were downcast but at last she looked at him, asking where he had learned such dances for she would not have thought them of him, alone with his herd, then saw the answer in his eyes, for the response to that query was contained already in the story he had told her, and she looked away, and the question went unanswered.

✦ ✦ ✦

He danced her to a corner, where they stopped to lean upon a fence and cool in the night. "I'm sorry," he said, apropos of nothing. She rested upon his shoulder then noticed a man staring at her from across the old corral.

She experienced a moment's vertigo, a sense of dread. She could not have told you why. Perhaps there was something familiar about the man, or something in his manner, a decided malevolence, she concluded. Still, she could not say that she truly recognized him and in the end she turned away.

"Do you know what they're singing about?" she asked.

"Marijuana, the border patrol . . . I catch the occasional word . . ."

"Each song tells a little story," she said, then undertook a translation of the song in progress, a tale of two drug runners, a man and a woman. "The man is an illegal, the woman a Chicana from Texas. They are smuggling marijuana from Tijuana to Los Angeles. After making the sale, the man informs his partner that he is taking his share of the money to visit his girlfriend in San Francisco, but by now his partner is in love with him. In a fit of jealousy she shoots him in a dark Hollywood alley and leaves with all the money."

"There must be a moral," Fahey said.

Magdalena smiled. She checked to see if the other man was still watching but found that he was no longer there. She was not sure whether to feel relief or concern. Fahey asked if there was anything wrong.

"There was a man. He's gone now."

"What kind of man?"

"I don't know. One of the cowboys? I didn't like the way he was looking at us."

Fahey looked over his shoulder, but saw nothing. When he turned back to Magdalena he was in time to see her reaching for the fence, as though to steady herself.

"Maybe we should go," Fahey said.

"I guess. All of a sudden, I got dizzy."

"Hey," he said. "We've seen what we came to see. It's late and you've been through a lot. You should sleep now. It's time."

Magdalena nodded. Apparently he was still looking out for her. By this time tomorrow she would be back on her own, on her own side of the fence.

They went out the way they had come in, along the neck of the guitar, past the circle where the bull that seemed to have vanished at the coming of the dancers had reappeared once more, minus both his tail and his tormentors. The animal stood motionless, then snorted softly as they passed as though to register some comment on the day's humiliations. They passed among the trailers mounted on dunghills and the hole in the fence from which the longhorn had watched them come in and searched once more for that skeletal face hung upon the night air but could not find it, and came finally to the road and the dead grove beyond it and so to the mouth of Smuggler's Gulch, where already a ground fog had appeared beneath the trees—a blessing to what pilgrims the night would bring, a curse to the border patrol sworn to stem their tide—a job now undertaken in the name of homeland defense though it was unlikely there would be any among this night's sad offerings with darker agendas than food for their tables or a little something to send home to the ones who waited . . .

Fahey noted these things and made mention of them as Magdalena stood in the dirt roadway waiting as he unlocked the doors of the old Toyota then ushered her in and walked round to the driver's door to get in beside her. He executed a three-point turn on the narrow road. The lights of his truck fell among that remnant of cadaverous trees, dead these twenty years, but he said no more about it and they rode on through the night and the valley that in one manner or another had begotten them both, each now alone with such thoughts as they were wont to entertain, yet never knowing that as they went, another had observed their passing, a crab man at one with the shadows, in ostrich-skin boots whose rightful owner lay still warm, dead aboveground. He stood outfitted with cheap Tijuana bridgework and garish Western wear, his shirt untucked and only half buttoned, the loose ends of this article spreading apart as he climbed atop a fence post to see in what direction the truck had gone, and this movement enough to reveal the large Aztec sun tattooed across his abdomen—homage to such fierce progenitors as it pleased him to imagine, despoilers of virgins, with a taste for the still-beating heart . . . and which mark, if only Magdalena could have seen, she could have recognized, and the road she and Fahey would have chosen would have been quite different from the one taken. For that led not toward the lights of town, but deeper into the black heart of the valley, toward the old Fahey worm farm, a sight already noted for its dark excess, even here, in a land steeped in malfeasance.

27

THE FIRST of the Pickerings had died quickly, more or less decapitated by Nacho's stroke. They had tried torturing the second in hopes of obtaining information about the big man with the worm on his cap but the woman had been less conversant in Spanish than the man and seemed to have undergone a kind of seizure even before the onset of the inquisition. The entire episode had ended badly, ankle-deep in gore, and even Armando was eager to drive the details from his mind. A well-stocked liquor cabinet in the Pickering kitchen had gone some way toward satisfying this desire and in the end all three miscreants had staggered from the property, barely able to find their own car in the gathering darkness.

Once inside, it was decided, inasmuch as anything was ever decided upon within the ranks of Armando's gang, to return to the rodeo. The light, after all, had failed them. Armando was drunk as a sailor, Chico a lover of the dance, and tomorrow was another day.

And so had Armando led his crew from the scene of the crime, never knowing that his Madonna had passed within shouting distance or that in driving the rutted dirt road in approach to Smuggler's Gulch he was following upon her trail, or that in two hours' time she would pass yet again, within the very bounds of Garage Door Tijuana, where Armando would lie in drink, at work in factories half remembered and half dreamed, yet the circles of their respective orbits drawing ever tighter, as if gravity itself had taken some hand in the proceedings.

He lay among the onions, affixing the leather covering to a steering wheel already coated with glue. The fabric of his shirt was drenched in sweat. His eyes burned, even in sleep, or what passed for it, the music of a hundred ghetto blasters rocking the very air he breathed. The wheel was uncooperative, its shape shifting even as he worked, the glue already setting up as suddenly he was aware of the women in the stitching area. He could smell their sex, wet beneath leather miniskirts and blue smocks as they looked on with eyes both aloof and painted, though indeed every eye in the factory seemed bent upon him at just that moment, as if he alone was responsible for its workings . . . as a hand began to rock him gently against the ground.

His eyes opened slowly. His head felt split in two. Yet even then it was his Reina he thought to see, the open doorway of their cardboard shack framing her with stars . . . or perhaps her face, anxious amid the polished hallways of the hospital in Reynosa . . . What he got was Chico, sequins winking at the tips of the little arrows that formed the pockets of his shirt caught in the light of a bare bulb somewhere overhead, and himself at rest in an onion bin, his head upon a scrap of tire, his body covered with a piece of plastic sheeting, which as he moved upright amid the reek of onions and cow manure slithered away as though bent upon escape, vanishing into the darkness beyond his boots. He watched it go with no small degree of wonder before turning to this figure now squatting there before him like some jackass at the window, possibly of no more substance than such phantoms as had proceeded it, for such were the boundaries between his worlds. But the figure spoke to him by name. Fire lit the bowl of a glass pipe. The pipe found its way into his hands. He took a hit. A voice whispered in his ear, telling him that it was time to get right. It was the voice of the cowboy with the red convertible, his partner for a day. *"Es tu Madonna,"* the voice said to him. *"Está aquí."*

28

FAHEY CUT westward through the valley, Chet Baker on tape, faint yellow light seeping from the illuminated face of an ancient radio, the numbers etched in plastic worn to illegibility . . . "I thought surfers listened to some other kind of music," Magdalena said. "You know . . . 'Wipe Out' . . ." She was trying to make light of things, to end with a smile.

Fahey just looked at her. "Not on your life," he said. They had arrived at the farm and Fahey stopped the truck to get out. Magdalena touched his arm. "I meant what I said at the rodeo."

Fahey could not quite bring himself to look her in the eye. He guessed at what might be contained there and it was not anything he wanted to see. He watched the dogs on the other side of the fence, then nodded and got out of the truck. He swung the gate wide on rusting hinges and drove them inside, after which he parked and went back to the gate one more time to lock them in.

She was out of the truck, waiting near the trailer as Fahey walked back across the yard. He had nearly caught up with her when he heard something in the darkness at the edge of the fence. The dogs, circling at his heels, heard it as well, Jack taking off at a dead run, Wrinkles going stiff-legged some ways behind. It was too dark to see more than a stirring in the night, yet Fahey went with some instinct latent within him, taking Magdalena by the arm, steering her into shadow, for she had been standing in the light where it pooled at the foot of the steps. He had no sooner done so than a bullet hit the trailer door—the crack of gunfire at one with the appearance of a black, puckered hole. He saw the muzzle flash of the second shot, and then the old hound, dropping like a sack of flour. More shots and the terrier blown sideways, tumbling across hardscrabble dirt like a paper sack torn asunder, caught upon the wind, white against the blackness of the yard. Bullets peppered the trailer, head-high. These were accompanied by the sounds of breaking glass.

Fahey made for the corner of the room he had built at the side of the trailer. Magdalena went with him. The trailer was longer than the room by a good ten feet, raised upon concrete blocks, with space beneath it.

"Roll under," he said. They had rounded the room and were kneeling at the side of the trailer. "Crawl to the other side."

She did so and Fahey behind her. They emerged in darkness, beyond the reach of bullets. Fahey went to the butane tanks at the trailer's tongue, on his stomach in the brittle grass, straining to see—some hulking shape out there in the dark, and then a sound, cutters at work on the fence, the twang of snapping steel. They would be in quickly, and Fahey's gun still behind the seat of the truck on the far side of the trailer, halfway to the fence where the men were coming through.

He was aware of Magdalena at his side, her breath a stifled sob.

Were he alone, he might have risked a mad dash to the truck, ending it one way or the other in a single stroke, at which point it occurred to him that he could not remember if he had ever reloaded the shotgun after killing the dogs. In the absence of such surety all such notions were at once made null and void and yet even if this were not the case, even if he knew for certain that the gun was loaded, the odds would still stand against him and he had her to think of now—twenty-three years old, all beauty and life unlived and one false move on the part of Samuel Fahey enough to end it here and now, to place her at the mercy of such creatures as were already cutting their way through his first line of defense.

Fahey took quick stock of his options. There were but two gaps in the fence that surrounded them—the gate already lost to them, and the old outbuilding that had come with the land, ten by twenty, set longwise at the very edge of the property so there had been no room to run the chain link behind it. They'd run it instead to either end and so made of the building a part of the fence but the structure had been old even then—single-wall clapboard and much of the wood warped and cracked from the years of sun and sea air, its interior a repository of old farming tools red with rust but suitable, Fahey reasoned, for the busting out of enough clapboard to make good their escape, and surely, he thought, a better option than attempting to scale the fence before men with guns, or to face them barehanded among the windrows of his farm.

He saw no good reason to believe the men who had come for them would not see them enter the barn, or hear them at work on the wall. Still, Fahey reasoned, if they could just get clear of the property they might stand a chance, for it was his intention to do as every other migrant, drug runner, and fugitive in hopes of eluding capture had done before him; he would make for the river and he would hope to outfox them. He would make for the mouth among canopied trails because it was there the river was most treacherous and once upon the beach the tide would be in their favor. He had Jack Nance to credit for that, or at least for his knowing it. For in tracking the swell he'd tracked the tides and he offered in silence a word of thanks then felt in his pocket the book of matches from Woody's at the Pier. With these came a rude plan that he guessed might just afford them some head start in this race to the sea, and he'd no sooner settled on it than he felt her hand as it touched his arm. His course set, he moved back from the tanks and turned to face her. She held his eyes with her own, but any such questions as she might have asked were already contained therein as were the answers contained in his and so left unspoken.

They had for the moment the old trailer still between themselves and the invaders. A metal storage shed sat back of the trailer as well, a few yards away, closer to the fence, and there were a few barrels of worm tea stacked out in front in steel drums that gave off a dull shine in the light of the moon as it snaked among the branches of the trees. Fahey told her to get between the shed and the fence and to wait there in the shadows, then went to his elbows and knees, crawling back to the front of the trailer, where he severed a hose with a pocketknife. The act was followed by the hiss of butane upon the bone-dry grass. He rolled away, struck a match, lit the book, tossed it beneath the tanks, then ran to join her.

The fire spread quickly. He could hear voices on the far side of the trailer, raised in alarm, coming through the garden. He thought he heard the door of his truck, the popping of the driver's door upon its hinges, and took this as a bad sign, for they would now have the gun he had been unable to reach.

"There's half a tank of butane up front," Fahey told her. "Fire gets hot enough, I believe it will blow. With luck, one or more of these bastards will be too close. Failing that, it might scare them off. Failing that, it will definitely get their attention."

"Or bring the border patrol?"

"Eventually. But we're not gonna wait around to find out. That thing blows, we make for the barn." He pointed toward the out-building, thirty yards away, some of those yards screened by clumps of weed and cactus, head high, some exposed. Magdalena nodded.

They waited in the dark, Fahey counting off seconds, wondering which would come first, the explosion or the men, whereupon the tank went off. Flames shot fifty feet in the air, igniting the limbs of a cottonwood. Fahey put a hand in the small of Magdalena's back and propelled her toward the barn.

They went among the weeds, came to bare ground and covered it at a dead run, the last fifteen yards, nothing but windrows between themselves and the fire and Fahey already knowing the artifact he wanted, the bloodred blade of an old plow he'd known since childhood . . . and then the boards, dry as old bones, coming apart as the blade struck through them, exploding outward in a shower of dust and flying splinters and Fahey out behind them and the girl with him.

They ran through a field of grass and weeds gone dry and brittle with the end of summer that crackled like sticks of kindling put to flame as they passed, stumbling on the uneven ground, the sharp-ened ends of broken weeds pulling at them as might the residents of nursing homes, reaching out from cloistered senility, half deranged, tearing at them with clawed hands till they had run free and come to the slight rise of an old levee erected by farmers in anticipation of coming floods and upon whose summit they went exposed for some short distance in the moonlight. From this van-tage point they looked back in the direction from which they had come and saw the men clearly for the first time, the men who chased them. They were three in number and they came loping through the waist-high brush in the fashion of lycanthropes and now one looked up and saw Fahey and the girl and whooped and was answered in kind by at least one of his fellows and a shot rang out, though where it passed by, Fahey could not say. There were not fifty yards between themselves and the men. Fahey pulled her among the trees and down along the muddy bank where the reek of toxic brew, as potent as one was likely to find, rose to meet them. Sweat beaded at his brow and ran into his eyes. He used the back of his hand to wipe it away. "Shoot away," Fahey said. "Call the border patrol . . ." though he doubted even they would follow here and picked a path in the cloying dark, for by such ways had he eluded enemies more times than one could count, humping dope back in the day, and the trails not so different then as now. It was the stakes that had gotten higher, and he led her as far down the bank as he dared to go, until the black muck was sucking at their shoes, then turned to the west, entering almost at once upon a little clearing where the trees gave way and the river lay naked to the night, emerging from shadow as had they themselves, its wind-rippled surface shimmering with uncounted points of light as though dragging within its oily depths a third of heaven's stars. For such was its poisoned beauty, the Tijuana River on its way to the sea.

29

HAVING REACHED the river, Fahey considered his options for the last time. They were two in number. One was to make for the mouth, as had been his intention. The other was to hide. Each had something to be said for it. They might try to bury themselves in the bush. Their hunters might pass them by. There were motion sensors scattered throughout the valley and somewhere upon the mesas the border patrol might well detect their movement, might have done so already, might in fact be on their way even now, by the four-wheel motorcycles they used, known as quads, or by horseback like the proverbial cavalry. It was, however, Fahey's experience that the border patrol was much like any other unwieldy branch of government, unpredictable at best. Unwanted, they would arrive en masse. In need of help, one might well bask in their absence for hours on end. In short, the border patrol was nothing to bet a life on and if he and Magdalena attempted to hide and were caught, they were done for. And then there was this: he had seen them kill his dogs and invade his land. It was more than fear that drove him. Anger drove him as well and there was a part of him that wanted these men at the river mouth, on the beaches of the Tijuana Straits, where some measure of justice yet might be brought to bear. At the very least, he thought, it suited his mood to try. Nor, if the truth were told, did he think himself physically capable of staying long in one place, of lying low in this muddy reek for what might prove to be hours on end while men with guns beat the bushes looking for them, perhaps even firing indiscriminately. No, he thought, he had been right at the farm. It was the headlong rush that was called for, the mad charge into some final reckoning . . . And he chose now as he had chosen then. He chose to run, to gamble at the river mouth on such skills as he possessed, if indeed it came to that, for in truth he would try to do both, to hide and to move at the same time. And so they pressed on, through the little clearing where bats now swirled like dust motes in a shaft of light above the black, moon-spangled river.

He led her among the willows and it was there he stopped to face her, to tell her of his plan. His breath came hard in this close place and hers as well, for he could hear it in the darkness, shallow and fast . . . Their faces were only inches apart and he could mark her features in the murky light. She's yours, he told himself, yours to save or to lose, and it was not the first time in this life that he'd taken such counsel.

Two sets of trails ran through the valley, some north from the border, others west toward the sea. The north-south trails were narrow and winding and were used by smugglers and migrants. The east-west trails were wider and straighter and these had been cut by the border patrol, laid out to intersect the smaller trails and open enough to accommodate both horses and quads alike, for rarely did the border patrol pursue on foot. And such were the trails Fahey now thought to use. He would use the border patrol trails for speed, the migrant trails to vary their course, but in general he would follow the winding path of the river and he told her how it would be . . . "We're going to move fast," he told her. "Zigzag, south to north, then east to west, then back again, over and over . . . Just stay with me. Step where I step. Turn where I turn. Stay up, right on my heels, all the way out to the beach. We'll use the ocean to cross the river . . ."

"The ocean . . ." she said, but Fahey stopped her, his hand on her shoulder. "It won't be like it was before," he told her. "I'll be with you. If we can put the river between us and them it will be very difficult for them to follow. Trust me to know how."

There was little she could do but nod some form of assent and afterward they were off once more and she tried to do as he had said . . . stay hard on his back, the flowers of his Hawaiian shirt moving in and out of shadow, the mud sucking at her sandals, particularly when she misstepped, for in no time at all she could see that this was something he had done before. He kept to what lines of vegetation he could find at the edge of the muddy bank, pickleweed and cordgrass, and she found that when she stepped as he did, the footing was firmer and the speed was greater and the speed was their friend . . .

It was never so dark in the valley that she could not see where to step. There were too many lights on the high ground all around them, the great urban sprawl of San Diego County becoming one with the disaster that was Tijuana to the south and on this night there was a moon as well so that the valley was dusted in light. It tipped the leaves of the trees and lay upon the blades of grass like a jacket of frost. It came in shafts through gaps among the branches, even upon the canopied trails, and when by chance they broke into some clearing, they were afforded views of the river's tributaries—like cords of braided silver or the tentacles of a living thing crawled from the depths to search among the marsh of the great wetlands. And even deep among the willows it was never so dark as to lose sight of one's hand in front of one's face or of the ground beneath their feet and though this absence of complete darkness would aid them in their speed, she knew that it would aid their trackers as well.

And so they went, Fahey holding to his plan, navigating these two sets of trails. The migrant trails were sometimes barely there at all, narrow and twisting, close among the branches of the willows, among castor bean and giant cane like stalks of bamboo growing in dense clumps and once, breaking from one such trail and onto a broader road, they encountered an entire family of migrants, perhaps a dozen in number, and these came on in utter silence. They ran barefoot in this foul place, their shoes and other belongings carried in plastic bags over their shoulders, and Fahey and Magdalena passed right among them as though they had entered upon a gathering of lost souls set to wander, and not a single word was spoken one to the other and within seconds the migrants had vanished among the cane and Fahey and Magdalena were alone once more, on a westerly path made downright brilliant in the moonlight, and they followed this for as long as Fahey thought wise before cutting back toward the reek of the river and the black shade of the willows.

As for Magdalena, the border patrol trails were more to her liking and each time they broke upon one she would hope to encounter at least one, if not more, of its makers, but each time the trail was empty and they would follow it for some short distance before turning back toward the hateful water.

It was roughly a mile and a half from the farm to the sea and they moved through this terrain by stops and starts, now at a dead run on hard-packed dirt, now at a slow crawl among the brush and the branches that tore at their clothing and the skin beneath, and down along the riverbed, where the bats came for insects and the shadowed dark made the footing more treacherous. And from time to time Fahey would stop in one of these locations and look back and it seemed to him that the men were indeed following, coming by some instinct for tracking latent within them as within any such beasts of prey, and once he heard their voices raised above the soft rush of water and once he saw them plainly, a hundred yards back upon a border patrol path, and saw to his consternation that two carried lanterns and cursed beneath his breath, for such light would facilitate the tracking and cursed too at the very brazenness of it, here, where no migrant or smuggler worthy of the name would risk such a display, and he guessed that the luck of the unrighteous came with them. Either that or there was other mischief about, in other quarters of the valley, and the attentions of the country's guard petitioned in more places than one.

They went on. In places the air was thick and sweet with the abundance of plant life close to water and in others rank as the exhalations of a feculent swamp and always the wheeling firmament above their heads, appearing as might the starry bottom of such canyons as the living trees had cut from the sky, as though the world they traversed was a world inverted, but there was little time for such observations. For the most part they went in silence, in single file, till that place where Magdalena's shriek pierced the air and Fahey stopped in his tracks to find her tumbling away from him, the red dress dragging across the mud and her with it, for she had been spent even before this chase began and in her weariness her foot had slipped from some bit of vegetation and into the mud and from there had shot from beneath her as surely as if planted on ice . . .

She hit the ground on her hip, sliding down the last of the

embankment as though it were the tilting floor of an amusement park ride, feet first into a kind of bog where she could no longer say where the earth ended and the water began and sank almost at once to her waist in this reeking sediment, unable to struggle free, indeed, sinking further with each new effort.

Fahey came after her. Heedless now of any sound his voice might make, he called out, telling her to be still, that to struggle was to speed the descent, as farther up the bank he sought frantically for some means by which to free her, for the time would come quickly when she was too deep to save and the earth would have her, and in all likelihood Fahey, too, for he was determined to pull her out or sink in the attempt.

He slid down the muddy bank, one leg thrust before him like a runner taking second base and one tucked beneath him in an effort to control his slide, at the last moment catching hold of a low-lying branch he'd glimpsed from above, trusting the article to hold, gambling that he would come close enough for her to reach. And indeed the branch took his weight with a low groan, bending downward so that Fahey's legs came within her grasp and there was no need to tell her what to do.

She took hold of his ankles and began to pull herself from the mud that sought in turn to keep her for itself. But she pulled hard and Fahey pulled too, hand over hand back along the branch and the branch held until at last they lay panting like spent lovers, so caked in mud, one might think the stuff in which they lay was the stuff from which they had been formed—the primeval couple. And it was from just this vantage point, one atop they other, that they looked into the shadows and saw the horse. And each in turn lay speechless, for such was the sight of this doomed beast, already up to its shoulders in a far corner of the brackish pond that was one with the muddy bog into which she had fallen. The animal was dark with white markings on its face and they could see it looking back at them, wide-eyed but silent, as though it was the ghost of the animal already gone that watched them from the gloom.

"My God," Magdalena said.

Fahey wondered how long the animal had been here and what had become of its rider, if indeed there had been a rider, for the horse was without bridle or saddle and at this stage of the game one would need a crane to rescue the beast and perhaps the horse reckoned this as well for the animal maintained its stoic silence in the face of its own end. When he had thought about these things long enough, he took Magdalena by the hand and helped her to her feet and told her that they had to go on.

She did as Fahey asked but she continued to stare at the horse till they had lost it among the shadows and stared at it even then in her mind's eye, and guessed that she would stare at it often in that cloistered place—this creature with whom her bones had so very nearly been mingled had not Fahey saved her yet again. Though to what end he had saved her was hard to say for between her screams and his shouts they had made a good deal of noise and the mud had taken her sandals and left her barefoot as any migrant. But Fahey sat on the ground and took off his own shoes and gave her his socks and told her to put them on, as they would be better than nothing at all. He added that he would give her the shoes as well but that these were too big and would only slow her down even more. She came to his side on the ground but had no sooner added the socks to her costume than some new wonder was visited upon them and the entire bank bathed suddenly in a brilliant light.

The roar of engines came quickly upon the heels of this display. Fahey's first thought was that the border patrol had come at last. Still, he thought it best to be certain and flattened himself to the ground, whispering for Magdalena to do the same, and each of them still so covered in mud it was unlikely that anyone would have been able to tell them from it at a glance.

Which in fact was a good thing, for the machines in question were not the machines of the border patrol but two-wheel dirt bikes with Day-Glo accessories and the riders came dressed in army camouflage and wore such helmets as might be found on the sets of movies and these decorated with skulls and crossbones and naked women with pendulous breasts and they carried weaponry slung low on their thighs in fancy plastic sheaths and diving knives strapped to their calves and the engines roared and the tires blew chunks of mud like bullets and before such grotesqueries Fahey and Magdalena lay silent as mud dolls. Only when the riders had passed did they dare to move, slithering like water moccasins deeper among the trees and finally into the arm of a narrow tributary cut among the cane. They followed this for some distance then waited for signs of pursuit. And for a while this seemed almost a possibility as the engines continued to roar in the general vicinity, without moving on. Nor, on the other hand, did the engines get any closer to where they lay.

"Vigilantes," Fahey whispered.

"Would they help?"

"It's impossible to say." Local high schoolers had been known to engage in such extracurricular activities, ROTC students from San Ysidro, Chula Vista, or National City, relatively benign. But so had assorted meth chefs and drug runners been known to traverse the valley, as well as racists in search of fragile prey. Fahey had a woman in tow, lovely and just about half dressed in the aftermath of the mud. Who could gauge the minds of such men? Who would count on their help?

In the face of such uncertainty the counsel Fahey elected was his own and his choice was to move on. A good deal of the valley was already behind them and in another few minutes of following the muddy little stream they came to the very edge of the trees and the last of the sheltering vegetation. Ahead of them lay the cordgrass of the great estuary, ending among salt pans and marsh grass and beyond these the dunes white as snow-capped peaks and past the dunes the beaches where it had all begun, the beach and the mouth of the river, and Fahey knelt now in the mud and looked out over this last stretch of ground that separated them from the sea, roughly half a mile in breadth.

Magdalena knelt at his side and he told her what to look for as they made for the dunes. "You see there are patterns in the grass, patches of light and dark. Where it's dark the ground will be firmer. Where it's light, the mud will be even worse that what we just got out of."

But as they were about to move on, a series of gunshots rang out behind them and they went to their stomachs yet again, wondering at what this new racket might portend. There were two distinct bursts of shooting and when the second died away the valley fell silent once more, save for the pounding of the surf.

"What do you think?" Magdalena asked him.

It was Fahey's guess that the riders had crossed paths with the men who chased them but there was no way of knowing this for sure and it was not his intention to investigate the outcome, or to wait long enough to see who, if anyone, would emerge from the trees.

With as much speed at they could manage they made their entrance into the short grass. And though the moonlight fell about their shoulders, the mud had rendered them as one with the night, and so they passed, little more than shadows, toward land's ending, toward the mouth of the river and the waves beyond.

30

ARMANDO HAD thought the place simple. But in this he had been mistaken. The valley was a labyrinth, a trick done with mirrors. The lesson was learned early in the chase, revealed in the strategy of the worm farmer. It began with the blast, which he had to admit was clever and sent him diving for cover—a belly flop near the wheels of Fahey's truck—and this the resting place from which he had glimpsed his Madonna, as Chico had so described her, a vision in red, running upon the heels of her companion straight into the gaping mouth of an old barn. He'd thought to trap them there but it was only the beginning of the worm farmer's tricks, for by time Armando arrived, the wall had been turned to a doorway and both of them gone into the night. He'd followed for a short distance before seeing them once more, now fifty yards away, nearing the trees at the summit of a shallow embankment.

From there he'd sent Nacho back to the car for such lanterns as they'd thought to steal from Garage Door Tijuana while he and Chico searched for the exact place where the others had vanished. His first guess was that they were trying to do no more than hide among the trees but with the aid of the lanterns he saw that once again he had underestimated the farmer. The lights revealed footprints, flattened grass, and broken bits of brush and he saw that in fact they meant to run, his Madonna and her farmer, in what appeared to be the general direction of the sea and he swore to himself that he had underestimated this man for the last time. He cursed aloud, making such oaths to himself and to anyone else willing to listen.

For Armando there was no question about how to proceed. He had her before him, in this place, in the dead of night. The very thought accelerated his sobriety. He would not lose her again. Chico expressed some concern about the border patrol, but Armando wasn't hearing any. His blood was up. The chase was on and he would see its end. And though he would have preferred to have taken her to his site in the desert as he had planned, the labyrinth of the Tijuana River Valley would have to serve and so he went on, like a man possessed, which to some degree he was, driven by such devils as his life had thus far engendered . . . through brush and bog, moving at a fevered pace and the others following in his wake, from one trail to another in endless crisscrossing steps like the Day-Glo footprints he'd once tracked through some dimly remembered funhouse of his youth . . . and no fewer wonders contained in this dark place, amid the reek of sewage and the flurry of bats swung like kites on strings affixed to the hands of lunatics. Yet none of these wonders was more outlandish than that which at last presented itself to them on the banks of a stagnant pool somewhere, by Armando's reckoning, at the very heart of this morass, halfway between the burning farm and the waiting sea, where a trio of gringos, dressed like Halloween soldiers, was engaged in trying to pull a horse from a pool by way of ropes run to motorbikes whose wheels did little more than tear great holes in the muddy earth, spattering the night with immense gobs of reeking manure so that in entering into the arena of this absurdity he felt that he had stumbled at last into the very eye of the proverbial shit storm from which he'd always hoped to absent himself, and he brought the gun to bear.

It was a wonderful pump-action piece, this gun belonging to the worm farmer. There had been extra shells in the truck and he'd stuffed as many of these into his pockets as he was able to carry and he shot now if for no other reason than to clear his mind, for the chase was beginning to wear and he did not stop till pretty much everything in the clearing was dead and down, the horse included, then paused to survey the carnage.

He was by then holding the shotgun in one hand and the pistol in the other, for each had played a part. The horse had gone to its side in the murky waters like a boat capsized. One of the Halloween soldiers floated nearby, facedown in the pool. A second soldier lay gut-shot, spilling viscera across the foul mud. One of the dirt bikes had fallen into the pool and gone silent, though its headlight continued to burn and so lit a portion of this grim scene from beneath the water—an eerie light tinted to an unearthly shade of green, rising up into the hoary willows whose branches reared like the arms of supplicants in the face of such decimation. Another of the bikes was still running, its rear tire still throwing mud and the entire contraption wiggling in creeping half circles where it had toppled to its side like a crippled insect, and Armando reloaded and fired at this as well, discharging three rounds before the offending machinery ceased its infernal racket to lie in smoking ruins that, deprived of motion, sank slowly into the earth.

Armando had embarked upon this slaughter in the belief that some measure of silence was required for the collecting of his thoughts. Clearly the farmer was leading him on a merrier chase than he would have thought possible and he was beginning to wonder if he had been mistaken in its undertaking. And yet he'd no sooner set about the consideration of such a conundrum and others like it when it occurred to him there was something else amiss in this hard-won silence. Whereupon he saw Nacho, or at least what was left of him, for the lumbering youth had somehow managed to fall into the same bog that had nearly taken Magdalena before him—though of this last bit of history Armando was still in ignorance.

Imagine a keyhole as might accommodate an old-fashioned key—a round hole up top, a longer somewhat triangular opening beneath it, for such was the configuration of this bit of topography. A stagnant pool formed the larger, triangular part. The bog was smaller and more circular in shape though each was joined to the other as has been described and existed amid a stand of ancient willows, half of them dead or bearded in some form of parasitic moss that hung like spiderwebs from decrepit limbs and all some yards from the main body of the river.

Nacho had fallen into the bog, early in the conflict it would seem, for the gunfire and roar of engines appeared to have concealed such cries for help as he may have uttered, and thus had he missed his chance entirely, for such cries were beyond him now. The mud had already engulfed the great tabernacle of his chest and much of his neck and there was little he could do by the time the others found him, save tilt that great head in one last effort to draw breath, so that as Armando and Chico reached the edge of the bog, all that actually remained of their companion was his face—as if that appendage had been flayed then spread upon the muddy ground in performance of a ghastly ritual. Or perhaps that scarred visage had been no more than a Halloween mask all along, fallen now in the aftermath of some reverie. But this sank too, even as they watched it, the mud closing over it, until all that lingered were a few unctuous bubbles. And finally these too were gone and everything that had been Nacho was gone with them, taken into the earth even as the bubbles were taken into the air, yet to what depth and station of hell he might descend, there were none there to say with certainty.

The entire spectacle seemed to have worked some adverse effect upon Chico, who now went to his haunches, gibbering in the midst of this carnage, at the side of the foul bog. His speech was difficult to discern but it appeared to Armando as if he was asking to go home.

Armando slapped him on the back of his head with the flat of his hand. "How will they write your corridos," he asked, "if you show weakness now?"

"How do you know she is still out there?" Chico said. The slap seemed to have gone some way toward clearing his mind.

"Where else would she be, *cabrón?*"

Armando squatted by his side, then noticed something upon the surface of the mud not far from that place where Chico had gone down. He rose, looking around till he'd found a dead branch with which to fish this object from the mud and when he had done so he saw that it was a sandal, too small to be any but hers.

Armando held it out for Chico to see. "Maybe this is what Nacho saw," he said. "Maybe it was this he was trying to reach." The news was both good and bad. Nacho was gone to his reward, but the girl had passed this way.

"Maybe she is down there too then," Chico said. By which he meant the center of the earth.

"And the worm farmer?"

Chico nodded. "All of them," he said.

But Armando swung his lantern among the shadows until he had found that place where Fahey had extended himself to reach her and he read such signs as were there to be read—the great limb, close to the ground, every twig broken upon its surface, muddied impressions near the trunk of the selfsame tree. He interpreted these as men interpret Scripture, in accordance with the leanings of their own hearts. For the sandal that had held her foot was still in his hand. Leather that had touched her skin had now touched his own. He would not admit to her absence. "She fell here," he announced, finally. "She fell and the farmer pulled her out."

He began a frantic search of the general area until he'd found the place where Fahey and Magdalena had gone to their stomachs with the coming of the dirt bikes before crawling away, drag marks and flattened pickleweed to mark their passing. He followed these into the arm of the tributary, where all such traces vanished, but came shortly into the cane, where he picked up the trail once more, and by this route came finally to the end of the trees and so stood looking across the last of the valley, to the dunes beyond and the lights of Imperial Beach at the northern edges of the beach. "He's going to town," Armando said. And so he reasoned it. The farmer had used the trails along the river to slow them down, to disguise his true destination. Once upon the beach, it would be a straight shot for help.

Armando now studied the dunes and the flickering lights and gauged their distance one to the other and his own from each, and it was his considered opinion that Magdalena and her farmer were not so far ahead that he and Chico could not still catch them on the beach and in fact took some pleasure in this for he found in the scenario grounds for hope. If he could dispense with the farmer on the beach it would be an easy thing to simply reverse direction and cross into Mexico by way of Yogurt Canyon, possibly even taking the Madonna with them, as far perhaps as that place already prepared for her coming and so in the bargain be done with this valley altogether; he said as much to Chico, this and more, and goaded and chided and in the end they went on together.

This was not exactly to Chico's liking. In truth he was afraid to go and afraid to stay. He was also afraid of going back to Garage Door Tijuana, where even to his own limited powers of observation it seemed that they had most likely worn out their welcome. In truth he could find no way out of this complexity superior to another so that in the end he did as Armando had asked, he sucked it up and soldiered on, at one moment gibbering at the prospect of some imminent demise, in the next insisting that he had never shown weakness, that his corridos would indeed be written and sung, of the women he had raped and killed and of other atrocities both real and imagined. And none of it with any claim at all on the attention of Armando, who was on the move once more, uppers in one pocket, downers in the other, and the resulting combination turning the valley to colors heretofore unimagined outside of desert raves. He might as well have been exploring canals on the surface of the red planet. Insects scuttled up and down his arms like passing trains. He viewed them as one having an acquaintance with such afflictions yet clawed at them nonetheless, and in so doing was viewed by Chico with mounting alarm, for he could see nothing about the other to illicit such antics and so suffered beneath the premonition that he would most likely die out here, on the wrong side of the border, in the company of a lunatic, and in that he was not altogether mistaken.

As if in response to Chico's paranoia a helicopter appeared in the night, hovering it would seem above the ruins of the worm farm, but it came no closer to where they stood before veering off into blackness.

They made no effort to track here. The way to the beach was clear enough. Moonlight made their lanterns superfluous and these they abandoned in favor of speed, following upon the main body of the river, pressing hard for the dunes and the sand beyond. They had by now learned the knack of where to step in order to avoid the deepest mud and the cordgrass swayed and bent with their passing. Armando broke into a run and Chico behind him, cursing as he ran, and it was in this fashion that they came upon the last of the three dirt bikes they had seen among the trees but forgotten about upon the discovery of Nacho and his ultimate demise. And yet here it was before them, sunk amid a swath of darkening grass like some failed aerodyne fallen from the sky and near to it a rider.

The man was sitting bolt upright in the grass, one leg bent beneath him at an unreasonable angle, a puckered hole below his collarbone leaking blood. But he was still alive and there was a weapon in his hands and before Chico and Armando could do more than register his presence he had fired, and upon the report Chico staggered backward, clawing at his face, his hands going blue with some substance Armando at that time and place was willing to take for Chico's blood, perhaps more toxic than even his own. Chico ran blinded from the scene of his own shooting. He went for some short distance calling out for mercy and forbearance then tumbled headfirst into the main branch of the river, taken whole beneath its vitiated waters.

Armando had not yet gotten off a shot when a burning point of flame erupted somewhere in the vicinity of his own sternum, giving him to understand he too had been hit, and he shot back in return. The phantom rider toppled into the grass and Armando stood looking down at himself in amazement. His chest was as blue as Chico's face. He went forward to examine the weapon that had produced this wonder. It was, he concluded, not really a gun at all but a device for shooting paint balls and was indeed little more than some elaborate toy. Nor was the murdered rider old enough to be properly called a man. His face was marked beneath the eyes with greasepaint after the fashion of television commandos and sitting slantwise upon his head, a black plastic helmet as might be found amid the *Star Wars* paraphernalia in a toy store catering to the rich. In fact the helmet had come in a box, with a sticker attached that Armando would never see, reading Made in Mexico. And indeed the same could be said for much of the rest of his outfit and that included a plastic scabbard, a fancy belt, and a Day-Glo watch. It was the stuff of the maquiladoras, as might be said for Armando himself.

He removed the helmet from the boy's head, which was very nearly severed from the rest of him, as the blast had not taken him dead center but had hit off to one side of the throat yet killed him dead enough all the same. Armando guessed he was no older than seventeen. In fact he was an officer-in-training from a local high school, dead in an incident that would lead to a banning of the ROTC program at that institution, though like the sticker that had accompanied the helmet, this too would go unknown and for Armando the boy and his costume were bound to remain as he'd first perceived them, one more enigma brought forth from the American night.

The helmet was covered on one side with blood and little pieces of flesh and bone and Armando knelt at the bank of the river to wash these away then placed the helmet still dripping upon his own head. He took the boy's plastic scabbard and the belt to which it was attached. He placed the farmer's shotgun into the sheath then looped the belt across his chest with the gun and scabbard at his back. The pistol he'd brought from across the border was still thrust into the waistband at the front of his jeans, and so bedecked he set out once more, at a steady lope, much as he'd once run the streets of the old red-light district, in his days of training as a fighter above El As Negro, the river at his side.

31

To Fahey's eye the dunes had never risen at such a distance from the last of the willows, nor had the salt marsh lain so flat and brightly lit beneath what at best was only half a moon. A hundred yards into the estuary they again heard the report of guns. Surrounded by vegetation no higher than their calves they feared for themselves as easy targets and so came to the sand on hands and knees, as still more shots rang from the darkness at their backs.

They heard the distant wail of a siren, the beating of a helicopter, and took some hope in these things, but the sounds came no closer to where they lay, at last dissipating altogether, and when the sounds were gone they got to their feet and passed through the last of the dunes, which seemed now as battlements before the onslaught of the sea. The beaches they found littered with patches of foam and uprooted kelp and these arranged in positions that might have passed for bodies of the slain. A heavy shore break pounded the sand and across the black faces of waves there were flashes of light, blues and greens, fun-house colors of a delicate luminescence culled from the mysterious deep.

Lines of white water were visible a hundred yards out and these gave evidence of both the swell's direction and of such waves as were marshaled in its coming. And those waves broke unseen, thundering like heavy artillery, and Fahey was eager to put the river between themselves and any who might be following. For even though the beach seemed shaken to its core, the tide was as he'd called it, still low enough to permit a crossing, and he took her by the hand and told her what it was they were going to do.

He'd brought her back to the beaches that had nearly claimed her and he could read the fear in her eyes. He took her hand in his, felt her fingers tightening around his own. "You have to trust me on this one," he told her. "I've done this before. I know how it works."

Magdalena could do little more than nod, but she guessed that at this very moment, if she was going to trust anyone, she would trust Sam the Gull and she got to her feet, for she had been kneeling on the flank of a dune, and Fahey rose with her and led her down.

For the most part, the beaches at the edge of the valley were steeply banked, plunging almost at once into a deep trough and a powerful current, the direction of the current depending upon that of the swell. Fahey laid it out for her as they went. He said that beyond the trough there was a series of long, inside sandbars running the length of the beach but that at the mouth the bars were more plentiful, extending well into the break, and that even the trough grew shallow here, filled in with sand so that they might wade across it. Once through, they would pass on the bars, north to south, till they had rounded the mouth, where they would make for the beach once more. He said these things as they walked, until the white water was snapping at their feet, then Fahey stopped to remove his shoes and Magdalena the socks she'd worn. She held them in one hand and Fahey in the other. The water rose to her waist. The current tugged at her legs. Memories of Las Playas came like the cold, running to her core. But Fahey was already on a bar. He gave her a pull and she stood beside him, suddenly in water no higher than her ankles.

They went out another twenty yards before turning south. They held to the bars, some more shallow than others, but never again in water beyond Magdalena's knees. It was a simple-enough trick. All you had to do was know it, yet many had been drowned here who had not.

"You see how it is," Fahey told her. He was fairly shouting to be heard above the roar of the sea. "If you fall, if you lose my hand, if you hit a deep spot, swim south. The waves will carry you in. Just don't fight them." But she had no intention of losing his hand. He led her in a wide arc, always south, through lines of white water made impotent by the shallow bottom, returning at last to the beach on the southern bank and the mud not even washed completely from their bodies.

"My God," Magdalena said. She couldn't stop smiling.

"What did I tell you?" Fahey asked.

Magdalena laughed out loud. She fell to the sand but Fahey urged her on. They covered ground not that far from where they had seen each other for the first time, with little thought to nesting plovers.

The dunes fell away near the mouth of the river then picked up again a short distance away and Fahey seemed eager to reach them. As they walked he looked steadily over his shoulder, following the silver bead of the river as it wound back among the salt pans and marsh and finally into the small grove of trees, where he had followed her on the first day, where he had killed the dogs, but the elevation was poor here and there was little to see save darkness.

When they had come to the first of the southern dunes they went up for a look. The view was better but neither could detect any movement between themselves and the trees.

"We've made it, then," Magdalena said. They went up a few more steps. A red smudge appeared in the east, the tops of a few trees silhouetted before it.

For a moment neither spoke. "Your farm," Magdalena said, finally. Her voice was soft. She put a hand on his arm.

"It might be no more than the trailer. You'd think if the house had gone . . . there would be more . . ." He paused, as if something else had just now occurred to him. "Your files were in the trailer," he said.

"You did what you had to."

"Maybe they were worth more than you thought. Maybe they would have told you who's out there." He nodded toward the valley.

Magdalena thought of the cowboy from the *charreada,* vaguely familiar. Did it matter if his name had been among the workers of Reciclaje Integral? There was no denying it. But the files were gone. "What now?" she asked.

Fahey was some time in answering, for in crossing the river it had occurred to him how simple it would be to just keep walking. Twenty minutes would take them to the border. The woman Magdalena worked for had come home. The amparo could be replaced, the battle rejoined on the other side. He said as much to Magdalena. He watched as she touched the back of her hand to her forehead. "That's it, then," she said.

Fahey declined a response.

Magdalena waited.

"Or," he said. "We could also wait right here, see who shows up."

"They have guns."

"We would have to be careful. The trick would be to lure them in." He pointed to a sandy bank not fifty yards away, where the river narrowed, transcribing an elongated curve, the water like smoked glass. "It looks like a good place to cross, but it's the worst place in the entire valley. The water's fifteen feet deep, sucking out like a bastard. As the tide rises the banks will crumble. It's a hell of a trap, you work it right."

Magdalena was about to answer when she caught sight of something moving on the valley floor—a lone figure loping from among the trees. She was aware of Fahey at her side. She felt him start. "There's only one," she said.

"Maybe." There was a long beat of silence between them. "You should stay here," Fahey told her.

Magdalena just looked at him. "But we're safe. He'll never cross." It was half statement, half question.

"He might try."

"But it can't be done."

"Not unless he knows how to use the bars."

Magdalena looked at the man, moving now among the long, dark lines of cordgrass and pickleweed. No good could come of it, she decided. The man was armed. He would stop at nothing. Time had shown it. Yet Fahey had already moved a few feet down on the side of the dune. "You said we could walk," Magdalena told him.

Fahey stopped and looked back. "You still can," he said. "If anything goes wrong. Do it."

The words did little more than stir presentiments. A moment passed. "We were home free," she told him.

Fahey stood just below her, the angle of the dune making them nearly equal in height. "They killed my dogs," he said.

He left the dunes, jogging barefoot toward the sandy beach he'd shown to Magdalena. Along its southern border was a series of salt pans, some edged by clumps of bulrushes and cattails. The pans themselves appeared as shallow craters sunk into the valley floor as though meteors had fallen here in a remote age, and he meant to use these as cover.

The other man jogged to meet him, in apparent ignorance of Fahey's presence—a mud effigy not unlike Fahey himself, coming at a half trot on the opposite side of the river, following its bank, passing the flats white as snow. A broad belt crossed his chest, in caricature of a Mexican bandido, but his head was encased in some manner of outlandish helmet, for Fahey could see its black, shining surface cut into sharp angles, glinting in the moonlight. In other circumstances the man's dress might have been comical. In the present situation it suggested dementia and other unpleasantries. Fahey watched as the man broke stride, drawing something from behind his back. Moonlight struck the shortened barrel of what Fahey could only imagine as a Mossberg riot gun, lifted no doubt from behind the seat of his own truck where it sat on the farm, still smoldering in the dark well of the valley.

He stared into the darkness from which the man had come but there were none following and he guessed that the men who chased them had indeed crossed paths with the men on dirt bikes, that gunfire had marked the encounter. And if such was the case then it must be that Fahey's plan had worked already and needed only for Fahey to show himself to ensure its completion.

And though Fahey had come to the place he'd aimed for and the final trap was all but set, his thoughts turned to Magdalena among the dunes, to their intended walk, to a parting at the border. He imagined these as things already transpired the better to indulge them, then set about his little act—feigning panic, calling out for Magdalena to run though she was already well sheltered from any line of fire.

He watched as the man came to an abrupt halt, snatching the outlandish helmet from his head as though it was suddenly an impediment to his sight, moving toward that narrow part of the river, and Fahey not thirty feet beyond it, raising the gun as he came.

Fahey showed himself a moment longer, surprised at his own daring before diving for cover. Yet he had nearly played the part too long, for the shotgun's report shattered the night even as he dove and buckshot grazed his shoulder. In fact, he'd managed to get himself shot.

He lay facedown on the floor of a crater, crusted in salt. He waited for a second report but there was none forthcoming. He examined himself for injuries—two pellets that he could feel, on the outer part of his shoulder, hard beneath his fingers. His heart thumped upon the ground. It was answered by the pounding of the surf. Cursing his insouciance, he called out from the prone position, in what little Spanish he'd managed to retain, a handful of insults from his youth and the Island Express. He was answered with silence. He belly-crawled to the far end of the crater, shadowed in a stand of cattails. The growth offered cover and he rolled into a second crater then chanced a look. The man had come to the very edge of the water, where he stood peering into the shadows, and Fahey saw him clearly for the first time.

In the absence of any helmet Fahey saw moonlight on a balding skull and beneath that pale dome a physiognomy of such haunted intensity as to set him, at least momentarily, upon his heels in simple wonder, like someone who had come face-to-face with first things, in a time before words, yet found in their presence the shock of recognition.

Time passed. The men were only yards apart. Armando stood in full view, washed in moonlight at the river's edge. Fahey remained in shadow, where, once the initial shock engendered by such a countenance as Armando's had begun to wear off, he wondered yet again at such motives as had driven this man from across the border. For in place of something better, he was willing to believe that he was one of the men who'd set upon Magdalena in Tijuana and that she had been badly advised when told such men were no longer a threat. If this were the case, it might also be true, as Magdalena had originally surmised, that the man did not act of his own accord but came in the service of another to whom failure was not an acceptable outcome. It was difficult, however, at just that moment, for Fahey to imagine the owner of such a face as that hung opposite him, as though provoked from the very darkness, as indentured to any save what demons were entirely its own. And yet whatever the reasons, for those were superfluous to the moment and might be considered at some later date, the man had come, his prey now close enough to smell, his thoughts transparent as a child's. For he was studying the river before him and even as Fahey watched, the man squatted, extending a booted foot, tapping the placid surface with his toe, about to take the first step, when Fahey's attention was caught by some movement upon the salt pans just east of where he lay, on his own side of the river.

He turned out of bleak necessity for there could be nothing there he wanted to see. And indeed by time he had done so a second man had risen fully formed from the salt pans and cordgrass and was coming at a fast trot, a figure even more befouled than Fahey himself yet with just enough of a garish Western shirt visible in the moonlight for Fahey to make some guess as to his identity, for he remembered there had been a man at the rodeo, a cowboy Magdalena had found reason to fear, though if in fact this was that man, and if so by what machinations he had been delivered here, Fahey had neither the time nor inclination to ponder, for already the man had seen him and called out, in rapid-fire Spanish. He was answered in kind by the man on the far bank—discourse of which Fahey could understand not a word and at the end of which the man gave out with a hoarse cry and launched himself into the flats, a rusted machete gripped in both hands and raised above his head, a grenadier from among the deranged.

Fahey's grand plan having made him for a fool, he had little time now for improvisation. In his efforts to ensnare the man on the opposite bank, he'd ensnared himself and Magdalena as well and the best he could hope for was that he might buy her some time. The first man was trapped by the river. If Fahey could best the second man, or at least slow him down, Magdalena might still outdistance him to the border.

Such were Fahey's thoughts as the man cleared the edge of his crater in a single leap, landing on one booted foot and one bare, the whites of his eyes visible above a toothless grimace and such skin as was not blackened with mud dyed to the color of tropic seas as though its owner had come in mad flight not from the rodeo at Garage Door Tijuana but rather from some darker and more ancient ritual, a thing infused with debauchery and the sacrifice of innocents. The machete was held aloft in both hands, the rusted blade rushing to sunder Fahey's skull.

He rolled clear at the last possible second, the blade striking the ground where his head had been. Shards of crystallized salt and pieces of earth cast up like broken crockery stung his skin. He spun on one hip, sweeping the ground with his opposing leg, catching the other man at the backs of his knees. The man loosed a guttural cry in keeping with his appearance, landing on his ass with enough force to bring forth small geysers of reeking mud from beneath the layers of salt. Fahey went for his throat, aware of the shotgun across the river, determined to keep the fight on the ground. But the man was quick. Fahey felt the bite of the old blade, catching him on the inner arm, thrusting forward to puncture the skin just above his collarbone. He drove it away with the butt of his hand. They had come to a kneeling position. Fahey drove his weight into the other man. Momentum carried them over the rim of the shallow crater and into the sand, in the direction of the river. There was nothing for it but to keep fighting. Fahey pushed a thumb into his opponent's windpipe. He was nearly blinded by salt and mud. The other man still held to the machete, which had on it a wooden handle and this topped by a kind of wooden knob like what you might find at the grip end of a baseball bat. Old man Pickering had made it so, fashioned it of hickory in his own toolshed when the first handle had come apart on him years ago, and fuck him for his craftsmanship, as it was this selfsame handle that at last made contact with Fahey's head, catching him flush in the temple. It could not be said that he saw it coming. His face hit sandy ground baked harder than a brick. The impact loosened a tooth. His mouth filled with blood and grit. A light show played somewhere in the darkness of his skull then faded to black. He went with her name on his lips. He wished her speed.

32

So it was that Armando had come to the very edge of the river. And so it was that he had seen Chico come back from the dead, brandishing the rusted machete they had taken from the farm of the old people, clearly an act worthy of such songs as Chico was wont to imagine, and he wondered briefly if they had not all become worthy of song, both he and his companions, and went so far as to imagine what these corridos might be like, such storied exploits from north of the line. But then Chico had ruined it all by calling out for Armando to shoot the worm farmer. Until that moment, Armando had taken Chico's use of the machete in place of his pistol as an act of machismo. But the other's pleas now gave him to understand that the jackass had simply lost his gun to the river and Armando cursed him for a dick and a clown. Still, he sheathed the shotgun and drew the pistol, reckoning the spread of the former too broad to hit just one of the combatants, if that was what it came to, but yelling at Chico even as he made the switch, telling him to use the fucking machete, for Christ's sake. In fact, he wanted to see how Chico would handle himself in a real fight. He wanted to see this because he imagined that one day he might be called upon to fight Chico himself and was curious about the other man's style.

Unhappily, it was a short fight, with Chico quickly upended but managing to club the other man in the side of head with the butt end of the machete, after which the big man lay still and Chico rose up over him, a pale apparition cloaked now in the salt of the flat and this adhering to clothes already caked in mud and wet from the river that had so delivered him, back from the dead. The machete dangled from Chico's arm. He gasped for breath, one hand on his throat. He seemed to be collecting himself for some final act when a stone struck him full in the chest. Chico cursed and cried out. He was answered by a voice from the dunes.

Inexplicably the voice called to Armando Santoya by name, in his own tongue. He looked toward the sea, to a Madonna descending. Her dress was red before the whiteness of the sand. Her hair was wild about her shoulders and the moonlight was on her face. She had filled a pocket of her dress with stones and she was throwing these at Chico and she was calling on Armando and asking for his help. He responded to these wonders in dumb astonishment, not only to her words but to the spectacle that she presented. She threw the stones overhand with considerable force. They were not so easy to dodge in the darkness. Taking one to the head might prove detrimental to one's health. A conclusion apparently reached by the cowboy, for once again he called out for Armando to shoot. When this did not happen he was ready to forgo the slaughter of Fahey in an effort to reach his attacker. A dive, followed by a shoulder roll, got him there. The move caught her by surprise and he had her by the arm. It was the way he'd once had her at the side of the road, above the beaches of Mexico, in Las Playas de Tijuana.

She fought now as she had fought then and for a brief time they whirled across the sand as if in dance. But she would not surprise him again. He was much the stronger of the two and as Armando watched, the cowboy released the grip on her arm and took her by the hair. He bent her back so that her throat was turned to the sky. His knee pushed the dress between her thighs and he slapped at her bare leg with the flat of his blade. In fact he had begun to toy with her. "See your Madonna," the cowboy said. "Get some while it lasts." He lowered his face toward her throat in the manner of a vampire.

Armando watched, fixated, beset by feelings of an immense complexity. Chico seemed ready to have her then and there, or maybe to stumble with her in the direction of the dunes and so remove her from Armando's sight altogether. But thanks to some movement born of her struggles, or perhaps out of choice, Chico raised his head once more, his shoulders swinging briefly toward the river, his faced turned in the direction of Armando, who read upon that painted visage a look of such naked and contemptible lust that he elected not even to waste such time as it would have taken to cross the river but shot him where he stood and so kept his Madonna in full view, not to mention preserving her for such ends as were all his own.

The bullet entered Chico's side near the bottom of his rib cage and came out through the front, where a broken piece of bone now pierced the skin for all to see and the cowboy stood looking down on it before letting go of the girl and staggering toward the water. He came with his face exposed to the moonlight and that simple organ twisted around such interpolations as were bound to go both unasked and unanswered, for the next shot issued from the barrel of Fahey's riot gun, taking the cowboy atop the head, and he fell with the skullcap blown mostly away and the contents spilled upon the mud, and the dance ended.

"The cowboy had a dirty mind," Armando said. He'd found it necessary to switch weapons one more time, apparently having discharged the handgun more times than he'd imagined, quite possibly in the slaughter surrounding the bog, where Nacho had fallen. In any event, the pistol now lay in the mud at his feet and it was the shotgun that he brought to bear upon Magdalena.

Still, with only such minor setbacks as those already enumerated, things appeared to be working out after all. He was a moment in contemplation, not only of his success but of his options as well. He could shoot her here. He could cross the river. She was his for the taking. In the desert, on the outskirts of Tijuana, the mineshaft waited. *"En la casa de mi Padre,"* Armando said, *"muchas moradas hay."* And didn't he know it. He had prepared the place. He would receive her home.

On the opposing bank, Magdalena heard these words, spoken it would seem to no one in particular, to the night itself. Their effect was as a cold wind in an empty room, a room in which she was finally alone. She staggered but retained her footing. She drew herself upright. She faced him across fifteen feet of soiled water, the shotgun pointed at her breast. *"En nombre de su esposa, Reina,"* she said. She might have said, *"En nombre de tu esposa . . ."* but this would have been a less formal way of invoking his wife's name. *"En nombre de su hijo, Immanuel . . ."* She could only hope that she had remembered the name of his son, that she had gotten it right. *"En nombre de toda lo que ha perdido. Por Dios, ¡piense! ¡Piense lo que está haciendo!"* It was not the first time she had so implored the peasantry, admonishing them in the use of such minds as God had given them. Reason had been always been her ally, or so she had imagined. On the night in question she was not altogether certain that reason alone would suffice and so went looking amid the farthest reaches of memory, and in these were contained the rustling of ancient muslin, stiff with time like death itself and the scorched scent of old metal, in cave-dark vestries the half-remembered verse . . . And always, the city hovering at the edge of this darkness, Mexicali, sun-blind pesthouse of afflicted humanity . . . *"Te pongo delante de la vida o de la muerte,"* she said finally, *"o bendición o maldición."*

The words came to her from somewhere among the pages of the Old Testament—such blood-soaked labyrinths now seeming to her quite appropriate, in both time and place. And hadn't he invoked the Word of his own volition? She had quoted a fragment but in another moment she would remember the text in full: "I do take the heavens and the earth as witnesses against you today, that I have put life and death before you, the blessing and the malediction; and you must choose life in order that you may keep alive, both you and your offspring." It had always seemed to her a simple-enough choice.

33

CERTAIN TOXINS, once inhaled, absorbed, or otherwise ingested, are thought by some to be stored in the fatty tissues of the body, released back into the bloodstream during periods of intense activity. A wide variety of psychotic disorders might well ensue, including both visual and auditory hallucinations. Among such toxins one could list benzene, toluene, xylene, and Varsol—known to the workers of Accessories de Mexico as yellow glue. Amphetamines would of course have their place on this list as well, as would alcohol and cocaine, together with certain opioids, sedatives, and anxiolytics, none of which were missing from Armando's considerable arsenal.

It is also thought, or so it has been stated, that every man carries with him some load in this world that is his and his alone to bear, much as Jesus was said to have born the iniquities of the race. In the case of Armando Santoya the iniquities were mainly his own, though it must be said in his favor that the world had given him little by way of succor and that whatever load had been consigned to him by whatever demiurge as would claim it must by now have reached to the heavens. And who could reckon its number, or otherwise imagine such ghosts and visitations by which the peasant from Sinaloa was at that moment beset, on the bank of the river that carried within its stream the very toxins he carried within himself, as though each had been made brother to the other and so united in blood? Sweat stung his eyes. The old valley was alive with geometric shapes heretofore unimagined, with afterimages and colors inappropriate to the time or place, and in the midst of which stood his Madonna, at the edge of the river, fearless in her beauty, in the face of his gun, able it would seem to walk upon water. The thought of shooting her and having done with it was never far from his mind, and yet her words fell upon him as might the invocation of a curate to some obscure order of which he was himself the lone petitioner, for they were secret words and carried within them the echoes of other voices, of times and places and things that were and things that might have been and the story they told was none but his own. She told him she was sorry for his son, though not the one dead unborn, but for the other one, whose name she had called forth, that tragic firstling, the poisons that would carry him away present even at the moment of his conception, in the blood of the parents, and that blood tainted like the very water at Armando's feet. And she spoke of the factories as well, and named them as a great monster come to suck the life's blood from that country beyond the fence, both hers and his, telling him that his life had been a tragedy, his and Reina's together, speaking names that he had not heard uttered by another in so long he had begun to consider them features of his own devising. Yet finally it was these very names that prompted him to speak back, to challenge her story— this delegate of the black arts. But she stood against that charge and others like it, telling him that he had gotten it wrong, even to the point of imagining a second son, a pure conjecture on his part for such had never existed save in his own mind and it was he himself that his wife had fled and the life she feared for had been her own. And she told him of her own mother, dead young, and of the flood that carried her to this valley, unknown and unburied, one of the disappeared . . . And that, she said, had been her struggle, to vindicate the life of a woman she had scarcely known, known no more of than Armando had known of his son. Yet each, she said, had been taken by the same agents of avarice and greed and it was against these very agents that she had taken up arms and she invited him to join her in this struggle, as it was his struggle too and before it all others were made spurious and of no account.

In fact she had made such speeches before, many times over, or at least variations thereof, each in accord with its own audience, and at times to none but herself, for such were her convictions, yet never at the wrong end of a gun, and the words came now in such a breathless rush she could scarcely make sense of them herself.

For Armando, however, the pace was dead on, lifting him to such vertiginous heights by which the world could be viewed in ways heretofore intuited though never beheld, holding him as if by spell, and before them he stood mute as a stone, gaping in simple astonishment as even the ground at her feet began to stir and his first thought was that some final reckoning was at last upon them and earth itself called upon to bring forth its dead. In another moment, however, he saw that it was none but the worm farmer. Having regained some measure of consciousness, he was now struggling to regain his feet as well.

Magdalena put a hand on the man's shoulder, speaking to him in English. In fact she was telling him to stay down but he would not be dissuaded. He rose by strength of will or simple confusion to stand tottering upon the bank, where he seemed to be trying to pull Magdalena away from the water, possibly in the direction of the dunes as the cowboy from Tijuana had done before him, and for Armando, the spell was broken. He allowed the barrel of the gun to drift in Fahey's direction.

Magdalena saw and moved to shield him from the gun but Fahey wouldn't have it. He moved along with her so that the two now stood side by side, facing the gunman from across the water, and so was Armando brought finally to a moment of choice. For in Magdalena's story he'd found himself contained, yet he was contained as well in such corridos as were sung in his honor upon the Mesa de Otay, and of these also he had been made witness, and in such shrines as he had dreamed in his heart. And yet he saw these stories as things at odds, as are warring arrangements of history. Yet who would deny that one must be claimed and one found wanting, or that any such judgment would have no bearing on what came next? For in one of these tales he walked upright as a man and in the other was only the wreckage of such, a thing meant for suffering, a vessel of pain. Yet he wondered if these stories were not of equal weight and veracity and if in the absence of one there might not also be some absence in the heart and so made a real effort to listen to that beleaguered organ, to hear what it might have to say, for he'd heard it said that knowing was not always in the head. But in truth he could hear little more than the sound of the surf. He found, however, that he could feel the beating of his heart. It seemed to reside in the very tip of his trigger finger as though it was the heart's intention to signal that appendage directly, by way of code.

And so he stood, as the seconds slipped away, as the gun drifted from one to the other, the woman to the man and back again. If she spoke again he did not hear it. His mind was fixed upon the enigma so encrypted, waiting to see what that appendage might yet do, even though it was attached to him and so in theory was not its own master, but was subject to the exercise of will on the part of whosoever would claim it. Whereupon the inevitable confluence of a rising tide and incoming swell at last lifted the river above its frail banks, even as the sand gave way beneath Armando's feet and he tumbled headlong into the water and sank beneath the surface and was swept to sea, just as Fahey had planned it.

34

H E WENT WITH the shotgun still clutched in his hands and no cry came from his lips, as the sand crumbled now on the southern bank and Magdalena and Fahey danced backward in advance of its collapse to stand looking toward that place where Armando had vanished. They looked downriver toward the mouth to see if he would regain the surface but the water rolled on unbroken and no trace was seen of him again, not then, and not in the days to come. For the body was never washed back to shore as so often happens along that stretch of sand. The sea had taken him and he was never seen again, not on the beaches of the Tijuana River Valley and not upon those of the country from which he had begun.

Magdalena now turned her attention to Fahey, taking stock of his wounds. There was a cut across one arm where the machete had gotten him and another shallow cut near his collarbone. The wounds were more like deep scratches than cuts, already lined with crusted blood. He'd taken a couple of pellets in the same shoulder and these would have to be gotten out and there was a knot near his temple and bruises across one side of his face. "You're like I was," she told him. "We've switched places."

"It's true," he said. "You saved my ass."

Chico lay close by, mouth agape, staring blindly into the night and none now left to sing his song. Fahey turned away but Magdalena looked long enough to see the Aztec sun tattooed upon his naked abdomen where the fancy Western shirt had fallen away. "That was him," she said. "The man from the road . . ." She looked toward the mouth of the river, the endless lines of white water crisscrossing in the night. "He must have been the other one," she said. "Armando. The one whose face I never saw."

"You knew him."

"He used to come to the center. He thought we had performed an abortion on his wife."

"That was why he followed you, all this way? It was why he came?"

Magdalena was some time in replying. "It's a sad story," she said.

Fahey could only nod, wondering aloud if in the end he might have tried to save him, but Magdalena put a finger to his lips and would not hear it. "You're hurt," she said.

"Not really."

"What about the water, the mud?"

"You live down here you keep up on your shots. I get home I'll take some of the Cipro."

"And your head?"

Fahey shrugged it off. "I can still count to ten," he told her. He walked along the bank of the river, studying its surface. Magdalena walked with him. She guessed that he was still looking for some trace of Armando. "He was beyond your help," she said. "Yours or anyone else's, for a long time now, I would imagine. I got to know his wife. I know something of his past. He could not have been long for this world. Believe me. The end for which you would have saved him would have been worse than the one he has endured."

Fahey continued walking. He did not ask to hear the man's story or to what end he might have come, then or at any other time, and would in fact go to his own grave without knowing it, for by his own measure the world was composed of sad stories and he saw no reason to learn another.

It was while they were still walking along the bank that a dark object, large enough to have been a man, was swept past them and into the sea. They caught no more than a glimpse, but in looking back along the way they had come, they could see that the banks had continued to crumble and that Chico was no longer there. He'd gone, it would seem, on the heels of the man who had killed him, a headless tracker set to wander, yet Fahey imagined the sea both wide and deep enough to sustain the chase.

"We should go on," he said. And those were the only words to attend Chico's final appearance in the land of the living.

They were by now standing on the beach, at the very mouth of the river, closer to the border than to the farm, or what might be left of it, and he was trying to decide which destination made more sense and to what exactly they should go on to when a pair of head-lights broke suddenly onto the beach from somewhere back of the dunes.

Above these headlights burned a rack of halogens more brilliant than the moon. The lights were coming toward them and Fahey raised a hand to shield his eyes from the glare and saw that still one more light had been added to this display. The new entry appeared to be handheld and was trained upon the sea, apropos of some drama no doubt unfolding out there in the watery dark.

Magdalena shrank back but Fahey assured her the lights could be none but the border patrol's. "The cavalry," he said, "right on time."

✦ ✦ ✦

Having nothing any longer to fear from such encounters, Fahey and Magdalena walked to meet the truck. It had come to a stop by the time they got to it and there was a young man standing at its side, a Mexican-American in the uniform of the border patrol, and he was indeed holding a spotlight and training it upon the sea.

Fahey and Magdalena were nearly on top of him before he noticed them and when he did his hand dropped to the pistol at his side but Fahey held up both hands, palms out. "It's okay," Fahey told him. "I live here."

The man did not seem immediately reassured.

"Really," Fahey said. "What do you see?"

The patrolman studied them a moment longer, then nodded in the direction of his light, and they followed its beam, which seemed at first to have found no more than the mist of an agitated sea, and this swirling within its narrow track like the coming of snow. In a short time however, they saw there was more. They saw what the light had found—a small boat swinging wildly among the huge ground-swells within a quarter mile of the shore and each knew it for what it was, a smuggler running migrants, and each could envision only too well such ragtag pilgrims as any boat of its kind was bound to contain, of any and all ages, their worldly goods in plastic bags, afraid for their lives, in the face of a night beyond their reckoning.

"The next outside wave will swamp them," Fahey said.

The border patrolman cursed softly in Spanish then switched to English. "What do they think?" he asked. "On a night like this?" He was looking from Magdalena to Fahey and back again, as though either might provide him with an answer. When none was forthcoming he shook his head in some combination of disgust and sorrow. "*Loco,*" he said. "They don't think." He went so far as to wave a hand in their direction, as though warning them to move farther out—a meaningless gesture born of frustration, for the situation had gone way beyond anyone's ability to control it—and even as the patrolman spoke, there came a deep booming that could be heard even above the general roar of the surf. The white water came within seconds, a roiling wall itself ten feet high, a quarter mile in length. The boat was set broadside to the impact and seemed to come apart even as they watched it. The patrolman groaned. Magdalena put the back of her fist to her mouth. By the arc of the patrolman's light, small figures could be seen spilling from the boat, vanishing in darkness.

The patrolman lowered his light and turned to his truck. He was about to reach for something inside the cab when he caught sight of Fahey at the rear bumper, naked except for his shorts, engaged in loosening the canvas straps by which a number of large metal containers were lashed into the bed. His shirt and pants lay nearby, where they had fallen on the sand. The patrolman nearly stumbled over them in his march to the rear of the vehicle. "What the hell?" he asked. But by now Fahey had freed the strap. He appeared to be measuring it for length.

"I need some kind of flotation device," Fahey told him. "Water bottles, antifreeze containers . . . anything that will float."

The patrolman began to shake his head. "I'm not sure exactly what you think you're doing but if you think I'm gonna let you go out in that, you're crazy . . ."

"You must have drinking water . . ."

"Forget it. And I've called for backup. The Coast Guard was supposed to have dispatched a helicopter . . ."

"It's not here," Fahey told him.

The patrolman just looked at him.

"Listen to me," Fahey said. "I've lifeguarded and I've surfed these beaches for thirty years. These people will die on your watch, mine too." The two men were by now eye to eye. "I can do this,"

Fahey said. "If the chopper comes, great, it will be easier for all of us, but these people don't have much time, not tonight, not in this kind of surf."

For a moment neither man spoke. Their silence was broken by Magdalena.

"I found this," she said. She was standing at the side of the cab, a plastic gallon jug of Arrowhead drinking water in her hand. "It was behind the seat."

In another few seconds there was added to this a plastic antifreeze container of roughly the same shape and size. The bottles were emptied of their contents then recapped, the canvas strap from the patrolman's truck run through the handles of each then looped about Fahey's chest, armpit to shoulder.

The patrolman looked on, unable to escape the feeling that in the end, he had, in some way, been had. He supposed it was the woman, as remarkable a creature as any he could remember, and he was yet to even scrape the surface of what had gotten her here, in the dead of night, wet and ragged, in the company of this man about to throw himself into the sea. But with the loss of the boat the clock had been set against him and if he was certain of nothing else he was certain of this: The man would not be dissuaded and there were lives in the balance. There was also the man's apparent confidence, together with his appearance. Deprived of his ragged clothes he had a solid-enough look about him to suggest he was at least up to the attempt, if not to its successful resolution, though given the conditions, that degree of surety would have been difficult to ascribe to any man. And yet the woman had chosen to back his play. Nor, finally, could the patrolman see any clear way to intervene in this adventure short of nightsticks and restraints and so busied himself with his truck's phone, calling yet again for the helicopter that seemed to have been detained, asking for backup, and all the while, his eyes on Fahey, on the beach, as he prepared to enter the water.

Magdalena stood nearby, rigid as a stone, one hand affixed to the open door of the truck. She took this as a necessary precaution, enabling her to remain on her feet, for she felt that in a manner of speaking her legs were gone, and it was this last bit that had done it. They had come so far, she thought, she and Fahey. They had bested the men who hunted them. They had come so close. Yet she did not trust herself to say any more than she had said already, in presenting him with the plastic bottle, in giving him her blessing, for she had doubted it as soon as it was given. She knew at once too much and too little, too much of his past and too little of what chance he actually had of making this rescue. She thought perhaps that if she could see his face . . . maybe there she would find a way to judge, but his eyes were turned toward her for no more than a heartbeat and even then he was asking the patrolman to swing his truck around and put the halogens on anyone he could find and failing that the wreckage itself and with that he was gone. She watched as he ran down the beach, pounding through the shallows. She saw him dive beneath a line of white water and vanish from view.

Fahey reckoned the boat to have broken up somewhere in the vicinity of Third Notch. What had gotten them was the Mystic Peak. One could not mistake its thunder. His hope would be to reach them before it broke again—at this point in the swell's progress, an event that was difficult to predict. He was vaguely aware of someone shouting through a bullhorn as he ran into the shallows. He took it for the border patrolman. Perhaps he was trying to speak to the migrants. Perhaps he was trying to call Fahey back to reason. Fahey never knew. He made his dive. The sea gathered him in, colder than it had been in recent weeks, made so by the winds that had driven the swell, and though he had not said so, another in this deck of cards now stacked against the people he would try to save. The power of the first wave drove him deeper than his dive. He felt a sandbar scrape his chest, and then he was clear. He came to the surface, his head ringing. He began to swim.

The pellet wounds in his shoulder ached for a while as did his head, but in a short time each was numb and he swam and he dove until the shore break was a thing of the past and he was swimming in a great cauldron, amid darkness and flashes of moonlight, swimming in one of the rip tides that Hoddy had taught him to use. For with all that water moving in there had to be places for it to move out and knowing how to find such currents and how to use them was an old surfer's trick.

He was somewhere past the peak at Second Notch when a broad shaft of light came streaming from the shore—the halogens of the patrolman's truck—and it appeared that the man must have gotten his truck farther up on the dunes as the light seemed now to issue from some altitude, hitting the water another hundred yards out, and he turned toward it, breaking from what was left of the rip, angling toward the waves of Third Notch.

A trio of waves broke in front of him as he made his approach, one after the other. They were big open ocean waves it was necessary to elude. He was still pretty far out on the shoulders of the waves yet each seemed to take him deeper than the last. The dives brought cold, an utter blackness, and with each descent came a strange, almost overwhelming urge to dive deeper still, to push farther into the void, as though the blackness were a thing he might strike through. It was spooky little game, yet each time he came back and each time he was farther outside with the sea grown calmer, able to raise himself upon his homemade buoy to get his bearings, steering by the lights that streamed from the shore until at last he was swimming among pieces of wreckage and came finally upon the first of the migrants, a man in his thirties, already spitting blood.

The man was clinging to an orange seat cushion and Fahey was glad to see it for he had been counting on at least two things. He knew enough of these outings to know that at some point the migrants would have been planning to swim to shore and so might be expected to have at least some ability as swimmers. He was also counting on their having acquired something in the way of flotation devices, if nothing more than bits of the wreckage itself. In truth he had gambled his life on these two items, for without them he would stand little chance of making a rescue and a very good chance of being drowned in the attempt. The plastic jugs would not, by themselves, be enough to do the job. Still, he had wanted them. They served the theory that in any rescue, the rescuer must instill within the victim the belief that help has arrived, thereby gaining a psychological advantage. And so did Fahey hope to make use of the things he had brought. He imagined that they would not only make it look like he knew what he was doing, but would act as a rallying point as well, for it was his intention to gather such survivors as he could find into a single group. It was the theory with which he had begun and he was not about to abandon it now. He pushed the plastic jugs toward the man with the seat cushion then reached him in a stroke.

The man regarded him with rolling eyes. "Lifeguard," Fahey said. He was astonished to find that he had lost the Spanish equivalent. The man flailed about. Fahey got the bottles under the man's arms like a pair of water wings.

"*¿Cuántos compañeros?*"

The man vomited.

Fahey tried again. "*¿Cuántos compañeros?*"

"*Seis,*" the man said. He spoke between chattering teeth. "*Seis.*"

Fahey nodded. Already there were two more, a man and a woman, splashing toward him. He arranged these around the man with the cushion and bottles. He found another man a short distance away, trying to keep afloat on a scrap of wood too small to do the job. Fahey saw his head go under. He swam quickly to the spot, pulling him to the surface by the nape of his neck, then floated him toward the others. He felt certain they were beyond Third Notch, and he prayed that his luck would hold, that he might assemble his group before the Mystic Peak could fire again. He had four already and in another few seconds he had the last two, a boy and a girl, the girl a teenager, the boy younger. These had also found seat cushions and he grouped them with the others—everyone assembled around the man with the bottles—and he bound himself to them by the use of his line, to make of them all one great floating ball of humanity that the white water might drive toward shore, and he was no sooner done with this exercise than he heard it come, a deep thundering from out of the darkness, and in another moment he saw it—white water like the vanguard of a mountain in ruin—yet the act was done and they were bound for good or for ill, knit by flesh and line and the desire to live, and so were they conformed as the white water hit them.

The impact was tremendous and they were driven down and slammed and spun and Fahey could feel the combined weight of them all lashed about his neck from which issued a variety of weird popping and cracking sounds, leaving him to wonder if that extremity would hold or give way altogether, but he held to people he could no longer see with both hands and they to him and all of them holding on as Fahey had instructed before the white water could hit. For by such efforts would their combined buoyancy return them to the surface and so it happened, all seven heads, and Fahey's among them, breaking into the light. After this wave there were more, though of diminishing power, and in time the migrants were able to see what Fahey had in mind, and to mark their own progress, and so held to one another of their own accord, pushed steadily toward the inside sandbars to arrive at last puking and chilled to the bone upon the shores of America, where the border patrol was waiting.

To Magdalena's eyes, they appeared as a circus act from beneath the sea, or perhaps some creature as yet unnamed, so absurd in its formation as to beggar description and moving forward with such locomotions as would befit its appearance, for in fact the survivors could not stop clinging to one another and some were still bound by Fahey's line—an even half dozen altogether, not counting the man who had rescued them, so that in total they were seven, and five of these from the same family, a mother and father together with an uncle and two children. But as for now, all seven came on in the manner so described, crawling shell-shocked and half drowned, their arrival contained within the great glow of the halogens. And which lights, angled now from the dunes above, contained as well the sea spray of a thundering shore break, swirling upward within their broad beam as though the survivors had come ashore in the teeth of some tropical cloudburst though in truth the sky above was clear and dark, replete with moonlight, twin dippers, and the belt of Orion . . .

35

THE QUESTION now before them was how best to care for the migrants. Procedure called for them to be arrested before they were treated but this was a dangerous way to go as most were approaching hypothermia if not there already and at least two were badly injured. One of these was the man Fahey had first come upon in the water, spitting blood, the apparent result of a broken rib. The other was the young girl, who seemed to have sustained some kind of head injury in the course of the rescue. She was moaning and nauseous, unable to bring her eyes to focus, and in the end it was decided that they could be treated most quickly were Magdalena to have an ambulance meet them on the beaches of Las Playas, only minutes away.

She made the call from the patrolman's truck, which he admitted was irregular, but then he was a Mexican as well as an American and indeed had grown up in Tijuana and said that he would take responsibility for the decision in order to save the lives of the people now huddled in the back of his truck, wrapped in such blankets and towels and other articles of clothing as could be found. Fahey said he knew of a place to cross and the patrolman saw no reason to challenge him. The man, he concluded, was on a roll.

The injured girl rode up front, draped across the laps of both Fahey and Magdalena, who rode side by side with the patrolman, Magdalena in the middle, cradling the girl's head and shoulders.

"This has been the devil's own night," the patrolman said, speaking as he drove. "Let me tell you. There was a stabbing over there at Garage Door Tijuana. Then some fool tried to run a whole goddamn herd of horses though a hole up by Smuggler's Gulch. Things have been running all over the valley and us chasing them. On top of that there was a fire at that lousy worm farm . . . what's it called . . . the Fahey place . . . but then I guess we can live with that. From what I hear no one's going to miss it."

No one said much after that and for the most part they rode in silence, in approach to the great fence with its seemingly unending string of lights spooling out before them like a constellation in decline, though from time to time the patrolman would look over at Fahey, not without some degree of wonder, asking him if he was sure he was okay, and Fahey would answer that he was.

"I suppose you're going to tell us you can still count to ten," Magdalena said. She had one arm around the child in her lap. With the other, she was holding Fahey by the hand.

"No, but I can whistle," Fahey told her. It had been one of the tests for hypothermia Hoddy had taught to his boys, back in the day, lifeguarding along these selfsame beaches, yet he made no effort to prove this was the case just now but was content to ride, Magdalena's hand in his own, and to think back along such golden chains of days as these beaches now evoked. For it seemed as if he was remembering them afresh after some long hiatus—days of off-shore winds and bonfires crackling on the beaches, cooking up lobsters from Hoddy's traps, and the beer fresh off the ice in the old dunemobile. And when the beer and the lobsters were gone and stories sufficient to the day had been told, there was at last the long ride back in the rear of that selfsame vehicle—the Dog's forty-nine Merc with the seats gone and the trunk cut out and the roof too—steel posts now welded to the frame in support of a new roof, and this of bamboo and palm fronds, and the whole rig sitting up high on the airplane tires Hoddy'd managed to hustle from some engineer at Lockheed with a weakness for the straits. And they'd gone with the lights of Imperial Beach scattered before them, in those days faint as a child's birthday candles above the grasses of the great estuary and the lights of Mexico at their backs . . .

Such were the images with which Fahey rode. From time to time he would hear Magdalena and the officer exchange a few words in Spanish and once he heard Magdalena mention his name. He was aware too that neither seemed able to keep their eyes off him for long, both looking at him in a way that no one had looked at him in a very long time and maybe never at all, save perhaps one, and that would have been the old Badlander himself, in a time before remembering.

In minutes they were nearing the fence and Fahey directed them. They drove inland on hard-packed dirt then off-road, a short distance to the foot of a mesa, among grass and brush and a few stunted cottonwoods, where the patrolman's lights fell across the opening of the old pipe, nearly invisible among the vines that drew enough moisture from the cliff face to dangle across its entrance.

"I'll be damned," the patrolman said. They parked and got out.

Fahey had brought them to a place he'd done his best to avoid, even in thought, for more years than he cared to remember and yet so had events conspired—a chance meeting and all that followed, an ending upon the polluted beaches he'd known since boyhood with a length of line and two plastic jugs. Of such incidentals was a man reborn and such were Fahey's thoughts, standing by the truck that held the migrants, as Magdalena and the patrolman went forward to meet a small group just now emerging from the tunnel's mouth, a border cop and two paramedics, one of these with a stretcher beneath his arm.

The moment left little time for good-byes. Still she came to him as the migrants were led toward the border. The young girl was taken first, carried away on the stretcher. The others went under their own power, even the man with the broken rib, walking bent at the waist, and each of them pausing long enough at the foot of the cliff to seek out Fahey and to raise a hand in parting. Fahey waved in return. He was very much aware of Magdalena, holding back, standing at his side.

"I know a place," she said. She said it was south of Ensenada on the Pacific side, so there were waves, and a small hotel opening to a beach that was rarely crowded and that the owners were friends of hers. She was thinking that she might go down there. She was thinking about a little rest and relaxation. "It would be nice," she said, "if you came too."

Fahey hardly knew what to say. In the end he muttered something about the farm, the necessity of looking in on the herd, or what might be left of it, though in truth the glow of dying embers could be seen even from where they stood, a red stain upon the sky.

Magdalena saw it as well as he did. "I told you," she said, "you're like me. We both have to start over." And while it was true that in Magdalena's case she would indeed take up the cross once more it was also true that she would do so in perfect ignorance of the fact that she had already, in the course of this night, done what she had always aspired to do, that is save a single life. In fact she had done more, for in the undoing of Armando she had no doubt saved more than a few and in the death of Chico she had rid the mesa of its cowboy in the red convertible, the same who had killed already and would no doubt have killed again. She knew none of it as she stood with Fahey at the borderline. Her thoughts ran only to the fishing village on its crescent of sand, to its small hotel and its sparkling waves. She could see no farther than that and would not have promised otherwise. But that was okay, at least to her. She was alive and so was Fahey and she could not see why they should not buy out a little time and share it, just the two of them. And really, when one thought about it, she did not see why they should not go on together then and there, with momentum in their favor, and it was what she argued for, then and there, with the valley at their backs and the crossing before them . . . "There's that cowboy," she said. "That friend of Deek's . . . yours too . . . I bet he would look in on those worms. I bet he would watch the whole place, at least until you came back . . ."

Fahey smiled and went to the patrolman's truck. He found a pen and a pad of paper. He passed them to Magdalena. "Tell me how to find you," he said.

Magdalena just looked at him, but wrote on the pad—the name of the hotel and a pair of phone numbers. The others were waiting for her now and there was no time for that, and yet she had to admit to some puzzlement at Fahey's reluctance to drop everything in favor of such breathless spontaneity. It was, after all, the thing he'd once argued for, in the confines of his tiny trailer, in his insistence upon life in the ever-holy moment, and she would no doubt have done more in trying to persuade him had the clock not been set against her and the lives of the migrants placed within her keeping.

In the end she pressed the scrap of paper into Fahey's hand.

"This is where I'll be," she said. She started for the passage then stopped cold and looked back, as something both obvious and revelatory had at just that moment taken hold. "It's not the farm," she said. "It's the waves."

Fahey smiled once more. "There may never be another chance."

"There are other waves, other places." But these words rang false even as she spoke them. "I'm afraid," she said, finally.

Fahey looked into the dark mouth of the tunnel, where the others had gone, where the lone border cop waited for Magdalena. "There's no need for that," he told her.

She walked back to him. She put both hands on his arms then rose on her toes to kiss him once on the mouth. And then she was gone, back into that world from which she had come.

Fahey and the border patrolman waited until the sirens had sounded on the other side of the fence and these were answered by the yowls of coyotes, both in the valley and beyond, for to these creatures one side of the fence was the same as the other, and to their voices were added the dog packs of Tijuana.

They were getting back into the patrolman's truck when Fahey caught sight of something atop one of the mesas in the valley, on the American side—what appeared to be a naked man engaged in a kind of dance. "What the hell?" Fahey said.

The patrolman laughed at him. "You've never seen him before?"

"I guess I would have remembered."

"We see him now and again, guys out on patrol. They call him the naked runner. No one's ever gotten close enough to hear his story. Though I guess there's probably one there to tell." Fahey said that he guessed there was and when he looked again, the man was gone.

"It looks to me like he's doing that thing," the patrolman said. "Tai chi." And he laughed once more, and shook his head. In another moment he started his engine. "I guess you'll want to be checking up on your farm."

Fahey just looked at him.

"She told me who you were," the patrolman said.

The man took him as far as the intersection of Hollister and the dirt road that would lead to his home and from there, Fahey said that he would like to walk.

"You sure? You sure you're okay?"

Fahey nodded. "I'm good," he said, and so he felt. "I have some antibiotics. I'll stay on them for a couple of days. I'll get someone to look at my shoulder." He opened the door.

"That was a hell of a thing you did tonight."

Fahey shrugged.

"I mean it, man . . . that was one of the ballsiest things I've ever seen."

"We used to say it was all in a day's work," Fahey told him. He got out of the truck.

"I'm sorry about what I said," the officer told him. "Earlier, that crack about your place, I didn't know . . ."

"Forget it."

"I'm going to put you in for some kind of commendation . . . For what you did . . ."

But Fahey only smiled and raised a hand and walked off into the night, coming finally to the dirt road that led to his farm where he thought to bury his dogs and to see about what was left.

His first good look was through the hole Nacho had cut in the fence, and he was surprised to find that no more of it was gone. The trailer and a few trees were about all that he'd really lost, these and the fiberglass palings that had once been his quiver, now charred and broken like the teeth of dotards.

Not until he had entered the property, however, did he see there was something propped in front of the old house, some sliver of white among the shadows, and moving closer he saw that it was the gun he had shaped and finished for Jack Nance.

It would seem that a person, or persons, unknown had taken pains to save it, just in case the fire had spread, just in case someone might want to use it, saved it then placed it here, on the porch of the house, where Fahey was sure to find it.

He stood there for some time, in consideration of this occurrence, of the board at his feet, as the first shades of dawn broke from the summit of Cerro Colorado, on the Mexican side of the fence that divides the valley into halves, as quite suddenly and from out of the night there came a trembling in the ground beneath his feet, and within seconds he saw the horses. He took them for those brought in through Smuggler's Gulch, the same the border patrolman had told them about. There were half a dozen. They thundered along the unnamed road bordering his property, nostrils flaring, heads thrown back, browns and whites, one with a diamond pattern upon its throat, one a chestnut roan. They went wild-eyed, with sweat on their flanks and heaving chests, like a wind out of Mexico, and were gone.

36

As might be expected, Fahey was not the only surfer to track that great swell. Others had monitored its progress and by the dawning of the first day a group had assembled at the pier in Imperial Beach, not far from the memorial at Surfhenge, though few had any interest in the Plexiglas swizzle sticks or the names of the ancients set in concrete on the small bronze plaques and half of those spattered with the droppings of both seagulls and pigeons. These came with boats and Jet Skis and were part of a group of professional surfers who vied each year in something called Riders on the Storm Big Wave Challenge to see who would ride the biggest wave of the year anywhere on the planet and thus win half a million dollars in prize money.

They were on their way to Todos Santos, an island off the coast of Baja some sixty miles south of the border, but they knew of the Tijuana Straits, of the lore connected to them, and so thought to take the morning for a tow-in session at what the old-timers had called the Mystic Peak, though none among them had done more than hear about it. Still, they were athletes with big-wave experience that spanned three oceans and reckoned a session at the straits a good warm-up for what they imagined to be the larger waves of Todos Santos—which waves they also imagined would be increasing in size, as the swell was predicted to gain in power over the next forty-eight hours, and so set off from the pier that morning on state-of-the-art 1200cc turbocharged Honda Watertrax jet skis, three abreast. One ski carried a pilot and photographer, the other two carried one pilot and one rider apiece, together with the boards they would ride, six-foot needle-nosed thrusters with lead weights set in their middles to hold the board into the waves, for it was not their intention to paddle into these giants but rather to be towed in and from there to ride them as they had never been ridden before, with such carving turns and down-the-line drives as would be made possible only by the short, highly maneuverable boards.

A certain amount of fanfare attended their leaving, with a turnout of lifeguards and local surfers together with their attendant girlfriends, scantily clad, and some smattering of the indigenous citizenry, all come to cheer and ogle at the weary grace of these riders on the storm, many of whom were tattooed and pierced with their heads shaved and the names of their sponsors written large on the gleaming sides of their jet skis and the decks of their boards, and they laid down a few big roundhouse turns charging over the tops of such waves as swept the pier, engines blasting and the spray off their wakes dusting the boardwalk to the delight of the hooting crowd, then angled off toward the south, in search of the Mystic Peak.

◆ ◆ ◆

Jack Nance was up early that day as well, though he had no interest in seeing off the gang at the pier but made directly for the top of Spooner's Mesa. It was his intention to be up there for as long as it took and he went with two freshly rolled joints, a breakfast burrito, a quart of beer, and one pair of industrial-strength binoculars.

His only regret that morning was that his old partner Deek Waltzer was not around to join him. In fact the old cowboy's whereabouts were still a mystery and would remain so for the next six months until a team of fence-hole diggers sent in by a county work program would find his grave on the outskirts of Garage Door Tijuana.

Jack was at work on the burrito when the jet skis put in their appearance. He could see them powering across the backs of waves at Second and Third Notch, white trails of churned water lying in their wake and the fumes of their exhaust risen even to the level of Spooner's Mesa upon which he waited. The sky was yet fairly dark and there was ground fog in ragged patches throughout the valley and a great band of it out past Third Notch, hiding the Coronado Islands.

The waves at Third Notch were well in excess of twenty feet by that time and Nance watched as one of the crews towed in. The waves were classic straits—big, open ocean waves, perfectly shaped upon a low tide with a light off-shore wind brushing their faces— and the surfer rode them in great carving turns, top to bottom. Finally the second team towed in as well and this surfer rode as though a carbon copy of the first and after the rides the surfers were retrieved by the skis and hauled back out to the break and this went on for some time before it occurred to Nance that something was wrong with the picture. When he got it, he laughed out loud. "They think that's it," Jack said, to no one but himself. For a second or two he wondered if this was right but the crews continued to circle at Third Notch and he knew it to be so. With no real understanding of the lineups, the crews believed themselves to be riding the Mystic Peak, and yet clearly they were mistaken. They were still too far north and too far inside, even at three quarters of a mile out.

Jack got out of his truck and seated himself upon its roof, his boots upon the windshield, knees drawn up to hold his elbows to steady the big glasses, his cowboy hat tilted back above his sun-beaten face and him grinning like the demented sidekick of some cowboy matinee idol as the thing he had so recently foreseen had in fact begun to unfold, and Nance himself its lone witness . . .

It began with a wipeout on a big wave at Third Notch, the rescue ski moving in for the pickup, the second crew, together with the photographer and his pilot, circling in behind the first ski, intent upon the action, and so never picking up on those subtle hints which might otherwise have tipped them off—the eerie whistling sounds, let's say, that are said to emanate from the ocean floor, attributable to movement among the great heap of stones that lie there, gathered by time from the mouth of the river, or perhaps the sudden disappearance of the Coronado Islands, suggesting that the sea was on the rise, evidence that an outside wave of gargantuan proportions had begun to build. But then the noise of the machines would no doubt have drowned out anything so sublime as the singing of the stones, and the islands were already lost to them in the fog. What they were about to experience was the straits in all of their mystic finery, and it would have taken a Hoddy Younger to have plotted their escape. But Hoddy Younger was a long time gone from that lineup. The Riders on the Storm were alone with the roar of their machines, and this was enough to mask even the distant booming which, in the absence of all else, might at least have provided them with some hint, however belated, of what was to come. As it was, the circling crews were still fighting for purchase in the oceans of foam that lay across the water, feet thick, in the aftermath of the wave at Third Notch when the fury of the Mystic Peak came down upon them—a churning wall of white water fifteen feet high, exploding from out of the fog, chewing up everything in its path, and that, by this point in the game, was bound to include themselves, both skis and riders alike, and there was little they could do save dive for deep water, hoping at the same time to distance themselves from the heavy machinery that would in fact be thoroughly trashed and rendered useless for the rest of the trip so that new stuff would have to be brought in, causing them to miss a good deal of the swell, which was peaking earlier than expected, as evidenced by the avalanche now upon them.

Yet even this was only a fragment of the story, just as the white water was only that part of the wave already broken. The unbroken part ran on for another hundred yards, twice the size of anything they had yet ridden, though of this wonder they were afforded but a glimpse. And some saw it not at all as they were in the midst of their dives. But for those still on the surface, it was a vision they would carry to their graves, for such were the lives they had chosen, and such was the grandeur of what greeted them. The face of that immense wave was turned to the light of a still-rising sun and was in and of itself a vast enough surface to capture such light, even amid the fog that was already beginning to thin, as though it had advanced only to mask the approach of the wave, and to cast that light back, so as to imbue those morning airs with the ambient radiance from which a solitary rider was only then seen to emerge, in full trim, surfing in from Outside the Bullring, and drawing there such lines as would please the eye of any so schooled and of neophytes as well, for that was the degree of artistry exhibited—a thing little seen now, even in those watery quarters of the world where such feats do not go unnoticed. And he rode at times with his arms at his side, as though what he did required no effort at all, and at other times with these same arms outstretched, rather, one might think, like a gull in flight. On the high ground of Spooner's Mesa

Jack Nance executed a little dance atop the hood of his truck, such as would have him removing dents for the next six weeks, while among the brush and stunted pines overlooking Yogurt Canyon a second man stood in mute observation, a spectral figure, dressed in rags, one arm outstretched as if in salutation.

37

MAGDALENA SPENT several days at the hotel in Baja, alone, watching the waves from the balcony of her room. The waves were followed by unseasonable rains. Her room leaked and she moved to another. In it she sat one evening by candlelight and arranged her hair as she'd worn it the night of the rodeo, fixing it with the combs that Fahey had given her. But Fahey did not come.

On the following morning she packed the combs away and left, a full week earlier than planned, driving the car she had rented back along the highway to Tijuana, passing the very place where she had collided with the cliffs above Las Playas. One might have thought there would have been some sign there to suggest the violence of what had transpired, burnt rubber or scarred ground, but the highway appeared unmarked and the face of the cliff where she had hit it no different than at any other point along the drive. She even turned around and drove back, then turned and passed it again just to be sure, but there was nothing to suggest anything out of the ordinary had ever taken place. A handful of small, purple flowers were coming into bloom at the edge of the asphalt and above the beaches of Las Playas the sun had broken from the clouds and the sea was blue beneath it.

She was back at work within the week, seated at her desk in Carlotta's offices, her face all but healed, her night classes resumed, her world acquiring its familiar shape. Upon leaving the hotel, she had informed its owners that there was a very slim chance a man would arrive looking for her. But there had been no word of his whereabouts, not from that quarter and not from any other. She was staring idly from a window when Carlotta appeared in her doorway.

"How you holding up?" the older woman asked her.

Magdalena said that she was holding up just fine.

"You've heard Luis Cardona got the appointment to PROFTA?"

Magdalena had heard. Luis Cardona was an academic, an environmental activist, newly appointed to the policy arm of Mexico's environmental agency.

"A small victory."

"Take what you can get, sister."

Magdalena smiled. She supposed that in the long run, it was how things would proceed, if they were to proceed at all.

Carlotta continued to stand in the doorway then crossed the room to Magdalena's desk. "Also, there was this," she said. "I was wondering if you'd seen it."

She held a San Diego newspaper in her hand. She turned it to an article about a surfer from Imperial Beach. The man had died of some obscure infection. The headline read: BIG WAVE RIDER'S DEATH BLAMED ON WATER-BORNE ILLNESS. Magdalena was some time in picking up the paper. She sat staring at the headline. Carlotta stood above her. "I thought I recognized the name," Carlotta said.

Magdalena crossed the border, by car, on Monday of the following week as a small ceremony was scheduled to take place in downtown Imperial Beach, at the sight known as Surfhenge. She went alone.

The day broke beneath coastal haze but by noon a stiff onshore wind had scattered the clouds, and driving along the eastern edge of the Tijuana River Valley she could see the ocean, a startling shade of blue flecked with wind chop. She exited the freeway on the Dairy Mart Road in order to see more of the valley and so came on paved roads, past the Oaxacan enclave known as Garage Door Tijuana and following closely upon the path taken by Serra and Piatro came finally into the town itself, wherein maybe a dozen people had gathered beneath the Plexiglas arches near the entrance to the old pier. Parking the car, she could see that a third of these were city workers come to jackhammer a hole in the sidewalk for the admittance of a freshly cast bronze plaque.

Jack Nance was there, recognizable as one of the cowboys, as was the border patrolman who'd driven them from the beach. The three stood together and exchanged a few words. Jack told them of the morning that had followed that night in the valley. He told them of having seen the wave from the top of Spooner's Mesa. He also told them of having visited Fahey in the hospital. He had seemed, Jack said, to be of remarkably good cheer and was getting better. But then his fever had gone off the charts for reasons the doctors were still not sure of and he had died that same night, alone in his room.

Jack Nance had no sooner finished with this story than Magdalena was approached by a plump, gray-haired woman of indeterminate age who seemed to have some interest in claiming her attention. Magdalena put her hand on Jack's arm then moved off a bit to hear what this person might have to say.

The woman identified herself almost at once as the worm woman of Perris, the same who'd once sold Fahey the mechanical harvester of which he was so proud. It seems that she and her husband had received an e-mail from Mr. Fahey shortly before he ah . . . passed, in which he had offered them his entire worm farm, as he was planning to leave the valley. It seemed that their own farm had gone under, which was why they had been willing to sell him the harvester in the first place, leaving them more or less homeless, in a cousin's trailer in the Coachella Valley. Fahey, of course, had known about all of this. It was not long after his amazing offer that they'd heard of his untimely demise and later still of this ceremony that was to be held in his honor though one would have been hard-pressed, the worm woman concluded, to actually call it a ceremony. "Sidewalk repair was more like it," she said. Yet here they were, the woman standing plump and goggled-eyed in the midst of the gaily colored swizzle sticks while a man Magdalena took for her husband sat nearby at the wheel of a battered pickup truck and even from this distance appeared uncomfortable, as if the meager formality of the occasion together with his general surroundings in some way distressed him.

"Then he meant not to stay," Magdalena said. She spoke softly and just about half to herself.

"Mr. Fahey?" the worm woman asked.

"Yes, Mr. Fahey."

"Oh no, I believe not. He said he was going to Mexico and would forward an address, so we could reach him, to arrange some modest price for the sale of his land . . ."

Magdalena looked away.

The woman continued, her speech halting. "We're not sure now just how to proceed with all of this . . . It doesn't look as if there were any heirs . . ."

"No," Magdalena said. "No heirs."

The woman accepted this news in silence then added that she had not expected any. "I suppose we'll need an attorney," she said finally, "someone who specializes in these sorts of things . . ."

Magdalena nodded. She supposed they would.

The woman sighed, folding her arms across her chest. "Yes, well . . . Roy, my husband . . . He's very good with these sorts of things. Legal things," she said.

Magdalena assumed that she was speaking of the man in the truck. She was trying to imagine Roy as a legal sophisticate when she caught sight of one more visitor to this obscure celebration, a man of perhaps eighty, dressed in a tattered suit. He stood stiff as a carved effigy, the wind riffling his dark gray hair, which appeared thick and unruly. His skin was lined and deeply tanned, like wood treated to endure the sun. She turned to the woman for the last time. "Well," she said. "You were the ones he contacted. I hope that it will all work out. I wish you the best."

The woman nodded. She was on again about Roy and his considerable achievements as Magdalena turned away. She did not wish to appear rude but she was afraid the old man was going to leave and she wanted to say something to him because, well . . . there was really no one else it could have been.

He was staring at the ground when she walked up. His eyes were blue and a little cloudy and seemed to have tears in them. Magdalena touched his arm and he looked up at her somewhat startled. "I'm sorry . . ." she began, then stopped and started over. "I'd like to thank you for saving my life."

The old man studied her, then nodded and began to walk away. The workers were preparing to lower the plaque into the freshly poured concrete. There was a middle-aged man there from the

Surfrider Foundation and he had begun to read a few words. Magdalena hesitated then hurried to catch up to the old man. She spoke to him by name. He stopped and looked back.

"I was wondering," she said. "If we might walk together, a little ways."

The old man nodded. He executed this maneuver in a rather formal way but then she seemed to remember Fahey telling her that Hoddy Younger could go days at a time without a word even then, back in the day. She also remembered his saying that if Hoddy liked you, he would give you the shirt off his back, and if he didn't, he wouldn't piss on you to put out the fire. "He was going to come," Magdalena said, finally. "He was selling the farm."

The old man looked toward the sea, or at least toward that part of it that might be seen beyond the reach of sand, a band of blue, dappled in light. "I guess it was about time," he said. He watched as a formation of pelicans passed above the pier then turned and began to walk once more.

Magdalena walked with him. He seemed content in her presence and she was willing to take this as a good thing. She imagined Fahey, looking on . . . They went along Ocean Boulevard, in the direction of the Tijuana Straits, as at their backs, in the harsh slant of light falling among the gaily colored arches, a new plaque was lowered into the wet concrete, at the foot of an absurd bench few will ever contort themselves to sit upon, bearing a name that fewer yet will ever stoop to read. Surfhenge is, after all, hardly a destination. In fact it is little more than an eyesore, in a landscape steeped in such, two miles from the Mexican border, where the sewage meets the sea, yet the names of the immortals are written there, Sam the Gull Fahey now among them. And one could say it was everything for which he might have asked.

ACKNOWLEDGMENTS

I am grateful to many people, on both sides of the border. I would especially like to thank Greg Abbott, Bill Spencer, Gene Muldany, and Brian Bonesteel of the Tijuana River Valley, Serge Dedina of Wildcoast, Mike "Duck" Richardson, Big Tony McCormick, Jeff Knox, Carla Garcia and the courageous women of Factor X. I would also like to thank Colin Harrison for his thoughtful readings.

ABOUT THE AUTHOR

Kem Nunn is a third-generation Californian whose previous novels include *The Dogs of Winter, Pomona Queen, Unassigned Territory,* and *Tapping the Source,* which was one of three nominees for the National Book Award. A graduate of the University of California at Irvine, Mr. Nunn lives in Southern California.